TO BE SOMEONE ALL OVER AGAIN

MARYAM A.H

Copyright © 2024 by Maryam A H

All rights reserved.

No part of this publication may be reproduced, distributed, or transmitted in any form or by any means, including photocopying, recording, or other electronic or mechanical methods, without the prior written permission of the publisher, except as permitted by UK copyright law. For permission requests, contact maryamakhtar2098@gmail.com

The story, all names, characters, and incidents portrayed in this production are fictitious. No identification with actual persons (living or deceased), places, buildings, and products are intended or should be inferred.

For those who believe their sun will never rise. You are the light in the darkest of chapters.

This is for you.

PLAYLIST
A PLAYLIST FOR ASHER AND ALESSIA

IDK You Yet – *Alexandra 23*
Mr. Perfectly Fine – *Taylor Swift*
18 – *Anson Seabra*
Come Back…Be Here – *Taylor Swift*
You Are Enough – *Sleeping At Last*
It'll Be Okay – *Shawn Mendes*
Someone To Stay – *Vancouver Sleep Clinic*
Daylight – *Taylor Swift*
I'm Yours – *Alessia Cara*
There's No Way – *Lauv, Julia Michaels*
Cloud 9 – *Beach Bunny*
Nice To Meet You – *Myles Smith*
Yellow Lights – *Harry Hudson*
Sailor Song – *Gigi Perez*
I don't want to watch the world end with someone else – *Clinton Kane*
Paris In The Rain - *Lauv*
3am – *ROSÉ*
Number one girl – *ROSÉ*
Arcade – *Duncan Laurence*
We can't be friends (wait for your love) – *Ariana Grande*
See you later (ten years) – *Jenna Raine*
Lovers – *Anna of the North*
Favorite crime – *Olivia Rodrigo*
Are You With Me – *Nilu*
Watch – *Billie Eilish*
I miss you, I'm sorry – *Gracie Abrams*
The Man Who Can't Be Moved – *The Script*
Where's My Love – *SYML*
Killing Me To Love You - *Vancouver Sleep Clinic*
All I Want – *Kodaline*
Fall Into Me – *Forest Blakk*
Someone To You – *Matt Hansen*
Carry You Home – *Alex Warren*

AUTHORS NOTE AND TRIGGER WARNINGS

This novel contains themes that some readers may find distressing, including:
- **Grief**
- **Mental health struggles**
- **Suicidal ideation**

While these topics are explored with care, they may be triggering for some. Please read at your own discretion and prioritise your well-being.

To those who have chosen to pick up this book—thank you. Whether you're here for the love story, the emotions, or simply an escape, I truly appreciate you giving this story a chance. It means the world to me that you're stepping into Asher and Alessia's journey, and I hope my words resonate with you in some way.

With love and gratitude,

Maryam

PROLOGUE
ASHER

I beg death to take me, but even death won't greet me with the guilt I carry.

I open my eyes and choke on the water, desperately trying to be released. My lungs plead to breathe once more. I cough and try to lift myself up from the stones that are attempting to etch their way into my skin. I try picking away the remnants of stone left, trying to invade my existing wounds.

The river continues to morph around me, streaming effortlessly like nothing happened, taking streaks of my blood along with it as if to commemorate the moment. The smell of woodland soil flares through my nostrils. I try to stand, but it's no use. The current is sabotaging my balance.

Instead, I suck in a deep breath and dig my hand into the ground within my reach and dig my nails deep in the soil, trying to hold myself. I bite down on my cheek as I pull myself forward, ignoring the taste of blood leaking onto my tongue. I pull myself onto the ground, sweat beads trickling down my skin.

"Asher."

My name jolts me upright. How can someone be here now? It's

the dead of night.

"Asher."

This time, impatience masks the mention of my name, but I recognise it. I always recognise this voice.

"Leave me alone," I whisper. *Just leave me alone*, I silently plead.

"I can't help you if you don't let me," he says, his voice sympathetic and faint.

"You're dead. You can't help me. Now leave." I wave my arm through the air past me as if that's going to do anything.

"You can't join me if that's what you think." His words are coarse, and his tone is mocking.

If I could see him, I would see a smile painted across his face. I grin to myself, thinking wistfully about how I would make that smirk disappear, but you can't beat a dead man. "You're trying to help me one second, and now you're mocking me? Choose one. You're making my head spin."

I groan as my hands caress my forehead, pressing it hard enough to make the pain subside, even if it's just a little bit. But nothing seems to work, not while he's made an appearance. "I'm trying to get rid of you, not join you. Believe me, that's the last thing I want." He already knows this.

Well, whatever *this* version of him is knows this. I don't know how my best friend ended up being the person I started to hate more than anyone in the world when he was the person I once loved the most. I try to steady the trembling of my hands. It's always like this whenever I talk to him.

I know he's not real—even I'm not crazy enough to believe he is, but it's hard when I'm the only person who can hear him, when

I can't do anything to get rid of him, and the guilt that comes with him is ready to consume me whole. I have to make myself look somewhat decent.

There's no way I can go home like this. I need to wash my hands somewhere, my face, everything. I start to peel away the shirt clinging to my skin, sucking in a deep breath as every touch feels like scalding water, the shock paralysing every function in my body.

I finally manage to pick myself up as I try to walk, wincing as I stagger forward, leaving a trail of footsteps piercing through what was once a white sheet of snow.

"This wasn't meant to happen," I whisper, trying to make sense of the predicament I've put myself in.

My thoughts run wild, mocking me relentlessly at the little control I have to think straight. "If you go straight from here, you'll end up on the main roads, and you'll be able to sit down for a bit and head home easier." I roll my eyes, gritting my teeth as his voice evades my space.

"I know the way," I bite. He's acting like I haven't lived here most of my life. "If you're going to bother me, at least tell me something useful."

He means well, but it doesn't make him any less bothersome.

"Tyler," I say, trying to stop the lump forming in my throat.

"Yes?" he says.

"Do you have to stick around for so long? Can't you do us both a favour and go into the light or whatever it is you have to do to get lost?" I murmur. It sounded more polite in my head.

He laughs, not the peaceful kind, but one that kind of makes you want to throw him off a cliff. "You realise you're the one keeping me here, right? Don't you think I have better things to do? But now that you mention it, we did say if either of us dies first, we would haunt each other."

He's staring at me with his arms crossed over his chest. "Yes, but I didn't think you would take it so literally." I groan as I steady myself.

My eyes start to adjust, the gust of wind piercing through the little vision I have, filling my eyes with tears. I can't see a thing. The numbness in my legs forces me to come to a halt and let my body recover for a second, leaning against a tree, heaving.

I can't *breathe*. Gasping for air to fill my lungs, I begin to choke, coughing up more water as I hold onto my knees. I feel like I'm going to cough up my insides. I'm surprised I'm not puking up blood instead of trying to think of ways to relieve the agonising sensation coursing its way through my body.

I can't help but laugh to myself at how pathetic this is. I resist the urge to just let myself fall and sink on the covered grass. My head feels like it's going to explode any minute, and nothing seems to stay still. I ignore my sanity to wait for help and carry on walking through the hooded sky.

The trees cluster together to block out the only light I have to guide me, or perhaps that's my imagination. Sighing in defeat, I wipe my eyes, but still, nothing seems to be clear. Water squelches in my trainers, my socks drenched. If I die of anything, it's going to be pneumonia.

I've never been more frozen in my life. At least Tyler has shut up for now. I stop in my tracks as I finally focus on the snow-covered postcard streets. I hold onto the wall that separates the ghost town from the forest-like wonder. I gather up the courage to limp forward a little more.

I grasp onto the bench and lay myself down, feeling every ache throbbing as the sharp gusts make it their mission to leave me helpless. I let my tears escape me, no longer being able to keep them at bay and let out a quiet sob. *I don't know what I'm doing anymore.* I suck in a deep breath and wipe my eyes with my arm.

Realising I've smeared blood across my cheeks, watching as the droplets from my nose and lips drip onto the layers of snow, making it look like a murder scene, I dart my eyes around my shirt to find a clean spot. I take the hem of my shirt and try to wipe off the blood, and of course, there isn't one.

I look like I'm covered in crap. "Here, take a tissue," a deep voice reaches out his hand towards me, his wrinkled hand trembling.

I choke. What's with these people coming out of nowhere? Collecting myself, I clear my throat and shake my head in dismissal of his offer.

"Take it you're ruining the snow, and to be honest, you're not really doing much for the scenery right now," he insists, waving it like I'm a dog after a bone.

I can feel my face flare up. Nothing could be more embarrassing than this. I hesitantly take the tissue from his hand and dab my nose; the blood seems to be soaking it up.

I keep waiting and hoping for the world to swallow me whole and make me disappear. "You intend on freezing?" he questions. "The snow is beautiful. I don't blame you for sitting here when the world seems to go quiet."

He places himself on the far end of the bench beside me. Quiet? That's an understatement.

I fight the urge to roll my eyes. Tonight is anything but quiet. He's ignoring the obvious issue, my drenched clothes. I'm grateful. I wish he would leave.

"Are you a mute, son? I'm sure I've seen you talk before."

I shoot a quick glare in his direction. If looks could kill, I know mine would. He can't seem to take a hint.

He's wrapped up in a long brown coat, his hands buried in his pocket, and his black scarf placed around his neck. I can't seem to place him. If he's seen me, I've never seen him before. Perhaps he has me confused with someone else, or he thinks I just survived an attempted murder.

"Glad to know you're not deaf." He smirks, his smile forming creases across his forehead.

I didn't realise I hadn't said anything when I looked at him. I stared at him. "I'm not interested in small talk. I'm trying to mind my own business, so I would appreciate it if you would let me be."

My voice comes out hoarse and weak. I don't recognise the voice coming out of me.

"You wouldn't be interested in this?" he says, lifting a grey coat double the size of me, the hood oversized and weighted with fluff.

Honestly, I would. "I'm good, thanks." I bite my tongue as I immediately want to bang my head against the lamppost. I'm sitting here drenched from head to toe, covered in dried blood.

"You're too proud. I was going to dump this stuff in the charity bins not too far from here." He rustles the black bags placed on a metal trolley.

"I'm not your charity." This time, I don't mutter, nor does weakness soak my tone.

"I didn't say you were." He coughs. "But you're soaked for a reason, which is none of my concern. Neither is it my business, but you and I both know dressed like that"—he gestures to my questionable attire and appearance—"you will freeze. Plus, the blood will wash out of it if that's one of your worries. So suck it up, save us both time and take it," he scolds.

I still for a moment. "Don't look so startled, and don't look at me like I slapped you with a fish."

I ponder for a moment before I shake my head. "I don't want it," I lie. I can't stand the way he's being so nice to me. He barely knows me. I don't want it if it can go to someone better.

"It's called kindness, son. You should try it once in a while," he grumps. "What are you doing out walking the streets at this time anyway? It's three in the morning."

I'm sitting here covered in who-knows-what, I'm not even sure anymore, and he wants to make friends? Doesn't he realise I'm a stranger who looks utterly psychotic, and I could murder him? I'm not psychotic, but he doesn't know that.

"You have your little secrets, so do I. But I suppose we both like to watch the world go silent for a while," he says as he shuffles awkwardly, placing the coat on the bare surface of the bench.

"I told you I don't want it." I try to hand it back to him, but my body is aching and frozen, every movement feeling like a million needles stabbing me at once.

He places his hand on my shoulder and softly squeezes it. "Look after yourself, kid." He treads forward, leaving his footprints marking his path.

I give up and cave, sliding my arms inside the coat and feeling the warmth immediately embrace me. I watch as he slowly fades from my sight, leaving me again with nothing but complete silence and the sound of my shallow breaths. I dig my hands inside the pockets and feel something nab at my fingertips.

Pulling it out, I wipe away the snow that begins caressing the picture.

It's a Polaroid. A girl.

Why would the old man have this? I can't even give it back to him. I breathe slowly, brushing away the snow masking her identity. Her smile is beaming so brightly and clichéd, but it's true. I never understood the concept of someone's smile filling the room, but this moment captures exactly that, and damn, it's bright.

Her arms are held up, and her right arm is curved over her head. Her black hair falls so carelessly over her shoulders it brings out her hazel eyes and sun-kissed skin. How did the old man forget about this? I reach to put it in the bin. It seems too personal to keep.

I don't know if I can bring myself to throw this away. It's comforting to know that smiles like hers still do exist. The pure blissful happiness that makes it happen is real, and someone has it. *It's real.* One day, in some fucked up timeline, this could be me. That smile could be plastered on my face.

I'll be one with a smile so bright it'll be blinding, and you'll know I'm consumed by nothing but happiness. One day, I'll be thankful to live another day instead of trying to escape it. I won't be so guilt-ridden, I won't feel so heavy. I'll be light and free. I fidget with the photo and slide it back into my pocket.

I'll keep this for the old man. One day, he might miss it. I would.

Perhaps I'll see him again one day.

CHAPTER ONE
ASHER

My eyes shoot open, breathing heavily. I lay in the darkness, the soft streetlight trying to break through the grey curtains. I wake up properly, taking in everything around me. I'm in bed, unsure of how long I was asleep, or even what day it is.

Everything's blurred and scattered. I rub my eyes and watch the dots fade and leave, leaving nothing but the darkness that I started with. I don't know why I'm thinking of my mother. I haven't thought of her in a long while. I'm not sure why my mind tries to warp her as something my memories know she's not.

Sometimes, I think I hate her, but deep down, I don't think I ever could. I'm curious if she knows how it feels to see other people embraced in their mother's arms, nothing but joyful laughs cementing the moment, their smiles capturing a memory that will never be mine.

Because no matter where I look, mine is never in sight.

"Stop already. As if being dead isn't depressing enough, I have to listen to you," Tyler whines.

I squeeze my eyes shut, trying to force myself asleep. For once,

I want to be normal and not hear him whingeing in my ear. "It's a bit of a long shot for you, don't you think?"

I wish I had a gun right now. I grab my pillow and groan as I cover my face, hoping he'll disappear. He's right. It is a long shot because this is anything but normal.

"If I get rid of you, I'm one step closer." I lift the pillow so he can hear me, not that lifting it will make a difference. He can hear me all the same.

I could be choking, and he would understand what I'm saying. I sit up, my body throbbing less. At least the pain is bearable now, and I lean against the headboard.

"I really thought you'd be joining me this time," he jokes.

"I'm sorry my life is inconveniencing you," I utter sarcastically.

"No need to apologise, it's okay."

If only there was a way to punch the non-existent. Burying my head in my hands as I suck in a deep breath, I wonder why my mind couldn't conjure up someone less irritating. I'm practically doing this to myself. "You know I try not to be like this, right? I have tried to see that the 'brighter side' that you've preached about so many times exists. But don't you think you being here isn't helping my situation?"

I can't see him, but I can feel Tyler's eyes scanning me. Even in the dark, somehow, his brown eyes overshadow the bleakness of my room. He ignores me, the silence loud. "You sound like a broken record." His laugh startles me.

"I didn't say anything," I snap. I did before, but I didn't say anything else. I sound like I'm about to throw a tantrum. I straighten up and remember I'm past the age of five, and in essence,

I'm arguing with myself.

"You're thinking too loud, Asher," Tyler says, annoyed.

I always laugh at the irony of my name, considering my mother is the one who chose it, and it apparently means 'blessed' or 'favourable'. It's hard not to laugh when you think about it. I gaze down at my bare palms. The scars have faded, and I brush my fingers along the scarred flesh.

I'm starting to forget how they looked without the fading and fresh bruises. Sometimes, I have this anger I can't seem to shake off. It bottles up until I become a person I don't recognise anymore.

They say everyone is capable of murder to an extent, and I think that I am. There's nothing I can do to douse the fire before it spreads. I'm always getting into fights, thinking the aftermath will be different and I'll feel something normal again, something that isn't so intensely suffocating.

"I may be stating the obvious, but your hands would hurt less if you—"

I cut him off. I don't need a lecture from my subconscious. At least, that's what I think he is. I don't remember him being this annoying when he was alive.

"I'm fully aware, thank you," I remark.

My room isn't big, but it's decent: grey walls, a desk across my bed and a box full of stuff in my wardrobe on the left side of my room. It's pressed against the corner, white and old. My desk is black and blue.

"You never were good with colours, but I'm sure it was better than this," Tyler says as if he's reading my thoughts word for word. I get up off the bed and make my way to sit at my desk. I lean on my elbows as I repeatedly tap my cheek to focus.

"Can you reminisce later?" I say impatiently. "You're the one keeping me here."

If I knew where to glare at him, I would, as if I were keeping him here on purpose. "You can't be serious right now?" His voice is on edge. "Think about this, Ash—"

I cut him off, my voice raspier than I expected, "Don't you think I know what I'm doing?"

I'm tired of defending myself and making excuses so people understand. I'm tired of describing my demons, the numbness that makes every day look the same. Every breath feels like a chore. I'm tired of trying to make somebody understand. I have my reasons, and that's enough.

I turn the lamp on and reach for my pen, the clamminess of my palms making it hard to hold securely. I can't stop my hand from shaking. My dad deserves more, so much more than this. My big gratitude for everything he's done. Is it going to be a note?

He won't see it as my defeat. He'll see it as his failure.

I'm starting to think perhaps no words are best. I can't write anything to make this okay or justify it. Nothing I do will make his pain go away. "Your dad always made me laugh. He always made you feel like you were his own. It's one of the things I loved most about him," Tyler says fondly, smiling at the distant memories I'm sure are replaying in his mind.

"You're blessed to have him as a dad. I would never consider doing something like this to him. He doesn't deserve it." And just like that, it feels like he's shoved a knife through my chest.

But it doesn't change anything, and I can't bring myself to shut

Tyler down. Because he's right, he's always right, and I don't know how to fight with someone who knows the inner workings of my mind. I stand up and make my way to the exit of my room. I open the door and close it as quietly as I can.

I fumble for my keys to lock my room door but decide against it. There's no point. Creeping towards his room, the light from the streetlamps shines through the window. I approach his door and open it enough for me to squeeze through.

I let his heavy breathing flood my ears. I don't know why I came. I want to say goodbye somehow. His brown hair is loose on his pillow. His hair isn't long—well, not long enough to braid.

"I never noticed how much you look like your dad," Tyler says. I try to stop my eyes from rolling.

Obviously I look like him. I really don't know how I made Tyler dumber. My dad is average looks-wise to me, but he seems to get a lot of attention, not that he realises half the time. His brown hair, fair skin and piercing blue eyes.

I got his eyes, except mine are more of a deeper blue than his. My nose is smaller than his, and my hair is pretty much black. I wonder what he's dreaming of. I'd love to see in his mind for a second, see the version of him that he wants to be.

I hate it when I sleep. It's tiring, which never makes sense, but sometimes reality haunts us in our dreams.

"Are you sure you want to do this? To him?" I get what he's trying to do, but it won't work. He can try all his tricks, but he won't make a difference.

When Mum left, Dad went crazy, drinking every night. I'd have to pull him down the hall to his bed. He'd always end up on the floor if I left him on the sofa. But I would always wait. I'd wait until his tears dried and his dreams weren't plaguing him.

One thing I do believe in, with every core of my being, is love. He loved my mother with every part of his soul, and that wasn't enough for her. But he did love her truly. The fault wasn't with him. He did everything right. Mum woke up one day and decided she didn't love him anymore.

Conveniently, after the divorce, it didn't take her more than three months to find the 'love' of her life and move in with him. Two years later, they had two children. I was too young to understand why she would leave in the middle of the night and sneak in early mornings.

Why would you want to fall in love in the first place if this is how it ends? I've heard you can't help it, but I'll be damned if I fall into that trap. I'd rather die a thousand deaths than experience heartache like that. You don't know what kind of story you'll get, and I'm not willing to leave it up to chance.

I rest my chin in the palms of my hands, with my elbows resting on the windowsill. Tilting closer to the window, I lean closer, resting my upper body weight on my arms, looking at passers-by. The smiles that curve on their lips. Their laughter fills the air. It's a shame it's not contagious. I miss Tyler, the real one.

On days like this, I remember him the most. He loved this season, the beauty of it. He would take everything in, and I always bullied him for being so sensitive. I wonder if he still loves it.

"I do," he says.

I try to stop the stinging sensation paining my eyes. "I always appreciated this. I always took a second to look, just breathe. You would get bored sitting." Nostalgia masks his voice. "You always wondered what was so mesmerising about it, but I think now you finally understand."

I wipe the escaped tears rolling down my cheek and see his reflection in the window. My heart stills for a moment, my breathing turning ragged, his brown eyes peering at me, nothing but softness and empathy consuming them. Tyler. He still looks the same, with his dark freckles sitting atop his golden skin and dark hair that always turns lighter in summer. Considering he's dead, his skin doesn't look like it's missed the warmth of the sun.

"Thank you." Tyler gleams. *This isn't real.*

"He's not real," I mutter, and I see a hand reach out to touch me.

I quickly turn away from the window and somehow make my way out of the apartment in one piece without waking my dad up. I lock the door. I can't stop the pounding against my ribcage, and everything feels like it's tightening. I'm trying to breathe, but it's as if I've forgotten how.

"I'm sorry." I hold my head against the door and sob, the tears rushing out, and I can't stop them. *They won't stop.* He didn't deserve what he got; no one would, but he *didn't*. They say stuff happens for a reason, but I can't think of a single reason why it was him; the world needs people like him around.

It feels so empty.

I take deep breaths as I try to make sense of everything. My logic doesn't really make sense, but it's all I have. Deep down, we all have a choice. Not all of us are strong enough to hold on. I sigh, running my fingers through my hair. I'm not scared or nervous. I feel guilty.

Just for a moment, I want to feel nothing. I know I'm not alone that there are people around me, and I can't blame the world for how I've chosen to see it, or people for the facade I've created, but I don't want to be a burden anymore. It's been hours, and I haven't moved. Can I move?

It's not like I want this, but what choice do I have? It's getting light, and I'm running out of time. If I wait any longer, I'll have missed my chance, and I don't know when the next time will be and if I can get it right again. I thought I was getting better at one point, that I finally had my breakthrough to moving on.

Then I guess it hit me. Everything I blocked out, tried to control, and hide from came back at once. "Any normal person would take this as a sign."

Why can I see him? This proves I'm going insane. At least I get to stop myself from fully losing it.

"What? You're not talking to me now?" Tyler grins. I'm not going to talk to myself anymore. He's not real. He doesn't need a response. "Hello?" He waves his hand in my face, and I think I'm going to be sick. This can't be happening. How do I make him disappear? I walk around him and head for the stairs that lead to the roof.

The staircase doesn't seem to fucking end. It's old and rusty. "Are you really doing this?" Tyler stands in front of me.

"What do you want from me? Stop following me."

He claps. "The man finally talks. Didn't take you long." He looms proudly.

"Tyler, please," I plead, "you don't get it."

I can't believe I'm actually doing this. I've really fucking lost it. "Are you punishing me? Is that it?" Confusion consumes his features. "You're my brother," he says as if that's meant to be clear. The insult lingering in his tone is deafening.

"Then leave. Just go. Why are you here? Don't you think I'm crazy enough, now you decide to show yourself to truly convince me I'm insane?"

He steps down a step, and he embraces me, "I'm sorry, but you can't do this." I don't know whether I've truly gone mad, but I can feel his hold. He breaks free and looks at me, his eyes a shade lighter like honey.

"I'm here because you need me. You really need me this time, and you know it. You don't want to do this. I know because I know *you*. Why else would you see me? You haven't all this time. Why before you decide this time is really it? You're not trying anymore. You've given up."

He'll be okay. Dad will understand. Tyler isn't real. I continuously tell myself until it's concrete in my mind. I shiver as the reality hits me. I'm about to do it, sending chills down my spine. I pull my hood forward, trying to not let the guilt consume me, repeatedly telling myself, it's for the best.

I need this. I want this.

Pushing the door open, I take in the cold air, letting the wind hit me. The cold air is prickling my skin, and it feels like I've got a whole stack of needles thrown at me. The roof is huge. It overlooks the shitty parts of Cove Haven. There's this ledge. It's wide enough to not fall if you stand on it. Only if you move forward will you drop.

That's my plan. To fall. No one is around. I won't make a scene. My dad won't find me. Someone else will. I don't mind that. I make my way towards the ledge and throw my legs over the wall, trying not to look down.

It starts to snow lightly, and I can't help but smile. This isn't a bad way to end it.

"You can still change your mind." Tyler sits beside me, his voice soft and comforting.

"I know, but I don't want to, and that's okay. Everything will finally be okay," I say aloud, holding my hand out as I watch the snow melt into my palm.

"I got this, trust me for once. I will be free, and I honestly couldn't be happier. I don't know what will greet me, but I'm ready."

I can't help but peer to the ground where my legs hang free. I swing them back and forth, gripping the wall on either side.

I look up and take the last moments in. The world can be beautiful sometimes. Inhaling a deep breath, I stand up to position myself properly on the ledge, trying to balance myself.

If there is one thing I'm sure of, it's the way I should go. It should be the way I want it to be. I should be in control.

"I'll go with you," Tyler says hesitantly as he gulps, peering down at the distance.

"What are you scared of? You're already dead. I wouldn't be surprised if you floated up instead."

I would nudge him, but I'd probably fall through him. I exhale as I hold onto the strings of my hoodie, slightly pulling it so the hood comes down my eyes a little, peering down at the empty streets below me. This is it.

"Asher, please."

Ignoring his pleas, his voice starts to fade, and I'm in the moment. I reject any doubt that might convince me otherwise. I'm free. I'm finally going to be free. *This is it. This is what I dreamt it to be.*

It's time.

CHAPTER TWO
ASHER

"Um, I hate to be a killjoy, but I was just wondering who you're talking to...? Because I know it's not me, and there isn't anybody else here, so..."

I stand frozen, my body turned still. *This isn't my voice.* I look to the side, and Tyler quickly says, "It's not me." I glare at him, and he pretends someone else is calling him.

This can't be happening. Can't I have one moment of peace, just one? Why is that so hard?

"While we're on the subject... are you sure you want to drop this far? It seems too messy."

There's the voice again, and I know this is real this time, and I can't move. I'm unsure I want to, but I can't pretend this isn't happening.

Unless...

My thoughts start trailing and abruptly stop as I realise I can't be dead. I haven't even moved, and it's not like I could be in heaven. The voice doesn't even sound like it could be remotely close to anything I'd find soothing. If anything, it's a bit squeaky for my liking.

I try to think of everything, anything, to think of a way to make this encounter disappear. Instead, she mistakes my silence as a starter conversation piece.

"Hello?" Her hand waves beside me as she's leaning over the wall, trying to grab my attention. "Hello-oooo!" Her voice is light and irritating. I heard her clearly the first time.

I squeeze my eyes shut, hoping that it will somehow make this all disappear, make her disappear. Why couldn't I have fallen sooner? I had to be all dramatic and sentimental. "You know I can see you, right?" she says, unamused.

Does she not have a mute button? I mean, I see her point. Why did I think standing still would somehow make me invisible?

I open my eyes and ponder whether my life is truly a joke. I'm standing here like an idiot while some moron is waving at me like a bigger idiot. I guess I'm not dead, but why does this somehow feel worse?

I could be dreaming, but somehow, I doubt I would torture myself with someone as oddly perky as her. Why is she still waving at me? I think I'm going to be sick again. I don't get it. Am I meant to wave back at her? I lift my hand, give a weak wave, and immediately regret it. "Why are you waving at me?"

"I'm confused. Were you not just waving at me?" I state the obvious, but her expression changes, and she starts looking at me like I've lost it.

"Are you just going to stand there, or...?" she says, finally putting her arm down.

I'm still standing on the ledge, but it's reached that moment when it would be too awkward to get off. "So are we going to pretend this isn't happening? Can you hear me?" she questions. "You don't say an awful lot, do you?" Does she stop talking?

"Now I bet you wish I was irritating you instead," Tyler whispers.

"Shut up, I can't deal with two boneheads talking at once," I mumble. I need to get rid of her.

"What are you, five? Bonehead? Really?" her voice muses.

"Are you always so clingy to everyone you meet?" Why does my voice always come out so raspy? I need to move but don't know how to get there.

"You're the one standing there like an oaf," she casually says bluntly.

"An oaf? What?" What does that even mean?

"Well, I can't call you an idiot. You might jump. I have to be kind of nice to you," she says, her casualness alarming. Is this woman feeling okay?

"Is there a reason you're talking to me?" I bite, cringing at this entire thing. This is possibly the most awkward situation I've ever been in.

"Yes," she says, her voice flat. I wait, but instead, awkward silence fills the air. This would be her cue to say something, but she doesn't.

I thought there was more to that sentence. What kind of species is she? Just standing there looking confused and so amused by everything?

"Well then?" I finally lose my patience.

"Oh, right," she snaps out of the bubble she seems so wrapped up in. "I was thinking since I'm here, wouldn't I be like... a suspect for your murder?"

I clear my throat. "My murder?" Did I hear her right? Maybe it isn't too late to jump. I knew there was something wrong with her.

"You're jumping in front of me. Wouldn't people think I pushed you? I was trying to get some air, not to get framed for murder," she rambles.

Tyler quietly chuckles. "I mean... she has a point."

Somehow, I've never wanted him to be more real than this moment, so I could push him off the ledge instead. How is she speaking so normally to me?

"I'm sorry, do I know you?" Surely, I'm missing something here.

"No," she answers again bluntly.

"I'm confused. Why are you talking to me as if we're friends?" Doesn't she have more words in her vocabulary?

"Wouldn't this situation make us friends?"

"You're a freak." this time, I no longer feel awkward about getting off the ledge.

I have a feeling she might push me off instead. It's not too late to run. What normal person would say that? I need to think. Did she escape from somewhere? It would be my luck to end up with her. Instead, she steps forward, and I step backwards, preparing to run, and I forget the most important thing.

I'm standing on a bloody ledge. I quickly try to scramble over the wall, and instead, a sharp pain ignites within my body. It feels like my skin is on fire. I'm launched backwards as my body is thrown into a pile of bricks, a whirlwind of thoughts racing through my mind, none that I can make sense of.

A loud thud escapes beneath me as I hit the ground, my back

bruised across the floor. Am I bleeding? God, I think I'm bleeding. I slipped. I actually fucking slipped, forcing my right arm to steady as I attempt to sit up, pressing my hand against my head.

I feel so nauseous. It wasn't meant to be like this. It wasn't meant to end like this. I'm not meant to be here. Why can't anything go my way for fucking once in my life? My head is spinning, and I can't concentrate. A ringing noise is in my ears. I can leave. It's not like I'll ever see her again.

I don't know who she is. She doesn't know who I am. It's fine. "Okay... wow, that was—was something." Her shadow crouches, holding her knees as she tries to come up with some dumb shit to say next. Why is she still here? "Are you planning on staying on the floor all night, or...?"

She positions her body upright, kicking the heel of my shoe. Is she mentally okay, or am I missing something? "I would think you're unconscious, but I can literally hear you muttering to yourself. You're not being quiet." She coughs. "Have you forgotten how to stand? I can help you... Well, on second thought, I would offer, but I admit I'm slightly scared, seeing as you've spent nearly five minutes on the floor talking to yourself."

Oh, she's the scared one? In all fairness, I have been muttering to myself. I have to suck it up and look at her at some point.

I glance around, and Tyler is nowhere in sight. The man is dead, and even he couldn't take that embarrassment of a show.

"Aw, damn, have you got a concussion? I don't really know how to help you if you have," she admits, uneasiness in her tone.

Kill me. Please just shoot me.

This is mortifying, and I'm only making it worse. Not that

she's helping, lingering over me like the fucking Grim Reaper.

"Here." She puts her hand out.

"I got it. Leave me alone."

She tries again and ignores me.

"Are you deaf?" I question.

"No, but you look like you're in pain." She sounds sincere. I almost feel bad for being rude.

"Why do you think that is?" I snap.

"Yeah, because it's my fault you slipped and fell on your arse, isn't it?" she mocks. Never mind—just give me the gun. I'll shoot her instead. "Damn, you're really not a morning person, are you?" she says, as she attempts to step forward and steady me, but instead, her touch sets my body on fire.

"Are you kidding me?" I scowl.

"No, you're actually really moody," she says nonchalantly.

"I wasn't being—never mind."

It's official: she has no brain cells. Wincing as I attempt to lift myself off the ground, I accidentally let the strings of my hood get caught under my hand as I try to get up, choking myself.

I quickly let go, tumbling back down like a clown. I run my hand through my hair, brushing the curls out of my face to see if I'm bleeding, I don't think I am, but it feels like it.

How am I questioning her for lacking a brain when I just almost choked myself to death? I try again, using the wall to steady myself as I place my arm on the corner, gripping the brick wall and pulling myself back up. I let out a squirm as I lose my balance and lift myself again.

I hear her sigh as she watches me struggle, eventually snapping out of her daze to help me. I would appreciate it, but I think she's secretly trying to kill me. She pushes my arm out of the way, trying to stop her, and I stop refusing her as I begin trying to figure out if she's trying to break my arm or not.

She's holding it so tight it feels like it will snap. But I have too much pride to admit she's on the verge of possibly snapping my limbs rather than helping me. She notices my grimace, and I smile to hide the pain. I wish I was being dramatic.

"I'm sorry," she quickly apologises as she lets go.

She lets me fall on my ass once again. "I'm sorry!" She hurries forward to lift me yet again. Does this torture never end?

"Stop touching me, for God's sake," I heave.

"I thought I was—"

I cut her off. "I don't care what you thought you were doing. Leave me alone."

My blurred vision finally focuses, and I can see her clearly now.

I try to move, but it's not happening, as I contemplate throwing her over instead since Tyler isn't around. I fight the urge to smile at the thought of happily throwing her off a cliff. I grip the end of the cornered brick wall. Bits of rubble fall onto my face as I tighten my grip to pull myself up.

Focus. I'm unsure what I expected, but this isn't the case. Dusting the rubble off myself, she doesn't waste a second to not let her annoying voice echo. I shouldn't feel guilty for being mad. I have every right. But I know I shouldn't be taking it out on her.

But I don't want to let her think this could be the start of something. The way her eyes are studying intently, overseeing me as they glisten with the early morning sky. It sounds poetic as hell, but the hazel in her eyes absorbs the lights around us, getting brighter.

My stubble is softer than the wild strands of wire she calls hair. It's flying everywhere. She removes her hood and places the long hair locks caressing her face behind her ears. Her dark brown hair kind of reminds me of coffee. *I hate coffee.* Why do I feel like I'm meeting Robin Hood?

The hood reveal feels like something leading up to a finale, and you finally get to witness who the annoying fucker was all along. I peer down, and she's wearing slippers. It's cold, and she's wearing slippers, blue jeans, and a hoodie. I can't help but wonder how she hasn't slipped on her ass a thousand times.

"I was trying to help," she defends herself.

"What?"

Her voice interrupts my thoughts. "You're really rude, you know that?" This time, she really does look like she wants to kill me.

"Is there a reason you haven't left yet? If you didn't get the hint before, I find you irritating. Not only that, I don't remember asking for your help."

"I see." She scoffs. "You can be as rude as you like. It's not going to make me leave any faster. In fact, I'm really enjoying this." Amusement blares in her smile.

"You're insane."

There's an awkward silence, her eyes staring right into mine. Does she think this is love at first sight? Isn't this how most of those psycho movies start, where the girl becomes all obsessive, thinking they're in love, and tries to kill the poor guy? I'm going to die here.

I've watched too many horror movies and already know what will happen next. I can't even begin to imagine how ridiculous I look. I probably look so constipated right now.

"Can you not sense the tension?" I plainly state.

"I can, and I have to say you're not my type," her voice is flat.

"Right. Okay. I'm going to ignore that." I rub my temples. "Just leave." If she leaves, I can collapse in peace.

"No," she says, crossing her arms over her chest.

"No?" I question.

"Yes, no, I'm not leaving," she says sternly.

"So… yes, you are leaving?" I'm confused.

"I said no, I'm not leaving. Maybe you do have a concussion." Concern laces her voice.

"Then, I'll leave. Get out my way."

I don't have time for this or for people like her.

"Summers is my name—well, my last name." She stands in my way, dismissing my attempt to move past her.

My expression is blank. I'm trying not to lose myself in thought at the daydreams to stop fighting the urge to drop-kick her into a bin and lock the lid. If she thinks we'll get to know one another, she probably banged her head, too.

"I don't care about your name. Move." Why is she so persistent?

She moves closer, standing less than arm's length away from me. This woman really hasn't heard the term 'personal space'. This may be her ideal personal space, but I need more. Her expression softens, and I dread the next line from her lips, which recites every motivational quote she's seen on Google.

God, I need sleep.

"Get out of my way, please." I push her aside and shoot a glare that is anything less than welcoming. I didn't come here to make friends. I don't need to have a conversation with her, and she doesn't need to involve herself in my personal business.

It's quiet for a moment until she decides to open her mouth. "Look, I didn't mean to offend you or anything, but you don't need to be such a—"

I don't wait for her to finish. "A dick?" I let out a quiet laugh. "I really do." I don't like being like this, but I can't help it. It's better this way, anyway. Whoever she is, she's better off.

I should apologise, but I won't. I hear her let out a sigh, and I try to pretend I didn't hear it.

"I wasn't going to say you were a dick. You don't need to be so cruel to yourself." I stop and wonder if she's being serious.

I don't turn to face her. "What were you going to say then?"

I can hear the surprise in her voice, half expecting me to ignore her. I would have.

"I was actually going to say moron."

I can't stop my lips from forming somewhat of a smile. But I can't tell whether she is being sarcastic or not. Moron? Really?

"Summers, is it?" I question.

"Yes," she says. I can hear the hope in her voice.

"I hate to be the one to tell you this, but that's the stupidest name I've ever heard." It really is.

"And here I thought you were going to say something poetic. I was ready to have my heart melt." I don't try to hide my disdain as I turn to walk away. This time, I don't stop.

"So! I'll see you?" Hopefulness projects her voice.

"No. Have a good night, Summers. I mean this sincerely: I hope I never see you again."

Stepping inside, I pull the door shut. I realise I've probably locked her outside, but for now, that sounds like a problem she needs to figure out. I make my way to the door to my apartment and unlock it, letting myself in and inhaling the fumes from the paint I used a few days ago.

Dad wanted some life in the apartment, and painting was the way to go. Relief washes over me as everything is the same as I left it, and Dad's snores flood the apartment. Crashing on the bed, I let the warmth welcome me, I don't need to talk about what happened. I don't need to see her again.

I was ready. All my planning has gone to waste. Now, I have to find the time to do it again. I'm exhausted, and the last thing I want to worry about is Summers. She's the thorn I never knew existed. If prayers get answered somehow, I pray *I'll never see her again*.

CHAPTER THREE
ASHER

I had my shot and missed it, all because of a woman named after a season. I feel like I'm losing my mind. I keep thinking about what Tyler said about this being a sign, and I need some clarity. He keeps nagging that I'm one of those stubborn people who doesn't listen to anything or anyone.

I'm too wrapped up in my own ways to give anything else a second look. "I'm right, and you know I am." Tyler shrugs.

"Yes, because listening to you for the rest of my life seems like the obvious choice." I hate how whiny I sound. I'm making my head explode, constantly seeking reasons why everything is so bad.

Then I see Dad, how happy he is to see me, happy to see he's not completely alone. I don't want to think about how he'd be if I left. But of course, that's the one thing Tyler is insistent on reminding me of, trying to get me to imagine how I'd make him sink and no one would be here to stop it.

But I know he'd go off the rails for a bit, but he would never kill himself. He doesn't believe in that. He believes it's selfish to disappear on your own accord, how you only think about yourself and what's best for you. How the world is a beautiful place, and we just refuse to see it.

I used to believe the same thing; I could never comprehend the thought of never waking up. It feels like a lifetime ago I experienced that. Maybe he's right, we do refuse to see it. The wonders it could do for us if we let it. It's not that easy, though. It's never as simple as black and white.

I hadn't realised how angry I was at her. How she makes my blood boil and infuriates me. I haven't stopped seeing her. I went from being unaware of her existence to suddenly finding her everywhere. At least Tyler disappears at some point in the day, but it's like she's stalking me and driving me insane.

I can't escape the damn woman. At first, I thought I might have imagined her, and she isn't actually there, but I don't know why I would imagine someone so perky and annoying.

"What you thinking about?" Tyler asks, snapping my mind back to reality.

"What do you think?" I remark.

"Ah, the mind of Asher, so profoundly dull and yet entertaining simultaneously. I wish I had more than your thoughts of kicking her ass to keep me company because your presence isn't cutting it at the minute." I want to bang my head against a wall.

"Go for a walk," I say bluntly.

"Yes, because I could really do with the exercise, couldn't I?" he ridicules.

The one thing about this place is it's mostly green, a little town that's kind of in the middle of nowhere. Everyone sort of knows everyone. The lakes here are beautiful, somewhere you'd be satisfied if this was the last thing you saw before you closed your eyes for the final time. I live in Cove Haven. These days, I'm starting to wish it was bigger so I'd never have to see her face again.

"You could enjoy the rain?" The least I can do is irritate him if I can't get rid of him.

"Carry on, and I'm not going anywhere today." Tyler sneers, and we both know he's won. I sit upright, looking through the centre window. It's chucking it down with rain, and everyone is panicking, acting as if the rain will miraculously kill them, ducking down as if they could dodge the droplets pouring from the sky.

I'm drinking coffee. I hate the taste, but it keeps me awake, so you've got to do what you've got to do. I remember the first time Dad gave me coffee to stay awake because I'd been up all night. I couldn't sleep, and I had exams the next day. I was tempted to miss them and spend my days in bed.

He insisted I had it before kicking me out; he wouldn't, but it worked. I vomited, and he felt terrible and drove me to school. I was an hour early because he changed my clock so I wouldn't be late even though I was already running late. I used to think that one day, if I had children, I'd do the same for them.

It'd be funny watching them get pissed because they're consistently an hour early. There's this coffee place down the street from me. It's bright and kind of busy, but not always. It's white, and these huge glass windows replace the walls, allowing the part-time sun to shine in. The back walls are white.

I'm a regular customer, so I have my own seat at the back. They have seats you can sit four on, like your own sofa, with an unwanted invasion of your personal space. Obviously, there are tables in the middle, and the same seating is on the other side.

I suppose people who like to squeeze their asses together enjoy coming here. Especially big groups. One of them always fancies someone, so they use the excuse of the seating to really push themselves together, laughing and giggling about how they don't know what they're doing.

"When was the last time you shaved?" Tyler gawks. "You look homeless."

I fidget with my coffee and wonder whether he would feel it if I threw it on him. "And you look dead, but don't see me complaining."

The bell rings, and there's Nate. He looks towards his right as he smirks at the girls at the front.

I wonder if I would find him appealing if I was a woman. It's one of life's many unanswered questions. "What a weird thing to think about. How are you twenty-one?" Tyler scoots over next to me.

"Hey man, how are you doing?" he asks, sitting on the opposite side of me and rubbing his hands together to warm them up.

He sighs deeply as he slouches back and sinks into his seat. "He looks like he's got bigger. You should tell him he's doing a good job." He nudges me.

I shake him off, ignoring his live commentating in my ear. He says he works out but lifts weights for five minutes and calls it quits.

His blonde hair always seems lighter every time I see him. It's starting to hurt my eyes looking at it. I guess the one thing we have in common is he always has bruises on his knuckles. There's never a day he hasn't punched someone in the face.

He's pale but not so white that he looks about to pass out. He's wearing a brown oversized sweater with cream trousers, his usual combo.

"I'm good. I'd ask you, but I think I know the answer," I say, moving the half-filled coffee cup between my hands.

He laughs, not fazed by how his hair is starting to cover his eyes, letting his blonde strands cover his forehead. I wave my cup slightly. "Coffee?"

You would think with the amount I drink, I would be used to the taste by now. He doesn't waste a second as he takes it and pours it down his throat. "Fuck yes."

I asked if he wanted one, not to take mine. I guess that's what I get for being polite.

"He hasn't changed in the slightest." Tyler sits, staring at him fondly. Why is he pretending he hasn't been here all this time?

"I haven't seen you in a few days. Where have you been?" he asks, grabbing the napkin to wipe his lips.

"You know, here and there." *I tried to kill myself. It didn't work out, so now I'm here because some hippie decided to scare the shit out of me, so I kept falling on my ass continuously. Oh, and I'm pretty sure she's psychotic, and now she's stalking me.*

"Helping Dad out mostly, and work." I shrug as I shred the napkin in front of me.

"Hmm..." he says as if he already knows the truth behind my white lie. I didn't tell anyone I quit. At least, I think I didn't. I avoid making eye contact. I haven't thought of any answers to follow-up questions.

It hasn't been that long since I've been out of it. I still have enough money to last me a while. I've been saving my money since I was a kid, and I worked with cars, which came into use around here.

I wanted to be a psychologist first. It still makes me laugh thinking about it.

I didn't enjoy it anymore, so I went the opposite way. I got myself into cars and got pretty good at what I do. I was going to open my own place and be my own boss. I have enough money to, but shit happens, and life gets in the way of your goals sometimes. So, I quit. I guess I'm jobless.

It's my own doing. I can't be mad. I could always get back into it, but it wouldn't make sense right now.

"I'm proud of you for sticking with it," he says sincerely.

"Huh?" He catches me off guard.

He's proud of me?

"You know, switching careers like you did and being determined to get what you want. People say being stubborn could be one of your biggest flaws, but it's also one of your greatest traits. There's nothing you can't get with that head of yours." He leans forward to slap me playfully over the head and ruffles up my hair, sinking back into his seat. Somehow, that makes him laugh, and he looks at me like a proud father.

It's weird. He isn't normally like this.

"You good?" I say more concerned than meaning to. "Yeah? Just because I mentioned something decent about you, you think something's wrong with me? Shut up." He punches me on the shoulder, and I try not to show how it feels like my body is about to collapse in pieces.

That Grim Reaper really did a number on me. "We should do something." He tries not to seem so enthusiastic, but he looks like a child who's just been told they can pick out whatever they want. "I'm not going camping with you again," the words pour out before I have a chance to register them.

"Oh man… are you still pissed about that? It's been two years." He sounds like a kid.

"You weren't the one getting chased by coloured sheep when you wanted to take a piss."

He tries to hold in his laugh, but it fails. "I still remember how you ran and how you kept running in circles. You almost knocked yourself out."

I attempt to cut in, but as soon as he sees my lips move, he eagerly jumps back in. "Forget that!" he says, trying to contain his laughter. "Wait, wait." I couldn't move even if I wanted to. "Remember when you thought you were drowning, and this old man had to save you from splashing around in shallow water?"

I tried to block that memory out. I fell, and it looked deep, but it wasn't. I just needed to sit up and wouldn't have almost choked myself.

"Man, you really know how to make someone's day," he says as if he's watching a movie with all the best bits his life has thrown his way.

"Why did you wake up so early?" I cut in before he can reminisce more about my stupidity.

"It's almost 3 p.m.," he says.

"For you, that's early." I didn't think he knew what daylight looked like. It's like he can hear what I'm thinking, and he looks baffled. Or he's genuinely confused about his existence.

The guy has a memory of a goldfish. "Yeah, you're right, but I've got a date—kinda. I can't lie. I'm bored, so I'll see where this goes." We've been friends for a while, a long while, a good eight years, give or take.

The doors open, and the bell rings again. And there it is—the voice I dread the most.

Summers.

I just want one day, *just one*. I hang my head low and place it on the table. I'm tempted to bang my head against it. I'm not going to get rid of this girl, am I?

We've had extremely short conversations. She always shouts "Hey!" at me like I'm her best friend in the entire universe, and she hasn't seen me for decades. *Every single time.* I do my absolute best to ignore her, pretending I didn't see her, and it almost always seems to work.

I can't think of anything to get past her without being noticed, but nothing comes to mind. Maybe she won't notice me if I don't look at her. I could get up and leave.

"Yeah, because you're invisible, aren't you?" Tyler mocks.

"Why are you even still here? Don't you have an afterlife to get to?" I whisper.

"Did you say something?" Nate says, puzzled.

"No, I didn't say anything." I shake my head. I can't let Nate see her, but to leave, I'd have to walk past her, which would get her attention.

"I think Nate has already ruined your chances of not being noticed," Tyler says. I raise my eyebrows slightly for him to carry on.

"Idiot. Because she's looking right at you."

I immediately wish I wasn't so gullible as I lock my eyes with her. Could his date be Summers? My eyes dart between Nate and Summers, and I try not to look like I want to gouge my eyes out. My heart's racing, and my mouth is suddenly dry.

How do I warn him without her seeing? But on the other hand, this could be an opportunity. She's psychotic, and her focus would be off me, so instead, she'll stalk him. I take one last good look at him. Poor guy doesn't know what he's getting himself into. I ain't about to tell him.

"Why are you staring at me so intensely?" he questions.

Because it was nice knowing you, but better you than me.

"Nothing, I have nothing else to look at." Poor guy. "Just know you're a good man," I say, patting him on the shoulder.

"Thanks?"

I take a few moments of silence for him and the insanity he's getting himself into.

I wait for her to come near, but she doesn't come forward, and I take another look, and it's someone else. Thank God. I let out the breath I didn't realise I was holding in. The woman has officially made me lose it. I've never been this paranoid in my life.

I feel relief wash over me until I realise I'm still her target. I was ready to throw Nate at her. I already accepted his fate. I didn't see her leave, so she is still here. But where? This is my chance to leave, but if she isn't here for him, I will go, which means she could talk to Nate.

I do what I do best and try to position myself with my arm up, blocking my face and turning my body towards the wall to avoid her. Wherever she may be, I might be mistaken, and she hasn't noticed me. Perhaps Tyler's right—I am a little self-centred.

I don't know how she makes me behave like a complete child. I hate how childish her presence makes me. Why is my immediate reaction always to act like a fifth grader? Even they would cringe witnessing this ordeal.

"Hi!" She beams excitedly, rushing towards us, her hair wet from the rain.

I steal a glance towards the other side, moving my arm ever so slightly so I can see. I shouldn't have begun to wonder why I could hear her so clearly.

"Behind you, dumbass," Tyler says, his voice growing tired of my antics.

My train of thought goes off track when I notice her attire. "Yeah, because checking her out from head to toe won't give her the wrong idea," Tyler murmurs.

Hasn't she heard of a coat or something? Does this woman not like to invest in anything that she needs? She looks frozen, not to mention drenched.

Her gaze follows my eyes, intrigued, as a touch of pink starts overwhelming her cheeks, confused as to why I'm scanning her so openly. Isn't she cold? Her cough jerks my thoughts back to reality as I realise I haven't stopped staring at her. I honestly don't know what's wrong with me.

This isn't me. She constantly has me so on edge when I see her. I see my failure, and she knows it, too. It's a moment I didn't want to share, but in my darkest moment, this stranger was there, and now she's here. I don't know how to escape it. When I look at her now, she looks different from before.

Something about her seems warm, as if she's this light cloud trying to snuff out my darkness, but the severity of what she witnessed won't let it. *I won't let it.* Her hair looks tamed, but I think that's because it's wet. Her hair is light brown with strands of a chestnut red. Her skin is bronzed the way I remember it.

She has apple cheeks, the kind parents always talk about. When she smiles, they look defined, which is practically always the case. Her hair is loose, as her wavy strands try to come undone behind her ears, where she's tucked them away. I remember her eyes; they still look like they absorb all the light around her.

I feel like my life is one big series of unfortunate events, and everyone's laughing at me. It would make me feel better to find the director of my life and throw them off a cliff, too. I can't help but laugh at my own stupidity.

"Hey." Nate snaps his fingers in front of my face. "Did you hear anything I said?"

"No, sorry," I admit.

"Typical." He slouches and instantly sits up.

"Hi." A woman kisses Nate on the cheek as she slides down next to him, trying to shuffle him along.

"I'm moving, I'm moving," he says, reluctantly pulling himself along.

"Relax, you don't need to squash yourself against the wall," she says, resting her hand against his.

Guess this is his date. Three's a crowd. If anything would be a sign of my exit, this would be it. How can I leave when she's still here? They start kissing, and she giggles as he bites her neck.

"It's a bit creepy watching them, don't you think?" Does this man ever disappear?

"I didn't know you third wheel dates. Doesn't seem like you," she says quietly, trying to not make herself heard by anyone else besides me.

"Don't you know how unnatural your behaviour is? You know this counts as stalking, right?" I say, trying to state the obvious.

"Yes, because me walking into a coffee shop where you happen to be is stalking. Get over yourself." She scrunches up her face. She's lying. I flinch as she lets out a quiet giggle. She sounds like a horse. I don't think anyone's ready to hear that.

I'm glad the universe isn't choosing to punish me by making her laugh properly. I think my ears would bleed from the sound of it. "Then why are you here?" I say loud enough for her to hear. I don't want Nate to see her. But I feel like I'm whispering in Tyler's face.

"To get a coffee..." she says slowly, as if I wouldn't understand her if she said the sentence at a normal pace. I'm tempted to turn back around and ignore her, but it beats sitting with Nate. I could leave completely. Then I remember why that's not an option.

I ignore every instinct to escape whatever this is and do not sit by her, but Nate seems to be getting intense. I wouldn't be surprised if they said they were going to the bathroom. I turn back around, and she's still there. I don't know if that's a good or bad thing right now, but at least she isn't trying to introduce herself.

If I talk to her, she'll think we're friends. That's the last thing I want. Nate catches my glance and raises his brow, peering over the seat, but he gets distracted by the girl not appreciating his attention being drawn elsewhere.

"I'll leave you to it then, yeah?" I say, getting up from my seat.

"Nah, don't leave. We were going to head out, but thank you for the coffee." He smiles, and the girl moves out of the seat, standing as she waits for Nate to get up, too. "Catch you later," he says, nudging my shoulder. He waits for the girl to walk away first and follows behind her.

I get up anyway, but Summers quickly sits down opposite me, hope gleaming in her eyes that I might actually stay. I ignore her, and I can see the shimmer in her slowly fade as she plasters a weak smile. "Do you have to be so rude every time?" Tyler snipes.

He doesn't understand. She took my shot. She stuck her nose where it wasn't wanted, and now she's in my face constantly. We're not friends, but she doesn't seem to understand that.

"I don't know what you hope to gain by constantly doing this," I say, defeated, taking my seat back.

"I get that you think I'm odd, but I don't enjoy this any more than you do," she says, awkwardly shuffling in her seat.

"So why do it?" I'm not forcing her.

"Be nicer," Tyler urges.

"Can you shut up?" I snap.

Summers flinches. "I didn't say anything," she says, her voice weary and soft.

"No, I know, I was just... Never mind."

Tyler doesn't know when to quit it. I don't care about being nice to her, but why is he so intent on making me seem crazy in public? She swallows hard as she taps the table. "I'm not following you."

My face must be revealing what I haven't said aloud yet.

"I'm not," she insists.

"Alright, so what is it you're doing then? One minute, I have no idea who you are. The next, you're everywhere. You telling me I'm being paranoid?"

She lowers her gaze as her voice drops quietly. "Well, no, not entirely. This whole thing is blown out of proportion. I was initially, but then stopped. Because... well... it is weird. Plus, no offence to you, I can see you regard yourself very highly." Her hazel eyes peer up at me, contemplating whether she should carry on. "You're thinking I'm obsessed with you, but I do have a life. And despite what you think, it doesn't revolve around you."

I take my seat opposite her and lean my arms against the table in response, feeling more comfortable. "You live around here?" I question.

She takes a moment before sipping her drink. "You could say that," she says her words cautiously.

"Why are you saying it like that?" Why is she acting like I'm the creep?

If she lives around here, it would explain her stalking tendencies. "Do you want me to tell you the exact location of where I live? At least buy me dinner first," she teases.

"I'm never buying you dinner." I'd rather jump in front of a train.

"And they say romance is dead." Her expression is dissatisfied.

"This is anything but a blooming romance, more like how I met my stalker." What does she think this is?

"You really are a charmer, aren't you?" she says, taking a sip of her cup. How is she still drinking? "I hate coffee. I always drink hot chocolate," she says randomly.

"Okay? I don't care." Why am I still here? I could have left a long time ago. If anything, I'm giving her a reason to bother me more and mistake us for being friends. Summers taps my arm,

"Hello? You really daydream a lot, don't you? *Better daydreaming than looking at you.*

"Why are you covered in streaks of paint?"

She peers down at herself as if she forgot what she was wearing and shrugs as if being covered in paint is normal for her. "I was working on something, and I guess I forgot to change my clothes," she admits.

She's wearing a minty sage green overall embroidered with tiny flowers, a white shirt underneath, and white pumps. I'm surprised they're not covered in paint. "Do you not own anything more than black and grey?"

I don't actually think I do. Even my jeans are black or grey. She's strange, but in a vibrant way, not an 'I'm in a cult' way. I wouldn't be surprised if she was.

Nothing would surprise me at this point, especially with her strength. I'm still traumatised by her helping me. "Why are you here again? I don't remember you answering my question before."

She exhales deeply. "Because I like to drink hot chocolate. And I just happened to see you."

Summers' words roll off her tongue too easily, as if no one can see through her blatant lie. She sighs defeatedly. "I thought we went over this. Do I have to repeat everything to you?" Her stare is sharp enough to slice through me. "Listen, it is exactly that. It's a coincidence. It's not my fault if you think everything is one big conspiracy." She honestly drains me. I don't need to run yet; I need to clarify that I want nothing to do with her. If there ever was a right time, it's now.

"Well, since you're not stalking me, I'm going to leave, and you're not going to follow, understand?"

She looks as though she just ate something sour. "Do you want me to say woof or something? Why are you talking to me like you're training your dog?" she says, confused.

"Are you always like this?" My voice is unapologetic.

"I'm not going to follow you."

I don't say bye as I turn away from her and leave through the door.

I quickly glance towards her, and her eyes follow me. She looks exasperated. It's for her own good. She gives a wave, but I ignore her as I stare ahead. Now she'll know we're not friends and to leave me alone for good.

CHAPTER FOUR
SUMMERS

I can always hear him muttering what a psychopath I am, and although he thinks I relish in the reputation he's created, I couldn't be more mortified. It makes it hard not to want to run a mile in the opposite direction, and he always says it loud enough for me to hear. Or sometimes, straight at me with no care in the world.

I get his paranoia, but does he always need to be so rude? He must like me somewhere deep down, even if it is practically a dot. I'm rushed off my feet, and today seems surprisingly hectic for no reason.

"Hello...?" says Cyra, waving her hand in my face. "Why are you always so distracted?" she groans.

"Shush, I'm paying attention, I promise," I reassure her, playfully elbowing her as she purses her lips.

"Are you okay lately?"

"Yes, I promise you I'm fine." No one is more protective than her. "Is there a reason you keep watching the time?" I pull her along so we can start walking again.

At this rate, we're not moving anywhere. "My paintings, I'm on a deadline, and right now, I don't think I'm making it," I mumble.

"I thought you finished them," she says.

"I have, but you know, they don't feel complete, I feel like I'm missing something."

"You're doing great," Cyra says, practically a born cheerleader.

"I appreciate the optimism." I need a nap, a very long nap.

"I have to go, but I'll see you later." She quickly pecks my cheek. "See you."

She squeezes my hand and lets go, waving goodbye.

Cyra is my friend. I don't know why that's so awkward to admit, but she is, and I love her dearly. Since moving here, she has been the only person who has been nice to me. I wouldn't say she's my best friend. I don't do that type of thing, committing myself to people. Not because I'm scared but because I don't want to hold anybody to me. They may be important to me, but I don't label them as staying mine. It's a bit too intense to think about that when it comes to friendships, but I like to think things through.

It leads me to no disappointments, and I can live without any broken pieces I need to pick up. Disappointments are inevitable. But for now, I'm perfectly content with how things are, and I wouldn't change it for anything.

"Don't you watch where you're going?" a familiar voice invades my ears.

"Obviously not." I force a smile and peer up at Asher. "Now who's following who?"

He bites his cheek, his smirk betraying him to be seen. "Don't flatter yourself." He almost looks sick.

"If you say so." It's not hard to be offended. "I... Uh... I was hoping we could actually talk." I try not to let my nerves show.

"Because you actually asked me instead of following me, I'll talk." *Lucky me.*

"Great." I kiss my teeth.

We walk silently, and he grabs a table towards the back of the café, which seems normal.

This is a change from the regular insults, even if the silence is insufferable. He once told me that I make his eyes burn, and he's scared of going blind, so I should never stand directly within his eyesight for his health. That day, I 'accidentally' spilt my hot chocolate on him. "What do you want to talk about?"

He clears his throat. "I wanted to talk about this whole thing. We never really got a chance, and it's just past the stage of becoming awkward." I want him to conjure up another reputation besides being his renowned stalker.

"You can say that again." His blue eyes are so dull, beautiful but dull.

Even when the sun isn't out, his eyes are still glossy, but somehow, they still look so drained, as if there's a barricade behind them, and he's been trying a lifetime to get out. Some people believe there isn't a story behind the eyes, but I think there is. You just have to look a little deeply. "How are you?"

He looks caught off guard. "How am I?" he says, confused. "I'm managing, I guess?"

There's no life in him. I've never met anyone so faded before, so disinterested in his existence and everything around him.

Whenever I cross him, he doesn't smile—not the real kind, anyway. He's always vacant and irritable. "Are you going to tell anyone? About what you saw?"

"I wasn't planning to," I admit.

"Then why do you insist on making yourself a part of my life?" I've never met anyone more blunt.

"I'm not intentionally doing so. I'm just worried, I guess."

His expression shifts. "I don't need your pity. I need you to leave me be."

Why is he always like this? So defensive and on edge all the time? I can't help but notice now he's sitting in front of me, the strands of his hair covering his forehead.

His skin is fair, and his lips are not too big or small. They're pink and kind of red. They kind of remind me of raspberries, and they look sweet. His dark hair is dishevelled and wild, and he's so effortlessly handsome. "I never once said I pity you. Worrying and feeling pity are two different things. You need to stop assuming I'm this bad person. I haven't done anything to you."

He tugs on the sleeve of his grey shirt, wiping his hands on his black jeans. "You changed everything for me, and when I see you, I feel like my world is closing in on me. Like you're constantly mocking, flaunting what you took from me."

"I... don't know what to say." I didn't realise I was making him feel like that.

"I didn't think you would," he says. He didn't mean it maliciously.

"So... you don't like me?"

He looks at me as if I'm absurd for even having to ask. "If I'm honest, no, I don't."

"If you dislike me so much, why did you agree to talk?"

"Because you were right, we need to clear the air and talk. It's getting tiresome trying to avoid you everywhere now that you know for yourself you'll leave me alone. I thought I made that clear last time when I ignored you."

"I get it. You don't like me at all, but do you always have to be this way?" Doesn't he realise I have feelings too?

"I get what I say is hurtful, but I don't know how else to put it for you to understand." I suppose this is what I get for asking him to talk.

"I understand perfectly, but just because you're hurting doesn't mean you need to make everyone else around you hurt, too." I get that he doesn't want to talk and despises me. But he needs to learn that being hurt doesn't give him a pass to treat people like shit.

"Now you're offended, great."

He leans back as he opens and closes his fist, squeezing it tightly shut. I take a deep breath. "I'm not beneath you. You can't discard my feelings and make it seem like I'm the one with the issue."

He leans forward, his hands entwined. "That's precisely the reason I'm telling you. I don't have the energy nor time to consider your 'feelings', and honestly, I don't care. I didn't ask you to care. You decided to." He holds my gaze, and I momentarily break it as I look outside.

"Right. Is this who you are then?"

"Who am I?" His voice dares me to paint him how he wants to be seen.

I take a sip of my hot chocolate and wish I had drank it sooner, the coldness making it rubbery. "An asshole. That is who you are as a person. Everything you have to show for yourself, your upbringing, your demons, everything. All you have to show of the aftermath is to be an asshole. How original." I chuckle lightly. "Honestly, I get the cold front, I really do, but to be honest, it's really outdated, and this whole asshole facade isn't cutting it. Shit happens, and I'm not going to pretend to understand because I don't, but don't let this be the person you become, the person you've chosen to be." My words pour out more harshly than I mean.

"Are you done?" His voice is tired. "I didn't ask for a speech," he replies coldly.

"You think it's okay to talk to me like this?"

He opens his mouth to say something. "I'm not done," I cut in. "I don't care what you think of me or how I seem to be failing to meet your expectations of being human enough for you to talk to me like a person." His eyes grow wide, and a little smirk appears to be curving on his lips despite how hard he's trying not to let it.

"You're the most obnoxious, self-loathing man I've ever seen. Granted, you want nothing to do with me. Fair enough, but excuse me for wanting to ensure you don't do anything stupid."

He sighs deeply. "You don't see the problem here?" he says calmly.

"I do, it's you," I say without thinking.

Before I can take it back, his face darkens, his cheeks flaring.

"Yeah, and you want to make sure I'm 'fine' so you feel okay and can sleep at night. I didn't ask you to prioritise me like that. I didn't ask to become the centre of your fucking existence." He slams his fist on the table. I flinch, but I don't move to leave. "Don't use me to make you feel okay. You know how draining it is? To have to reassure someone else that you're okay so they don't feel like crap? I didn't ask you to care. I don't care about you, so why do you care about me? I'm not your responsibility; don't make me a burden." His voice is low, the anger fading from his tone.

"You're doing it again, and just so you know, you're not going to tell me what I can and can't do. I have every right, so I'm going to do as I please, and there's nothing you can do." I don't know if tears start welling up in my eyes or if my expression has changed dramatically because he changes his tone.

"Look, I'm sure you're nice, but I don't need you looking out for me," he says as if pleading.

"Are you done?" I say.

"Am I done?" he questions.

"Yes, with the whole speech about me being overbearing and whatever else. I get it; I can be annoying, but it is what it is. Nothing you say will make me disappear, no matter how hurtful you think you're being. I know you didn't ask, but I—"

He cuts me off. "I didn't ask to hear your speech, as motivational as it may be. I'm not interested. Just leave me alone." He begins to stand.

I don't know what I was expecting. I wipe a loose tear and avoid looking at him. He sits down and sighs. "This is what I wanted to avoid. We wouldn't be having this conversation if you weren't so persistent."

"Excuse me for caring," I growl.

"You're excused," he says.

"I don't chase people," I say, defending myself. He scrunches his eyebrows and makes a face to question everything I've been doing up until this point. "Okay, yes, I'm contradicting myself, but I'm not normally like this. I tend to keep this kind of stuff out of my life. You can't hate me for trying to see that you're okay," I say.

A moment passes and he coughs. "I wouldn't sit like that if I were you. That angle doesn't do you any favours," he says, concerned as he analyses my position. How does he manage to completely change the subject? I should probably expect more insults each time his mouth opens.

How does he manage to think of something new every time? Sitting up, I begin crossing my legs on the seat and holding them, shifting in my space and trying to get as comfortable as I can.

"You don't need to pretend you hate me," I say, following his gaze from the ceiling, and he looks at me dead in the face.

"Brave of you to assume I'm pretending," he says. Life isn't all bad. He just doesn't see it. He sees it for a moment, and it fades. He sees something, and his face lights up, and then the colour rushing into his skin vanishes as quickly as it came.

"I don't hate you" he shrugs.

"I don't get you," I say.

"I didn't ask you to try to understand me," he points out.

"Hear me out a little. If you really wanted to leave, you would have already. There's nothing I can really do to make you stay." His expression eases, and he sighs in defeat, sitting up properly and looking at me. "I'm listening," he says genuinely for the first time.

I try to hide the delight from showing and manage a small curve to feign a smile to say thanks. I could've sworn I saw him blush momentarily as he nods for me to carry on. "My point is you constantly look so hopeless, and you do everything to feed the despair you're feeling. You see an ounce of light and act like it's a disease. Did you ever think of maybe changing your outlook on things?" I don't know what mark I'm overstepping far, but judging by his expression, I know I'm not treading too far.

"I tried, but it didn't work," he says quietly.

"Did you think it might be because you never give it a chance to?" I wonder when I will hit his nerve, but he seems surprisingly calm. He will probably snap at some point. I feel like he's forgotten for a moment how much he can't stand me.

"I don't expect you to understand, but sometimes you have too many pieces that don't work anymore. You're too broken to be fixed." He takes a breath, anxiously fidgeting with his fingers. "The light?" he continues, "sometimes you have one too many cracks that just shine through you so that even the darkness isn't fazed any more. It doesn't break like it used to. Instead, it grows stronger, and you are the only thing that keeps it alive. Understand?" he says.

I didn't expect him to be so vulnerable. I try to tame my eagerness to not overwhelm him with so many questions at once. I didn't think I would get this chance.

Now that I've got it, I'm scared he will realise his vulnerability and switch off. Or maybe I may be overthinking it, and he doesn't care because he knows I won't share his secrets deep down. "I understand, but I don't think you're unfixable."

He laughs. "You don't know me. Believe me, I've tried," he scoffs.

"I believe that." I smile. "Just not hard enough," I say softly.

"Look, the point is, you don't need to worry about me." I can tell he's trying to be nice.

"You took the opportunity," I say quietly, "to kill yourself?"

I surprise myself with my own bluntness.

"You don't need to word it like that, but yes. I was ready, I had it planned, and it was the perfect night," he says. I wonder if he can hear himself talk.

"I'm going to pretend I understand what you're saying, but if you have to plan to do it, don't you think it's a sign to say maybe you shouldn't?" I question.

"Not really," he disagrees, "I think you should have an input on the way you leave." He's talking as if this is an everyday conversation.

"So you chose the messiest way you could think of?" I would hate to leave like that. I imagine the fear of falling.

"What if, halfway, you changed your mind?" I ask.

"I wouldn't have," he says confidently.

"But what if you had?"

He pauses for a moment. "I guess I'd be stuck, wouldn't I?" he finishes. "Can I go now? Or are you going to follow me?" He shifts awkwardly, waiting to see if I follow him.

"You can go. I won't follow."

It's embarrassing. I have to reassure him, but I mean it this time—for now, anyway. He clears his throat and hesitantly turns towards me.

"Don't care too much, Summers. In the end, it'll only destroy you," he warns.

"Should I be worried about you destroying me?" I ask, pondering on his last words.

"I don't want you to be hurt when this doesn't play out how you think it will." Wariness lingers in his words.

"I trust you," I say.

"Don't."

"Why?" I ask.

"I don't even know you. Besides, I can't even trust myself. How are you meant to trust me?" He has me stumped for a moment, and he knows.

"I don't know," I answer sincerely. "Bring me your worst. I'll prove to you there's a light you're just not seeing. It might not be the brightest right now, but one day it will be, and you'll have no choice but to accept it."

He hesitates for a second.

"You really have no idea how this is going to play out. How are you so sure I won't break you?" his tone is curious.

"It's my choice, and besides, it's inevitable to get hurt, but to break me? Give me some credit. There's nothing that could break me, especially not you." No one should have that kind of power over you, especially a man. "I won't bother you so much, and I promise not to 'follow you'," I say sarcastically. "We're friends, whether you like it or not. I think you like me a little more than you let on." I poke.

"Your friend? Really, Summers?" he mocks.

"Yes, really, don't sweat it. You'll warm up to me soon, and eventually, it won't bother you who I am to you," I say confidently.

"You confuse me."

I seem to have that effect on a lot of people these days. "I know." I giggle. This feels normal, like how we should be.

"Well, on that note, I'm sorry for how I've been speaking to you." He looks away, ashamed. "And…" He pauses.

"And…?" I question. He sucks in a breath.

"If you're going to keep bothering me, you should at least know my name. I'm Asher." I'm going to pretend I don't know his name. I've heard it plenty of times.

"I can call you Ash." I beam.

"No," he answers bluntly.

"Baby steps it is."

I know he likes me. He genuinely smiles, a small glimpse of hope appearing in his eyes as he takes his leave. He pauses momentarily, opening his mouth to say something but deciding against it.

"Yes?"

His eyes really do pull you in. "Nothing. Just see you around… Summers."

He walks away before I can say anything. I try to ignore the butterflies forming, and my eyes follow him. He makes his way out the door and puts his hands in his pockets, giving in to his temptation to steal a glance through the window.

I return his gaze as the colour appears on his cheeks, and he looks away and remains that way until he's out of sight. I did it. I squeal like a kid who just got given a fountain of sweets. This is my breakthrough. He *likes* me. No matter what he says, no one is beyond repair. I have to make him see that, and *I will*, no matter what.

I'm not making him a project. I'm not using him, but he deserves, like everyone else, to know there is more beyond his darkness.

I'll make him see what it means to live.

CHAPTER FIVE
ASHER

"So..." Tyler awkwardly wavers on the heel of his trainers, biting the inside of his cheek, grimacing as he reads my thoughts on ways he could meet other unfortunate ends.

"So? Again, and I really feel like a broken record this time, but don't you have anything better to do?"

"That's a new thing. You can sense my presence now, can you?" Summers rolls her eyes, tucking her hands deep into her white coat. Clearing my throat, I kiss my teeth, cursing my poor timing and a reminder Tyler isn't real. I really need to stop talking to myself in public. No wonder she cares so much about my well-being.

I let out a nervous laugh, and she eyes me suspiciously, probably counting her lucky stars that she's run into me in daylight with other witnesses to vouch for my psychotic breakdown.

"Yep. What can I say? Your presence really disturbs me," I murmur flatly.

Tyler leans forward. "Smooth," he mocks as he watches me squirm. I shoot him a dagger, wishing he had an off switch.

Summers follows my eyeline. "I kind of feel less special. I

thought your daggers were reserved for me. I didn't think I would have nature to compete with."

"Believe me, no one comes close to making my blood boil like you." I smile, returning her gaze.

"How sweet." She half-heartedly curls her lips. She debates whether to carry on walking but uncomfortably hovers.

"I thought we agreed you would stop following me?"

Tyler scoffs. "You should try humbling yourself," he mumbles. I still don't know why he hasn't disappeared.

"What can I say? How can I not stalk the light of my life? The bane of my existence?" She tucks the strands behind her ears as the wind wrestles to make her messy bun come undone. How does her skin maintain such a honey hue in the winter?

"I'm joking," she blurts. "It's not my fault I go for a walk, and you happen to be in my way. Even stalkers have lives, too." She turns to walk away, no longer being able to take the awkward tension threatening to suffocate us. Even Tyler is pretending to gasp for air.

"Wait." My words pour out quicker than I can cover my mouth. Summers hesitantly stops, turning around as she watches me carefully.

"Yes...?" she questions cautiously.

"Can I walk with you?" I surprise myself when the words effortlessly escape my lips.

"Okay?"

I run beside her to join her. If I'm going to be running into her as much as I am, I have to at least save myself from being an embarrassment every time. It's exhausting trying to make yourself unseen in case I run into her, which seems to be every day at least once a day at this point.

I still dislike her more than words can say, but if I'm alive, the least I can do is make my days somewhat more manageable.

"I'm proud of you. Who knew baby Asher knew how to make friends?" Tyler nudges me jokingly.

"Shut up." I try to fight the laugh, trying to erupt.

"I didn't say anything," Summers snipes.

"I know." I'm not looking at her, feeling her gaze scrutinise my sanity. Not that I blame her.

"Right," she says, low, unsatisfied with her analysis. We both walk in silence as the loud horns blare, and muffled conversations are cut short with our passing steps.

"I want to apologise," I begin, noticing her tense. "I shouldn't have spoken to you like that, but in my defence, I see you more than I see my dad these days, and it can get a little overwhelming." I nervously chuckle, unsure what to do with myself, sliding my hands down my jeans and trying to find my pockets.

"Where is Asher, and what have you done with him?" she jokes, staring ahead, not meeting my gaze. It's good. I don't want her to look at me. This is already weird enough as it is.

"I'm just saying, that's not me, and I don't want to be that person that makes people feel like shit just because I do. So, I'm sorry." Silence falls between us, and it doesn't feel unnatural for once.

I may dislike her somewhat, but that doesn't give me the right to make her cry. She almost loses her footing for a second, tripping over nothing, and I try to bury the laugh, trying to erupt.

"That's the most tragic thing I've seen in a while, and that's coming from me," she says as she scowls, her cheeks reddened.

"Yeah, yeah." I peer down, watching her steps, careful not to trip over the air. Her eyes catch the silver glint wrapped around my finger.

"You married or something?" Summer questions, not taking her eyes off the silver band on my finger.

"No." I peer at my hand, stretching my fingers. I don't know why I don't invest in gloves.

"It's on your ring finger," she simply says, stating the obvious.

"I see that." I laugh to myself at the thought of the possibility of being married. I wonder if I'll have kids. To be honest, I want a few. A house always full and warm, somewhere distant but homely. I cough, clearing my throat. There's no point in pondering a life that won't exist.

"Well?" she pushes, still not bringing her gaze up.

"You're very pushy, aren't you? It's not a quality I like." I don't wait for her to answer. "It's not an answer you'll be satisfied with," I begin. "But first, tell me why you wear that necklace." I point towards the silver butterfly she's fiddling with. I can't really see it well. She always seems to be grasping it.

"I asked you first," she says, annoyed.

"Well, what can I say? I'm not really a stickler for the rules," I mock.

"Don't make me sick," she scoffs, trying to tame her laugh.

"Well?" copying her.

"It was a gift, and I haven't taken it off since. I've always loved butterflies, but this really cemented it for me," Summers answers, short and sweet.

"I suppose it's my turn now." Why does this feel like twenty-one questions? "I... uh, don't actually know why I wear it. I just know I've kind of always had it. It feels weird not to wear it. It's hard to explain because I'm unsure why I'm so attached to it. But I am."

"I don't mind that answer." She finally lifts her gaze.

I wince as I waver for a moment, holding my leg. I hate that my leg does this to me sometimes. It always seems to flare up more these days. I feel like I can't do anything without the pain reminding me of my shitless failed attempts, which I'm assuming is the reason for it.

I've never really known. It's always kind of been there. I glance up momentarily, and the pain doesn't seem so strong, the amber pooling around her irises. Why am I noticing her eyes? The colour. Why do I care? Averting my gaze, I try to ignore the hues dancing around her eyes, the fusion of green and chestnut.

"I... uh... need to leave. See you around. Or not. I don't care," I stammer, leaving her baffled before she can protest.

I push open the door to my front door and sigh in relief. It's been a week. I haven't seen her. But I don't know why I keep going outside for long, stupid walks when I only complain about how freezing I am.

"Dad?" I call out, but he doesn't answer. I walk past his room and notice his door slightly ajar, a vodka bottle sitting on top of his dresser. My breathing hitches, and I try to shake away the sinking in my stomach.

Try to ignore the heavy lurch of my heart, trying to find a way out of my ribcage. I grab the bottle before I can stop myself and put it on the coffee table. He's drinking again? Since when? He was doing so well. I wipe my hands against my jeans, but they're still clammy.

"Buddy, you're back." My dad beams brightly. My eyes start to burn a little, and I keep my head low. I can't say anything. I don't know what to say. I push the bottle forward and bring my gaze up to meet his.

"Ah. I see," he says casually, sitting beside me on the sofa. "I ran into your mum, and I brought this. It was a reflex, but then"—he picks up the bottle, tilting it down, watching the vodka swirl inside—"I brought it home, and you know what happened?" he asks me. I manage a slight shake.

"I realised I didn't need it. I had it, and I didn't want to drink it. I didn't want to drown my sorrows. I kept hiding from it for so long, thinking I wasn't strong enough, cancelling plans with friends and dates, and I thought if I saw a drink, I wouldn't be able to put it down, but I did. I brought it, and I didn't want it." He puts the bottle down and puts his arm around my shoulders. His voice is soft.

"Thank you for being my rock, Ash, for being my son. Believing in me when I didn't believe in myself and standing by me. I love you son." He ruffles my hair. I swat his hand away, letting out a breath I didn't realise I was holding. I wipe my eyes with my arm and give him a hug.

"Anyway, I need to go. I'll be back later." He glances at his watch and pushes himself up. Putting a russet trench coat on as he hurries to leave. The door locks behind me, and I run to the bathroom. I retch, and Tyler watches me, sitting beside me as my guts threaten to spill out.

I grab some tissue and wipe my mouth, throwing it in the toilet and flushing the chain. I force myself to stand, washing my hands.

"If your dad can do it, why can't you?"

I scrub my hands harder, the water becoming hotter. "Tyler, please." I try to keep my voice steady. "Give it a rest for once." I splash the water on my face and let the heat attempt to shred my shame away.

"You make me laugh, you know that?" Tyler begins ignoring my plea. "You think you're all alone, and no one on this earth could possibly understand you." His laugh is disbelieving and cynical. "You have your dad. Do you think your dad wouldn't understand? You really are your own worst enemy."

"You see that feeling? The way you saw the bottle and you panicked? The way you started questioning everything? Yourself? Why nothing is good enough? Why you aren't good enough for him? Is that what you want for him when he finds your body?"

Squeezing my eyes shut, I try to make him go away, but when I open my eyes, red and burning, but he's still watching. Ignoring him, I go to the living room. Grabbing the vodka, I pour it down the drain and throw the empty bottle in the trash.

Perhaps if I ignore him, he'll disappear. I make my way to my room and slam my door shut.

"You still mad at me?" Tyler questions, his voice quiet. I ignore the twinge of guilt gnawing at my chest as I listen to the pelts of rain against my window.

"No." I sigh. I can't be mad because he tries to make me see past my ignorance. I begin to close my curtains, but I notice a familiar smile. The beating of my heart slows down a little. I unconsciously reach for my chest as my heart beats aren't as fast. My breaths feel collected, calm.

Normal.

Why is it normal?

I watch Summers walk with no care in the world. The breeze carries the curls of her soft chestnut hair draped over her shoulders. How does she do that, somehow bringing colour to the dullness that seems desperate to consume her? Tyler watches intently, following my gaze as he watches the world rush in warmth for a moment. I watch as she trips over a piece of broken concrete; this time, I don't fight the laugh. I run my hands through my hair, noticing my smirk in the corner of my mirror. I quickly close the curtains.

"Real mature," Tyler ridicules.

"Shut up," I muster.

What the hell is happening to me?

CHAPTER SIX
ASHER

The air feels more crisp lately. I love the cold, but I always feel frozen, even for me. I've been giving her a hard time, but she means well. I haven't spoken to her. I keep expecting to feel relieved, some newfound lease of life, but I don't.

"And, of course, you're blaming her." Tyler shrugs.

"I didn't say anything," I moan.

"You didn't have to, but you miss her, don't you?" His brown eyes gloat.

"No," I'm not arguing with myself.

"Yeah, right. Your long face says it all." He laughs. "Plus, you realise you can't lie to me, right? I feel the way your heartbeat flutters a little slower when I mention her name. The way you immediately picture her smile and stay in your daze for a little longer."

"You don't know what you're talking about. You're just making shit up." I try to keep my mind blank and not entertain him. I hate that he can see everything. It's not what he thinks.

"It's exactly what I think. It's amazing how much you can lie to yourself," Tyler taunts.

"Shut up," I mutter under my breath. How am I getting annoyed with a person that doesn't exist? It must have to do with being used to seeing her, and I expected her to appear, whether I wanted her to or not. It must be that proximity thing. When you're around a person a lot, you tend to like them. It doesn't mean anything. Not everything needs to be a big deal.

I didn't realise she had become a part of my routine, and now, my days feel incomplete. I don't mean that romantically. We don't talk, and if we did, it was me telling her I wanted nothing to do with her. I should be glad. I hate that I'm not. It's *weird* that I'm not.

"It's not weird to have feelings. It's perfectly normal," Tyler interjects my thoughts.

"I don't have feelings, for the hundredth time. I maybe got kind of used to her, and it feels a little weird without her, I suppose. I don't like how I spoke to her, though." Embarrassment creeps in, making my stomach sink.

I hate that I spoke to her like that. She was right. She didn't deserve the way I spoke to her. I was an ass. I even made her cry. She didn't deserve that. "You can say that again," Tyler murmurs.

"Yeah, alright. I said sorry." *Not that it makes it any better.* I hug my pillow across my chest. "We having a girl's night?" Tyler bounces on the bed.

"Get lost." I slam the pillow in his face.

"I thought I'd find you here." Nate casually throws his brown jacket across my room and slides down into the chair by my desk.

"I wasn't exactly hiding." I wait for him to say something to see if he caught me talking to Tyler. But he doesn't, and I ease.

Or he thinks I talk to myself, which is less crazy. "Ha-ha, I don't appreciate your remarks so soon. Give me a few minutes to settle." He throws his legs on top of the desk. "I just had the worst date," Nate exclaims.

"Is that even a thing for him?" Tyler whispers, and I bite my cheek to stop myself from laughing.

"Yeah, no, really," he answers as if he can hear Tyler. "I thought I was texting this girl for a while. I met her, and I thought I'd slept with her before, but it turns out it was her sister I had a thing with. I didn't bother apologising. I just left. Nothing could save me after her sister recognised me."

He pauses. "I don't even know why she turned up. It probably would have been alright if she wasn't there," he moans.

He genuinely sounds gutted, which is new for him. I'll give him ten minutes before his fascination turns to someone else. "Now tell me, what's going on with you?" he pries.

"Nothing new."

He looks annoyed. I can't say that I blame him. I'm so vague. I'd beat the shit out of me if I met me.

"You seem different," he says, scratching his neck. He only does that when he's nervous. "Has something happened?" he leans closer, ready to see through my lies.

"I met this girl…"

His face lights up, and he's trying his hardest not to get excited. I already regret this. It's not like I can take back my sentence now.

"Go on," he encourages, taking his legs off the desk and sitting upright.

"Why are you looking at me like we're in a counselling session?"

He laughs. "Sorry, I just haven't heard you mention a girl for a long while. Who is she?" he says, intrigued.

"Her name is Summers, apparently. I only know her last name. She won't tell me her first name yet. I think she's saving that for a special occasion." I laugh at the stupidity of that logic, but it makes sense to her.

I wouldn't be surprised if that's what she plans to do. Everything seems so grand to her.

"You didn't ask her what her name was?"

After the ledge incident, I didn't bother to find out her first name. I think finding out her name would make all of this real.

"I didn't think I needed to... I wasn't planning on getting to know her." I thought, *the less I know about her, the better.*

"And have you?"

"Have I what?" I say.

"Got to know her?"

I swallow as I think about every instance I've had with her, and none of our interactions have been pleasant, but that's because of me.

"At least you admit that," Tyler praises, and I wish he would stop his new hobby of commentating on my life.

"I haven't exactly been the most welcoming to her," I admit, and I can see him holding back from shaking me and throwing me against a wall.

"Why do you self-sabotage? If you like her, what's the issue?"

"I never said I liked her... like that, anyway," I remind him.

"If you didn't, you wouldn't be telling me about her."

Since when did he start acting like Dr Phil?

"I'm hungry." I search for my phone to order from somewhere. "You want anything?" I offer.

"Stop trying to change the subject and tell me," Nate says, grabbing the phone out of my hand.

"Come on, man. I'm starving." I'd snatch the phone back if I could be bothered. I want a food coma and to go to sleep. "You seem to like her," he says.

"I don't know... she's.... I'd say unusual, very unusual, but she isn't afraid to be herself. I suppose I like that about her." I laugh to myself, remembering her clumsiness. I don't think I've met anyone who falls all over the place more than her. I admit, it's kind of cute. She still looks like a moron, though.

"How'd you meet her? Better yet, when can I meet her?" he asks.

"Why?" I question,

"Don't you think I want to meet the girl who's got you laughing to yourself? You haven't been yourself for a long time. Even when we hang out, you're barely even here. So, if you've met a person who has you laughing the way you are, I want to meet her," he says.

I didn't realise I was laughing to myself. I didn't think I did that. "I don't think so. If anything, you would probably scare her, and it doesn't matter. She thinks I hate her," I admit.

"Why?"

"I sort of told her I do," I say quietly, low enough that I hope he doesn't hear me. It sounds dumb saying that out loud, properly. If he didn't want to launch me out the window before, he definitely does now. He growls, launching his trainer at my head. That hurts less than I thought it would. It beats flying out the window.

"Because that's exactly what you do when you meet someone you like." He frustratedly throws a pen he finds on my desk at me and somehow misses that, too. "What are you, five? Come on, man." I can't exactly tell him how we met. He would kill me, forget me killing myself.

"I'm not what she deserves..." I confess. My heart sinks a little. I forgot it can do that. "She's this... well, I don't really know how to describe her, but she's different. It sounds cliché as hell, but she is."

"Why her?"

"What?" This is really turning into a girl's night.

"You never do this. Me? Sure. But you? Never. What did she do?" *She made me feel something I thought I was too broken to feel.* I don't know what it is about her, but I wouldn't mind getting to know her better. I've made it out like I hate her. At one point, I thought I did.

I find her annoying, that's true, but I don't hate her. I don't even hate my mother. How can I hate her for trying to make sure I'm okay? I can't be mad at that. Lately, I've seen her, but I haven't approached her. I find myself wondering where she is or what she's doing.

I hadn't realised it before until I found myself doing it, but I watch her on the off chance. Then I start to find every excuse to go outside, and I feel a little gutted if I don't happen to see her that day.

I always make sure to hide myself well so she won't notice. I think I'm beginning to become addicted to the way everything seems a little less lifeless when she appears to be around.

I don't know when it started or how things began moving slowly. It's terrifying. It's fast, and I don't know why it's happening.

But she's so oblivious I could be standing before her and still wouldn't notice unless she's seeking me out. I notice everything, from her smile to how she takes everything. The lust for life she has. I find her taking photos of everything.

Summers can go past a tree with hardly any leaves on, spot a nest, and it'll make her day. She could be walking and tripping over her own foot. It makes me laugh so much. But I also question her safety and stability.

I didn't know I could still laugh like that. It still feels unnatural when I find myself laughing, knowing that sound is coming from me, that my stomach is hurting from barely being able to breathe because I'm laughing so much. I get strangers passing by giving me such odd glances.

I'm stood just out of sight, laughing. I didn't know I could laugh that much until I met her. She doesn't even realise what she's doing to me. *I don't know what she's doing to me.* I don't know what goes on in her mind, how she's so easily pleased and content, but I wish it was contagious.

The way she strides, with no care in the world, dresses so bizarrely, the way she stops and notices her reflection and beams in excitement, and how one of her curls has come out perfectly. Her aura is something I've never experienced before. I can't explain it and find it hard to figure out what I mean.

I know one thing: I can't get enough of it. Then it hits me, where I know her from. That Polaroid I kept. It's her—her smile. Of course, that light belongs to her. I still have it. I don't know why, but I can't let it go. Maybe she can help me find something to hold onto. Help me experience that kind of joy she felt, she feels.

"Hey, Romeo," Nate interrupts the silence, "you need to act like a man and admit you like the woman."

He's right. I know he's right. Knowing me, though, I'll screw it up even without meaning to, and how is she meant to take me seriously after all the shit I've said to her? She'll laugh in my face, or she'll probably run away thinking I've gone insane. She won't understand what's happening. I don't even know what's happening.

"What if she doesn't like me? I don't know if I can tell her without making it feel like a grand declaration. I don't want to tell her anything because I don't want to commit."

"You don't want rejection?"

Nothing I'm saying feels real right now. I hate how scared I sound. "I didn't say that," I utter.

"You didn't have to. You live one life, man. What's the point of dwelling on whether she'll like you back? Life is too short for that. Say what you feel and do it with no regrets. If it works out the way you want, great. If not, that's okay. It's life, don't take it so seriously. It's okay to have moments like these. It's okay to like someone a lot. Just tell her."

No, forget it. Burying my insecurities screaming to surface, I will tell her. She'll probably think I'm joking, but no, I'll tell her the next time I see her. Then, when the time is right, I plan on returning the Polaroid to her.

It's now gone past the point where I can casually return it to her without making it weird. Plus, with all the follow-up questions, she'll probably think I've been stalking her instead. I guess I should hold onto it a bit longer.

"I'll tell her." What's the worst thing that could happen?

I'm a ticking time bomb. The only reason I think I'm here for now is because of her. I'm curious about her. There's no harm in that.

"Really?" Nate says, unconvinced. He thinks I'm not going to do it. I don't blame him.

"Believe me, I'll tell her."

He studies me. "Good."

"Good," I agree.

CHAPTER SEVEN
SUMMERS

I've used my time wisely, I think. I've finished the painting I spent ages procrastinating on. Normally, when I start a project, I'm set for days, and that's all I do, but then Asher came along, and all my focus was on him. Even when he's not around, I'm wondering what he's doing, and it's so distracting I can't focus.

I'm not counting down the days I haven't seen him, but it feels like years, even though it's only been weeks. Is that even normal? I'm trying to make this whole situation normal, but it's anything but that. I've given him the space he wanted. I admit I miss getting under his skin. It kind of made my day.

This will show him I can listen and that I'm not as insufferable as he thinks I am. He needs to realise he's not exactly a ray of sunshine himself, but I hate knowing how he is and how he feels, and I feel so hopeless not being able to do anything about it.

I can't prove his point, though. I can't let him take over my life and show him his odd concept about caring is true. Letting someone in is okay, even if he doesn't think so. I put my groceries on the kitchen table and sort through it. I thought I'd try being healthier.

Cyra always goes about eating clean and tries to inspire me by telling me how great and healthy she feels. I think she's been hinting I've put on weight, and I think I have, but if anything, I think I look curvier. I'm not overweight, but I'm not under either. I guess I'm just right, and curves never hurt anyone. I like them, so that's all that matters.

"You seem busy these days," Cyra says.

I know she's suspicious, but when isn't she?

"Well, I've been working on my project. I'm bound to be a little busy." I try not to give into her trap. I'll say something I'm not supposed to, and she's got me.

"Hmm, if you say so…" Her nude lips curve as she grabs an apple from the fruit bowl that I forgot I owned. "You mean chasing someone," she says.

And there it is. She knows, or I'm getting ahead of myself. She hasn't even been here to notice anything out of the ordinary. "You know I love you," she says, twirling her auburn hair, long and thick.

Her dark eyes lose a glint of light for a moment, a black pool warning me to get my story straight if I'm going to say anything else.

"You got anything planned for tomorrow?" That is such a lame attempt to change the subject. "This isn't like you. That is all I'm saying." She keeps her focus on me, her brown eyes alight with scepticism.

"You know you look really pretty today." I attempt flattery and hope this goes away. But I'm not lying—she always looks beautiful.

"I know," she dismisses my attempt and shoots me a dagger.

I stop what I'm doing and pay full attention this time. "I know, I know." I sigh. I sit on the sofa and lie down. "I'll pay more attention. I've been a little distracted." I may not be telling the whole truth, but I'm not lying either.

"Yeah, I see that." She walks over, lunges on the sofa, and sits on the end, throwing my legs off.

"Easy." I catch my balance, and I almost plummet to the floor when she throws my legs off.

She bites her apple and laughs. "Are you going to tell me what's been distracting you?" I can already tell how this conversation is going to end, and I don't want to stress her out.

"Should I?" I raise my brow.

Obviously, I'm going to tell her. If I don't tell her, who am I going to tell? But I don't think I'm ready to share the whole truth.

"Oh, come on. I need details." She shakes me, nagging dramatically.

"Okay, okay. Well, you see, once upon a time—"

I catch the soft pink cushion she throws at me. "Stop playing," she whines.

"Gosh, okay. Well, I haven't met anybody, if that's what you think. I've been thinking more lately." Again, it was not exactly another lie.

"About…?" her tone was more serious.

"Where everything is going to lead us."

"But why?" she says, the suspicion in her tone snaps me out of my daze.

"I just am. There's no harm. I want us to do well, really well," I admit.

"I believe that, but that's not all there is."

"What do you mean?" Has she seen me? I've been careful, so she hasn't.

"He's back."

The silence is deafening. Can she hear the thundering of my chest, the slam against my ribcage? "I don't know what you're talking about," I quickly say. She knows, *damn, she knows.*

"You're willing to do it again?"

This is exactly what I wanted to avoid. "You mean well, and I love you for it. But it's not the same," I confess.

"Maybe not, but you are exactly the same. You've forgiven him?"

I understand her worries, but I'm fully capable of making decisions. "Can we not? Please?" I can't do this again. She doesn't want to see me hurt, and I get that, but she can't talk me out of this.

"You can't help everyone, especially those who don't want to be helped." Her voice is soft and urging.

"Please, just leave it. We both know it doesn't matter what you say. I'm not going to give up." If anyone knows that better than me, it's her.

"There's having hope, then there's being delusional." Her cheeks flush a burning red.

"Remember what happened last time? It fucked you up. Why are you doing it again? Is he worth losing yourself over?" I know she wants to scream. She's trying to keep herself from pulling her hair out. I know what I'm getting myself into.

Her dark eyes try to find anything to grasp onto to make me

see things like she does, but she doesn't. The silence that lurks after her sentence seems like it lasts a lifetime.

"I'm not giving up, and you can't make me," I finally say, my voice secure. There's nothing she can say or do that will sway me. Nothing is going to make me quit.

"I'm sorry. You know I—"

I begin to say, "Don't be sorry. It's not your fault. As I said, not everyone can be helped. Sometimes their urge is too strong that nothing you do is good enough, and if they don't want to be helped, they won't be despite doing everything."

Cyra lets out a heavy sigh as she brushes her fingers through her hair, fidgeting with the end strands. "You're going to end up getting yourself hurt in the process."

"Things change, people change." I don't know how else to say it without sounding like the bad guy."

In all the time I've known Cyra, she's always been like this. Cyra doesn't like to think in the moment. In whatever she does, with whoever she meets, she always looks ahead. She sees whether it's worth getting to know them and whether they're worth stressing over. Whether they'll be good or bad for her.

"Believe me, I've got this," I reassure her the best I can, placing my hand on hers and gently squeezing it. "Trust me."

I hope she does. She won't lose me.

"You had it last time too, and look where it got you." Her voice sounds defeated. She stands up, puts on her long black jacket, and removes her hair from the back.

"I'll be back later. I have stuff I need to sort out," her voice cracks a little.

"Cyra, come on," I say, trying to erase the tension. "You don't have to be like this. I promise you I know what I'm doing. You don't need to protect me." I can handle it. I don't need to be coddled. "I'm not a child, don't treat me like one. I get it. Believe me, I do, but there are some choices I have to make." My words pour out quicker than I can stop them.

"See you. Please think about it," she says, trying to tame the desperation masking her tone, and with that, she walks out the door.

"Cyra," I call after her, but the door slams shut, and I'm left in the silence I started in.

Cyra doesn't get back till late, but when she comes, she acts as if everything is the same. I couldn't have been more grateful, but I have no idea how long that will last. She used to bug me about being a hoarder and that I couldn't let things go.

So, I got my den instead. My room isn't big enough, but the den certainly is. She can't complain when she's not tripping over my art.

I put everything away and sit in my bedroom. I like to try to keep an aesthetic, but I think my room is beyond that now. It's colourful, though. My room is basically splattered paint; you'd think it looks messy, but it blends well together. I pick up the paintbrush and dab it in yellow paint beside the canvas stand.

I've had the same stand for years. I don't think I could complete a painting without it. It wouldn't feel finished. I gently finish off the strokes of the sunflower. The sunflower is halfway underwater; it's not completely whole, and the flower's upper side stays afloat with scattered petals.

Even though it's not whole, it finds a way to stay afloat regardless of how it is falling apart. It's by far my favourite painting. This isn't for anyone else; it's mine. I reach for the orange to mix the texture, and when I look outside the window, he is there, Asher.

I ignore him and continue dabbing my paintbrush, trying not to pay attention, but it's hard when he looks like a lost duck. *Should I go?* I ponder to myself. I want to, but has it even been long enough that he doesn't get sick of me again? I just about made it into his good books, kind of.

I hope I have.

Oh, forget it. I don't know why I'm contemplating like I'm not going to go; it's nice to pretend sometimes. I tie my hair in a loose bun and throw on a pink sweater over my blue jeans. I try to find my shoes, but I guess my slippers will have to do.

I peer through the door to see if Cyra is still there, but she's gone. I'm not sure when she left, but she's not here now. A wave of guilt is lifted. I don't have to lie to her about what I'm doing. I don't need to worry if she follows me or not. I rush out and try to act casual, and there he is, sitting on the kerb, throwing pebbles as if it's a river. *Just be normal; that's all I need to do.* I muster the courage and try not to startle him.

"Hi," I say, unsure whether he's planning to run or not. "Hey, of course it's you." To my surprise, he steals a quick glance towards me and doesn't move.

That's new. I sit down next to him. I don't know how to really start this. We kind of left it weird the last time we spoke. Even I find it awkward. "It's icy as hell, and you're wearing slippers? Do you ever dress appropriately?" He lets out a laugh.

"I couldn't find anything else," I admit.

"I see, so what? You saw me and ran?" he asks.

It's quite vain how he assumes that I came running, I mean, it's true, but it's still vain, and I didn't come straight away.

God help me.

"No, I happened to be passing by," I lie. "I needed milk because I ran out, and you know you can't have tea without milk." I ramble, internally kicking myself at not knowing when to stop.

"Where is it then?"

"Where's what?" My feet are frozen, and my hands are getting more numb by the second.

"The milk..." His eyes gesture to my empty hands.

"I dropped it." I hope he thinks the redness invading my cheeks is because of the cold and not my embarrassment. I won't admit I saw him and did exactly what he thought. I sneeze, and he looks concerned, or I'm so cold I'm starting to hallucinate.

"Tissue?" He pulls a spare out of his pocket and hands it to me.

"Thank you." I try to ignore the butterflies fluttering in my stomach.

"You should try dressing up to actually match the season. You're going to make yourself sick," he says. Is he actually concerned?

He scoffs. "Here, take this," he says, taking off his coat and handing it to me. "Take it." He gestures towards me, dangling his coat in front of me.

It's black. This man does know that more colours exist other than black, right?

"No, I'm okay, r—" I begin to say.

"Don't make this awkward. Just take it." He gestures for me to turn around. I do. he holds it up, and I slide my arms through, appreciating the immediate warmth. He smells so good.

"Why are you covered in paint?" Before I can answer, he wipes my cheek with his thumb. "It's fresh," he says. I try to hide the immediate flush in my cheeks. "Are you blushing?" he teases.

I knew my cheeks wouldn't hide it. I shake my head to deny it. If I say anything, I'll go even redder. *This is so embarrassing.*

"You like my touch, huh?" I spin to look at him, wide-eyed. "Would you like it if it wasn't my hands that touched you this time?" he says teasingly, leaning forward. "I have something I'd like to touch." His voice is low, stealing a glance at my lips.

I immediately look the other way; I don't understand what's happening right now. This can't be real, right? It doesn't even make sense.

How do I stop my heart from beating so loud? What if he can hear it? Why are the butterflies going crazy? Am I okay? For goodness' sake, why am I like this? He's just a man, nothing more. I try to convince myself to stop myself from swooning like a dumbstruck teenager. I try to say something, but my voice fails me because nothing comes out.

Honestly, I'm not even sure if this is happening. I want to pinch my wrist, but he'll see me, and that's even more embarrassing. He laughs and pulls me into his arms. "Relax, stalker, I don't want to kiss you, but judging by your looks, you definitely want to kiss me. Let me break it to you now. It's never going to happen." His voice is tender and warm.

I hate him.

"What's wrong with you?" I jokingly push him away. "Say what you like. You wouldn't suggest it if you weren't thinking about it," I tease, raising my brow a little, letting my smile cave in. Maybe that was a little too bold.

"Alright, now who's getting cocky?" He pulls my coat a little more forward, his emerald eyes not so vacant as usual. "So why are we sitting here?" I pull his coat over me tighter to feel the warmth. The least I could have done is wear socks.

"I came to be by myself. I don't know why you're here."

I scowl. "Oh, stop pretending," I moan, "and they say women are the indecisive ones. You obviously like me. Let's leave it at that," I mock.

I dig my hands in his pocket and feel something poking at my fingers, I pick it out, and it's a star. An old token, it looks like someone stitched it together a long while ago, the way the fabrics worn out.

It's a mix of red and yellow with some orange. It kind of reminds me of a sunset. It's cute. The holes, worn over time, reveal a metal star, the shiny kind of metal that reflects different colours when you tilt it.

"Ah, that. I'll take that." He quickly snatches it out of my hand. "Didn't anyone tell you it's rude to go through people's stuff?" Yes, they did, but in my defence, it was irritating me. "I'm not telling you what it is, so don't bother asking," he quickly says before I have the chance to ponder. He holds it so delicately, looking at it in admiration.

"It's pretty." I lean towards him, nudging him a little. "I'm not asking. I'm stating the obvious," I quickly say.

"You don't strike me as the sentimental type. I got to say I'm pleasantly surprised."

"I've had it for as long as I can remember," he says tenderly.

"Someone gave it to you?" I ask, pushing my luck, hoping he doesn't notice. "A long time ago," he says, brushing his thumb across it. "Don't ask me who," he says. I didn't say anything. Am I that transparent?

"Your painting," he randomly says, clearly trying to change the subject.

"My painting?" It's unusual for him to pay any interest in what I'm doing.

"What were you painting?" He wipes another streak of paint along my cheek.

"A sunflower," I say. I don't really feel like sharing the story behind it. He might think I'm trying to be all sappy.

"You paint flowers, then?"

I laugh. "I paint a little more than that. I'm an artist. It's what I do for a living," I say. Painting is what helps me get by.

"Can you show me?" he asks softly.

"You want to see my work?"

"I just asked, didn't I? Why do you sound so surprised?" he says, not bothering to hide the annoyance residing in his tone.

"I'm not... I mean, a little, but can you blame me?" I say, flustered. It's not that big a deal. I got this, it's fine. I'm all *good*.

"I guess I could show you, but it's a lot of unfinished pieces, though." I don't know why I bother telling him that. I haven't felt this nervous in a long time.

"I don't care. I want to see. I'm not really into art, but it would be cool to see what you do."

He seems intrigued. I admit it's slightly attractive that he's interested in seeing what I do. It seems like we're walking forever, I guess because I'm so nervous, and I have no idea why. You would think I would have my own painting studio where I live, but I don't. I mean... I do, but only what I'm working on. Then I move it into my little den.

I rattle open the door to what appears like an old shed, hidden in basically nowhere. It's near this bridge by the riverside. It's quiet and peaceful, and no one really ever passes by. It's practically abandoned. I'm surprised he actually followed me, even though it was a silent walk.

I think he thinks I'm leading him to his death because he seems hesitant to step inside the gate when I open it for him.

"Welcome to my humble abode," I say, opening the door and rushing inside. I start turning on the lamps that rest on the shelves, which look like they are ready to fall apart.

I suck in a breath and smile proudly, giving a welcoming gesture to come inside. He studies it for a few long moments, taking in every detail, noticing the warm, subtle lighting to the paints smeared across the canvased walls as he walks by my paintings one by one, not saying a single word.

He lingers on the black ribcage, with the colourful hands gripped on the bones.

"Here I thought you were all sunshine and rainbows, Summers," he says, while not taking his eyes off the painting.

"You like it?" I ask, and he seems to.

"I do. It's actually pretty cool. You're really talented." He notices the smile spread across my face and grins. I validate his approval. "It's beautiful. You really are more than meets the eye. That's for sure." He doesn't take his eyes off of me. "You must be pretty special to do something like this. I mean, I could never do this, but to have a gift like this…" His voice is consumed with admiration. "You really must be special."

There it is again, the stupid butterflies. I don't know how to react when he does this. Can he see how weak in the knees he's made me? I feel like I'm going to fall any minute.

Does he even realise what he does? How one minute does he hate me, and then the next he calls me special? At least the special I think he means. He must know what he's doing to me. He can't be that much of a fool.

"Teach me someday?" He has no idea what he's doing to my heart.

"You want me to teach you?"

"Do you have to repeat every question I ask?" he mocks. "I probably won't even come close to you, but I'd like to try." I try to stop my eyes from burning. He's going to make fun of how I'm such a girl.

"I'd like that a lot," I swear I see his eyes glisten, I mean really glisten, the kind that could spark a thousand fireworks inside you. "I look forward to it." His voice is gentle and kind.

"I'm glad you like it," I honestly admit.

"I'm glad you showed me." A softness consumes his tone. I hadn't noticed before.

"I'll tell you something now," he interrupts, the feelings running rampant inside me.

"Hmm?" I say, waiting for him to carry on.

"The star? It's my token. It sounds pathetic, but it saves me." It doesn't sound pathetic. I get it. "I've never realised, but I've always had it on me, and I always carry it, but when I think this is it. I feel like the star always saves me." His eyes are low. He hates showing this side of him.

"It doesn't sound stupid at all. It sounds like we could all use something like that."

He lets out a low laugh. "I guess so." He grins.

"Here was me thinking I had you all figured out." I grab a beanbag and stow it away in the corner. It's old and blue, but it still does the trick. "Who knew you were the sentimental type?"

I let myself fall onto the bag, and I push it in front of him. "I guess we both learnt something new today," he says, studying me as I try to focus on anything and everything besides him.

I try to pretend I can't feel him staring at me. He wants me to look, but I don't think I'll be able to look away once he traps me with those deep ocean eyes.

"Why do you do that?" he questions, sitting cross-legged in front of me on the old red rug I bought from a yard sale a while back.

"I don't know what you mean," I say, feigning obliviousness.

"Shy away each time I say something nice to you." I knew he was blunt, but he didn't need to put me on the spot. "I'm not used to you complimenting me."

"Would you rather I insult you?" he asks.

"Obviously not," I say.

"Then accept the compliments and don't shy away. I don't say it for the fun of it. I mean it." He fidgets with his hand, and his ocean eyes seem like the only thing that exists right now.

I wonder what things look like from his lens, what I look like. He looks as though he wants to say something else. He scrunches up his nose and chuckles nervously.

"Where have you been lately?" he finally blurts. He noticed. I knew he would, but I didn't think he would care.

Does this mean he genuinely likes me? I want to stop gushing like this, but I can't.

"I didn't want to invade your space." What else is there to say?

"That's never stopped you." I guess that's true, but he doesn't need to openly say that.

"Maybe I fancied something new for a change." My voice is slightly higher than usual.

"Ah, I see." I thought he'd have more to say, at least an insult or two. "Yeah." I've never closed a conversation so fast.

"Summers?" his voice is hushed. I can barely hear it.

"Yeah?" I say, trying to tame my eagerness.

"I think I would like it if you stayed by my side a little longer."

The flutters in my chest become unbearable as my heart is desperate to out me.

"I thought you hated me?" My breathing is a little heavy. I try to tame my breath to be normal.

"No, I just realised you're the only person I can really be myself with. I don't know why that is or when it started. I don't know whether it's because you're the only one who knows what I tried to do, but it's nice not to have to hide." His eyes don't shy away from mine as he holds my gaze, his ocean eyes daring me not to drown in them.

"I'm glad." I try not to let the raspiness of my breath give away the pounding against my chest.

"Oh, and Summers?" he says, standing up and walking towards the door.

"Yes?" I'm scared of what else he's going to say next. I don't think my heart can take it anymore. I'm sure my face has already confessed my feelings.

"I can't stop thinking about you." And with that, he closes the door behind him.

He can't stop thinking about me?

Wait, what?

They say absence makes the heart grow fonder, but I never knew it was this fond. "Wait..." I collect myself and rush to the door. "Hey! You can't just say that and walk away. I don't get it. Are you playing mind games with me?" He stops walking and turns around. "Why would you think that?"

He seems genuinely hurt. "Because it's—I mean—oh, come on. One minute, you hate me, and the next, you suddenly like me? You said so yourself you can't stand me."

"You're right, I can't stand you." He steps closer, an arm's length away, and it feels like there's no air between us.

"Ash—"

"Like I said," he cuts me off, "I don't plan on being here for long, and in the meantime, I don't plan on lying anymore, either. I don't see the point." He pauses for a moment.

"I don't understand," I say, genuinely confused.

"You wouldn't. I like you, but I can't stand you. You're this light that I can't seem to shake. As much as I want to hate you, I can't. I just hate myself for how much I'm beginning to like you, I don't want to hurt you, but I know that's how this will end. Nothing good lasts for me, especially something as pure as you. I can't stand that you chose me to be the one who hurts you because I don't want to be the one to break you."

"Asher, you need to—"

He cuts me off before I finish. "You don't get it. This"—he gestures with his arms all around us—"is everything I didn't plan on. I like you a lot. I don't know what it is or why, but I do. I feel selfish because I want you to stay. I say all these things, and I don't want you to leave because I plan on leaving anyway. And I feel selfish because I want you to be the one who stays with me until the end." I think I forgot how to breathe.

"Wait, you want me to help you commit suicide?" Suddenly, my heart sinks.

"No. I just… I'm sorry, I really don't know anymore. I didn't expect anything to happen. I haven't felt an ounce of something in so long. I've encountered many people, but none quite like you, and I don't know how to be or react anymore. You terrify me." His eyes are defiant and unsure.

"I'm not doing anything to hurt you. I don't mean to make you feel so overwhelmed."

I close the gap between us, and his breathing quickens in sync with mine. I didn't mean to do this to him. I don't even understand how I did this to him.

"No, see, this is the thing. It's not you, it's me. It's so fucking cliché, but I find myself wondering when you're going to appear. I feel comfort when I see you or hear your stupid voice. Or the way you dress, I find myself smiling when I think about you, and I didn't expect this. To like you. I don't know what I'm doing."

He runs his fingers through his hair and sighs in defeat. Stepping back, he turns around and leaves.

I don't say anything after him because, if I'm honest, I'm even more confused now than I was at the beginning.

This is it, isn't it?

This is how he's going to break me, and *I'm going to let him.*

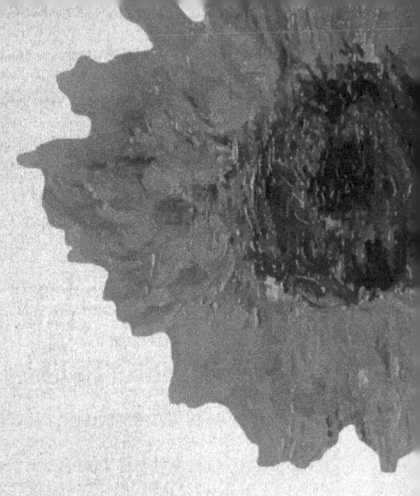

CHAPTER EIGHT
ASHER

"I'm hungry," Tyler huffs, his curls flowing with the breeze.

"Can you even get hungry when you're dead?" I question.

"What's your issue constantly reminding me that I'm dead? There is more to me, you know." He pretends to be offended.

"Please, for both our sakes, don't cry." We both chuckle, and I try to forget I'm sitting on a wet bench.

It's getting harder not to reminisce about whatever kind of outburst that was. I cringe as I remember how I walked away. I knew I should have taken drama in school. I would have smashed it. I don't know why I'm chasing her when I'm unsure about myself at the minute.

You'd think I would have run for miles, given how my legs are burning. I didn't even walk for that long. I hate that it hurts more these days. Maybe heights aren't the best thing for me, considering they never works out.

"You need to walk more; that's your problem." Tyler eyes me up and down, concerned.

"Thanks, Dad. I'll take that into consideration." How is he

always so talkative? I don't remember him talking this much when he was alive.

The throbbing in my head aches as I ponder on what to do next and how I can face her again after that. I manage to find my way out of that maze she's brought me into. I've never wanted to crawl deeper into a hole and let the earth swallow me whole.

I can think of many ways I could have done that so much better.

I wish I had some water. The thirst is starting to become nauseating. If I hadn't freaked her out before, I definitely had now. I have no idea how the tables have turned. Now I'm the one looking like a creep.

"So, you really like her, huh?" Tyler nudges me softly.

"I was beginning to appreciate your disappearance. Can't you do that again? I did miss you."

"I know you don't know how to cope without me," he says confidently, and it couldn't be more true. "Don't you think it's unfair to tell her all those things when you're planning on dying anyway?"

I hate how he's right.

"You realise the woman has feelings? That if she does like you, you're giving her false hope? That you might be something?"

I hadn't thought about that. "I didn't think," I admit. "I wanted to say how I feel." *Even if I could have done it better.*

"And that's okay, but at the expense of what? Nate told you, but does he know what you're always trying to do? No."

I haven't seen her again since. Not that I blame her. Tyler is right. What I'm doing is selfish.

"I want her light," I whisper.

"The Polaroid girl?" he queries.

"Yeah, it's her. I knew there was something about her, in the way she smiles, and how it makes the world fall silent for a moment. I recognised it. It took me a while to figure out where I knew her from, and now I remember. How am I meant to let that go?" When I saw her photo, her smile occupied my mind for the longest time. It still does. It's my favourite thing about her.

"I can't tell you what to do, but a person can't fix you, and it's cruel to only get to know her because you think she's the cure to your demons."

He's wrong. I would never use her like that. "I don't want her to fix me. I don't need her to fix me. I like her because of who she is and her warmth. Have you ever felt that? When you meet someone, and you're at ease? Your mind comes to a standstill, and you feel content, even if it's for a moment? You feel at home? She's funny and so fucking talented and kind, even when people don't deserve it, she's kind."

Tyler doesn't look at me, his gaze somewhere in the distance. "As long as you realise she's a person too." He clears his throat. "I'm sorry I'm not here," he utters low.

"What? You don't need to be sorry. You should be here. You deserve to be here, to live the life that was ahead of you. It should have never been you." I clear the lump forming in my throat.

"I'm always here." He places his head on my shoulder.

"Tyler?"

"Yeah?" He lifts his head.

"If I was normal, do you think I would be worthy of her?"

He looks at me and smiles. "You've always been worthy." I let the silence fill the gap between us. I try to find the den again, that shed of hers. It kind of reminds me of something out of *Doctor Who*. How it's deceiving on the outside, but when you step inside, it's unexpectedly bigger than you think. You know I live under a rock when I compare her shed to the Tardis. I think she owns this part of the land. She has to. It's closed off from everything. I wouldn't be surprised if she did.

"Didn't go well, I take it?" Nate smirks. "You haven't told me anything, but please prove me wrong, and at least tell me you didn't yell at her," he groans in defeat.

"Where the hell did you come from?" I look aside to see Tyler, but he's gone.

"Are you taking the piss?"

I want to say he's joking, but his expression suggests otherwise.

"No, I really don't know where you came from." I look past him, trying to figure out why I hadn't heard him. He pulls me up, and we start walking. My legs feel like they're going to cave. "I came with you." He slaps me around the head.

"No, you didn't," I say, rubbing my head. I'm gone, but I'm not that far gone.

"You literally have my phone in your pocket. I asked you to hold it, but you wandered off," he says, his expression unamused.

"Yeah, right." I look down at his phone in the bottom pocket of my grey jeans. I've lost it.

"Here you go," I say, handing him his phone, which I forgot I had in the first place. "Maybe you did come with me..." I say, embarrassed.

"Idiot."

"You can say that again," I whisper under my breath.

"Tell me, is it that girl you're dazed about? You're acting more dumb than usual." I can't argue with that. It freaks me out how well he knows me sometimes. I wonder if he secretly watches me, too. Or it could be the fact we've been friends for longer than I can remember.

Summers is right. I really do need to get over myself. "I did it. I told her," I quickly carry on before he has a chance to chime in. "She's really talented, though," I admit, trying to get off the subject of my failed declaration.

"Talented?" He peers over at me before carrying on straight, kicking a pebble in our path.

"Yeah, she paints. I asked her to show me, and I thought I was going to insult her about her work because if there's one thing I'm good at, it's offending women, but she's amazing," I exclaim.

"Now you've got dramatic yells out the way, why don't you try talking to her like a normal person and see where it goes with her?"

"I don't want it to go anywhere with her." I sound like a child, but I can't explain the entire thing to him.

He stops walking and pulls me by the arm backwards. "Wait. You don't want anything to happen with her?" he questions.

"No, I don't. I like her, but I don't want anything to happen. I like her. There's nothing more to it than that."

He hesitates, scrunching up his face, trying to figure out what to say next. "Let me get this straight…" He pauses. "You gave her this whole speech about how you like her, but you want nothing to do with her like that?" he questions, trying to make sense of my dilemma and whether he should find something to knock me over the head with.

"Yes," I admit. It sounds confusing, but I'm standing by what I said. I don't want anything to do with her. I'm not here for a long time. Just because I like her doesn't mean my entire world has changed. I already went over this once. I can't be bothered to do it again.

I'm still the same broken mess, and I happen to like her without meaning to.

"Then why tell her?" His voice is sharp.

"She needed to know."

"I'll never understand what goes on in that head of yours." He scrunches his face, clearly worrying about my lack of common sense.

He clears his throat and walks on. I follow closely behind him, struggling to keep up as my knees threaten to collapse.

"You were never good with women." He shakes his head. "The number of times I've had to save you."

Nostalgia seeps into my thoughts. "Save me? You're the reason I need saving in the first place."

Once, he convinced me to try out this restaurant. I was super busy, and I didn't have the time or care for it in the slightest. Anyway, long story short, I arrived, and he was nowhere to be seen, nor were these other guys who were supposedly meant to be there, but this girl he set up with me.

He thought I liked her because I didn't know how to keep my jaw shut when I saw her. It wasn't her. I could smell the food from the window she was sitting by, and each time I'd walk into the coffee shop, there'd be a new stall outside, and it always had me drooling because I was so hungry all the time.

He sat there the entire time and watched as she got offended by how I didn't know who she was, that my playing hard-to-get act wasn't cute and was insulting.

I really had no idea who she was. I told her I'd pay for her bill, but I had to leave, and she slapped me and stormed off, saying I was the one chasing her.

I had never been so confused in my life. The moral of the story is that you shouldn't look at anything when you're with Nate. Cupid will kick in and guarantee you a slap by the time he has worked his magic.

He howls, pushing me into a bush full of nettles, landing flat on my ass. "Sorry, my bad." He tries to contain his laugh. "I forgot you have no balance," he says as I wince, pulling the leaves off my arms.

"How many times have I told you to stop slapping me like a fucking seal when you laugh?" He should have a warning sign when he finds something funny. "How did you know I was here anyway?" Even I don't know where I am.

"I'm glad you fucking sat down. I was walking around in circles trying to find you." He slaps my arm after pulling out his phone from his jeans pocket. "I'm coming round tomorrow or later. I'll catch you in a bit."

He pushes me again, and I go flying into a bush.

This bastard.

"I swear I didn't mean to that time." He yanks me up, and I throw him in it instead, kicking him in the crotch. "Dickhead, fuck, I'm going to kill you," he yelps in pain.

"See you later." I laugh, and I start walking off. I don't bother looking back. He'll be fine.

I give up and take a seat on the bench. Either I've put on weight, or this is really old, and that's why it feels like it's going to fall apart. Either way, I don't move. If my ass lands in mud, so be it. "I have to ask, are you lost, because you've been going around in circles." A soft voice giggles.

"I'm fine, thanks," I lie. Not to lift my gaze.

"I'm heading to a café if you want to follow." She realises there's more than one, right? "You coming?" she asks, flicking her auburn curls over her shoulder. I reluctantly look up as she smiles. "I'm Cyra."

I don't remember asking her name, but okay. "I suppose there's no harm."

I don't want her to get ahead and see me following behind her. She'll probably scream. "I'm okay with that," she perks up, tone polite.

"Okay…" I nod my head and give a weak smile.

"Not much of a talker, are you?" she says, trying to make the walk tolerable.

"I don't know you," I say flatly.

"It's called having a conversation." she laughs, "have you never had one before?" Something tells me this won't end as quickly as I want it to.

"I've had one… I'm particular with who I have them with."

She purses her lips and smiles, the dimple in her cheek making an appearance.

"Is that so?" her voice teases. I glance in her direction, and her brown eyes are trying to read me, alight with a challenge.

"We're literally only talking because you're forcing it out of me," I say in an attempt to shut down anything she hopes to spark. "You look really yellow, kind of nauseous. Are you okay?" I'm only asking because I don't want to have to carry her, not that I would anyway. I would probably leave and, for her sake, hope some passer-by makes sure she's okay.

"I've just been on a run, I don't sweat like this for nothing. You would never catch me wearing this outfit for casual wear." She gestures to her athletic attire. I wonder if she meant to match the scenery, being surrounded by green and wearing green.

"That's nice." I really don't know what else to say to her, but at least we seem to be getting somewhere, more than I was.

"You from here?" she asks.

"Yeah, you?" I reply, treading lightly.

"Yes, I don't live too far from the coffee shop." Again with the café. "You say the coffee shop as if there's only one around here." I really need to broaden my horizons. How small does this town need to be to know where everything is?

"It's the only one worth getting your coffee from." She's not wrong there, silently agreeing. I don't think I've seen her before, but then again, there are a lot of locals I could swear I've never seen before. "You look confused," she pries.

"It's just my face." I've been told I always look confused in everything I do.

I could be sitting and minding my own business, and I'll get a concerned passer-by asking if I'm okay and if I need any help. Then I get confused, and they sympathetically look at me in awe and remind me that it's okay and that I don't need to be embarrassed.

It would seem I look like I need a lot of help. I don't get what everyone else sees. I think I look fine. Apparently, that's hilarious because she touches my arm, laughing, "You're cute."

"Okay." If she touches me again, I'll find a bush similar to where I threw Nate to push her into.

"You want to do something later? It's a bit random, but it could be fun." I guess I can cross her being shy off the list.

"I'm a stranger, and you haven't known me longer than a few minutes, and you already want to do something?" Is this how people make friends now? Seeking out random people to occupy your time with?

"What? Are you telling me you might be crazy or something?" she teases sarcastically.

"I might be," I say.

"I'll take the risk." Her cheeks flush with a little colour, and I'm scared she thinks I'm flirting. I was trying to make a point.

"I'm covered in mud, and I'm sure I still have nettles hanging off my shirt somewhere. That doesn't concern you?"

"Is it meant to?" She laughs. Now, I find her alarming.

The hairs on my arm stand up, the wind pressing harder against my skin. How does it manage to get colder every time I come outside? But how is any of this attractive? I can't even say it's my personality because I'm pretty sure that's also failing me.

Unless she's one of those girls who like the rude guys. Would it kill me to be nice for once in my life? Where's Summers to make everything awkward when you need her? I can hear Nate cheering for me in my head. He would be so proud of me, congratulating me for still having *game*.

"You seem shy," her voice is barely audible with the chaos looming in my head.

"Yeah, that's me, shy," I lie. I want to vomit.

"There you are."

We both stop to see Nate holding his knees as if he's just run a marathon. "This is a little sooner than I said, but I took your keys by mistake when you pushed me." He throws them to me, and I catch them.

I would've been waiting outside for days. Dad isn't home. I convinced him to go on a little vacation and take a break. It was hard, but he left eventually. At least he's starting to trust me now. Cyra barely even acknowledges Nate, and he doesn't seem to mind.

"I know the way from here, so I'll leave you to it." He gives a quick wave and walks off before anyone can say anything. It's weird for Nate to not say anything. He practically dies after anyone with a heartbeat. She's not my type, but she definitely is his.

My mind drifts to Summers, the woman named after a season. Somehow, her name fits her perfectly. She never told me her real name, so it's about time I asked that. I don't need to make anything happen; nothing needs to happen. Not everything that happens needs to go somewhere. *I'm okay with that*, I remind myself.

I can deal with being friends for now. As long as she's in my life, I don't mind. I hope I didn't scare her. I'm allowed to like her. I'm allowed to notice everything about her from the second her eyes get a little lighter. I can think about her and still be friends. I won't confuse her. I hope she's okay with that.

I hope she stays *as a friend.*

CHAPTER NINE
SUMMERS

I'm talented. Me, talented? I'm great. I'm already aware of that, but he loved it, really loved it. It's hard not to fangirl, especially when his vocabulary has been hurling insults lately. The way he was observing my pieces so attentively made me melt.

I've never had someone look at my art and understand the story behind it how I see it. We don't see the same thing when we all look at something, no matter how beautiful or tragic it may be. It looks different to each and every one of us because we don't look at it in the same way. We couldn't.

But Asher, the way he looked at them... I didn't need to tell him the story behind them. He knew. He knew *me*. It seems like everything is happening too fast, and I can't seem to slow it down. I can't decide whether I should be scared or kind of excited.

Things could go horribly wrong. I'm not being oblivious. It could end up like Cyra warned. There's a possibility of getting hurt, but I read somewhere that it's inevitable, but at least you get to choose who by. I'm not trying to lose myself; I don't want to end up like I did before.

But if things do go wrong, I didn't jump into the deep end

fully blind. I don't want to be a hypocrite and convince myself otherwise. I owe it to myself to not ruin myself for somebody else. Even if that somebody else is him. But if it ends the way Cyra thinks, that's the ultimate ending.

There really is nothing I can do to change that. I'm terrified to think I won't make it in time one day. It scares me how he seems restless and constantly defeated as if he can't wait to be erased. But I saw hope, even for a moment; it means things can change, that he can *change*. He isn't in pain; he is just him. The part of him he finds so hard to believe exists. Deep down, he wants to live. He wants to escape because he feels too burdened and doesn't know how to see past it. I'm not giving up on him. He'll find his way out. It's just a matter of time.

The snow is starting to melt, cueing everyone to slip everywhere. I tried to help a lady who fell by the trash and ended up falling myself, knocking it all over her. But the rain, that you can't beat. There's something calming about it that makes you feel instantly at ease.

Even though I feel like it's laughing at me when I come out wearing my summery dresses. I feel like I'm having an endless battle with the weather, one I know I'll never win, but still, it's fun. Outside, the den, which is basically a massive shed, has surprisingly lasted me several years. It cuts off from the river.

It's a private piece of land, there's open space everywhere, it's beautiful. A woman owned this property, and she needed some help to get to the end of her years. I was more than happy to make her days more manageable. When she passed, I wasn't expecting anything, but she left all this to me.

I don't live here. I wanted to, but things happened. Something about the rain makes it stunning, the little details you would miss if not for the drops falling off the leaves and flowers. It's like a painting, one I will never tire of replicating.

The sunset is breathtaking. The setting is never the same. I could lay here for hours, and I wouldn't notice how time has passed me by, and *it's all mine*. Since I started taking care of it, more butterflies have come by. They're my favourite, and I don't know how anyone could be afraid of them.

I tried some DIY a long while back and tried to make this bench. I got tired of the pebbled path which goes across sticking to my butt when I stood up. It was painful and unnecessary. At least I don't have to water the flowers today. I planted a mixture of random plants. Mostly asters and even a few roses, some whites and reds and even a few pinks with a yellow here and there. When I first came, it was more of a hideout spot; when bad shit happened, this was my refuge, my safe place. It's my second home, if not my first. If I ever got married, it would be here.

It would symbolise the commitment and refuge I hope to have one day. I'll make a path in the roses; I've already started it, so there's no gap, but I want the background to be beautiful. I'll make a path, a pebbled path with roses surrounding us, in the autumn, leaves blowing past us, and I'll get to make the commitment of my life in the place that gives me the most comfort. Closing my eyes, I let the droplets hit me, trickling down my face, one after another, letting my head hang back as my neck rests on the frame of the bench.

My hair hangs down as the rain defuses my waves, and I inhale a breath, closing my eyes. Letting myself drift, letting my dreams overtake me, and I rest.

"Hey... hello?"

Drowsiness is trying to pull me back into a slumber, and I can feel a hand rocking me profusely. I know this voice. Hesitantly opening my eyes, I see Asher hovering over me, his hand placed on my shoulder, pushing it back and forth, his face seeping in worry. Does he think I'm dead?

I should've kept my eyes closed and seen what would've happened. "You're drenched, you're dripping." Looking me up and down, he begins saying something too quietly for me to hear.

"Is it that obvious?" I groan, stretching as I rub my eyes.

"What?" he almost chokes.

"I wasn't even doing anything to imply I meant it that way, you perv." I cough, swinging my legs off the bench, gently patting down my dress, all crinkled and soaked.

He sits beside me as he examines my clothing. "I knew you were weird, but come on, I think you're pushing a bit too hard on that quirky side of yours. I don't think it's a trait you should invest in," he rants. "Seriously, who falls asleep in the rain and in the middle of nowhere on their own?" he asks, baffled, as he takes in the surroundings and pushes me aside, taking a seat beside me.

"Why are you moaning? You realise you're getting just as wet as I am, right? At this rate, we're both going to die of pneumonia."

"I see that, but at least I used my head to bring an umbrella," he ridicules, looking at me as if he's just run into an escaped patient and considering calling a psychiatric institution. He stretches his arm out and holds the yellow umbrella above me. I look up at it, and I can feel my face burn, and I don't feel so cold anymore.

"Don't look at me like that. It's just an umbrella. At least you won't get any more drenched than before. I can't promise you that you won't get ill, though. It's freaking me out, and your eyes are red. Do you really not see the way you look sometimes? Haven't you wondered why you make kids cry?"

"I do not make kids cry!"

"Oh, but Summers, you really do," he teases.

Well, I hope he's teasing. "If it makes you feel better, it looks like you just climbed out of the sewers."

He grimaces. "How would that make me feel better?"

"I'm not sure, but I know it makes me feel better."

He nods. "Do you enjoy making yourself sick? You haven't even got a coat on, and why have you got random bits of grass on you?" Irritated, he begins picking the random bits of grass off my green cardigan.

"I have no idea." I peer down at my attire. "I wish I knew myself."

I help pluck the last few pieces off me. I didn't realise I was nudging further away. I sit cross-legged on the bench, no longer sitting under the shelter he gave me, facing him as he faces forward.

"Here you go." He pulls off his hoodie, revealing a black shirt underneath. "Wear this. What's with you and your obsession with getting yourself sick?" He moves closer and stretches his arm as he holds the yellow umbrella above me again, filling the gap I created.

He hands me his hoodie. "Put it on, will you?" he says eagerly, his voice calm and gentle, with an underlying urgency that makes me forget the world's existence for a moment. All I can see is him. I watch as the rain begins to soak him, and his dark hair is so carelessly fumbled.

Locks of dark curls rest on his forehead as he wipes the trickles of droplets running down his fair skin, a little paler than usual. I think it's too late for him not to get sick. Is it possible for him to become even more radiant every time I look at him?

"What about you? Won't you get sick if you're wearing just a shirt?"

It's hard not to stare as the shirt begins to cling to him, the structure of his body, his chest rising and falling ever so slowly as it feels like everything is starting to cease to exist.

"Don't worry about me, it's fine. Rather me sick than you," he says warmly. "Now, please put it on Summers."

He lays down the umbrella and grabs my hand, opening my palm as he presses his hoodie against it, closing my hand. No words will come out, and I'm thankful for the rain because I can't hide if I start to cry. His smile is so familiar and contagious. Does he really not realise the effect he has? How much brighter he makes everything? He holds his umbrella back up and locks his gaze with mine. His ocean eyes refuse to look down past my eyes. It wasn't my brightest idea to wear a white dress. I thought it went really well with the oversized green cardigan.

But now that it's wet, it doesn't leave much to the imagination. I remove the green cardigan, daring him to look a little further, but he resists the temptation and keeps his eyes fixed. I put his hoodie over my white dress, wincing at how ridiculous I must look. Out of everyone, Asher is seeing me like this.

He takes a quick glance around. "Don't you feel weird being here on your own? You're practically in the middle of nowhere," he questions, as he places his hands in his pockets and looks around, wondering how he even made it here in the first place.

"Not really, it's hard to explain, but I feel at home here. If I don't make sense, it's because of you," I joke,

"I'm sorry for making sure you're okay," he says, tired of my remarks already.

"It's okay." I smirk. "But I'm tired, and you woke me and now, come to think of it, I'm frozen," I say, shrugging. "Plus, it can't be in the middle of nowhere if you found me."

"Barely."

"Wait, you were actually looking for me?" I'm taken aback at his honesty.

"Yeah, you're impossible to find, you know that?" He runs his hand over his hair and wipes his eyes as he peers up at the rain hitting us hard. "Here," I say, moving close to him and taking the umbrella out of his hand, putting it above the both of us.

"How's this?" I say, nudging closer, trying to stay dry.

"This can work," he says, tapping his knees awkwardly.

"What? You've never sat so close to a woman before?" I tease.

He rolls his eyes as he grumps. Before I can protest, he puts his arm around me, pulling me close.

"Asher—" I begin to say,

"Don't say anything. Just let me be."

His touch is gentle, and I don't say anything as I lay my head on his shoulder. We both let the silence embrace us, and his warmth wrapped around me. It's familiar, and this feels like how it should always be. I cough and can't help but curse at myself for ruining the moment.

"Where do you live? I'll walk you home."

He must be worried if he's offering to walk me home. I almost say yes as alarm bells begin ringing, making me see sense, and I realise I can't do that. It's nearly impossible to get out of this without making it weird. I'd rather not share where I live with him just yet.

He's just starting to like me. This will set us back to square one. "Come on, tell me, where do you live?" he persists, realising I haven't said anything.

"Don't worry. I can walk myself," I say, hoping he doesn't take it the wrong way, but I can't see any way where he doesn't.

Before I can stand up and he can say anything else, this old couple, no more than I'd say late sixties, strolls past us. I wonder if they realise they're not meant to be here. I don't even know how Asher found this. His memory isn't his greatest asset.

They stroll by, studying him as he stares at the ground. He leans forward and doesn't seem to realise he dropped the umbrella, so they can't recognise him, but it seems to be late as the couple seem to realise who he is and exchange looks, whispering.

He starts to breathe heavily as he begins playing with his hands. They're not loud enough to be heard to be sure of what they're saying, I can't hear them, but he starts clutching his hands. Asher looks uneasy as he begins breathing fast and deep, sucking in air as if he's just been running a marathon.

"Are you okay?" I reply towards him as I try to see his face, but he won't look up.

"Look, do you want me to walk you home or not?" he snaps as he picks the open umbrella off the ground, standing up. To think, this guy thinks I have no social skills. He's not exactly charming himself.

"Oh, um, yeah... sure." I take my place next to him as we walk silently on the way home. I honestly don't know how this is going to work. He's going to see where I live. How am I meant to explain myself? Where to begin? I should probably stop panicking before he thinks I'm trying to plot his murder, which doesn't seem like a bad idea right now.

I'm kidding.

I think.

I don't really have any other option. I reach out to take the umbrella from his hand. He shoots me a glare and holds it over me completely. I want to say thank you, and I will once we're past the river, or I have a feeling he might push me in. He has the emotional tolerance of a five-year-old. How does he keep switching?

"Don't you want to join me under the umbrella?"

He peers down at me and shakes his head. "I'm fine, and it's not big enough for me to fit under. You would get wet," he says, his voice gruff.

"I'm fine with that." I don't mind the rain. It's not as if I'm not already wet.

"You may be, but you're already going to get sick. I don't want you to get worse," he says.

Why does he keep making my heart flutter? Our walk was silent.

I was trying to think of ways to maybe initiate the conversation. He kept giving me one-word answers. Each time I brought something up, it was either 'yes' or 'no'. I wanted to ask who that couple was.

The way they looked at him, it wasn't as though he had done something wrong. It was sympathetic.

"Um, we're here," I announce as I slide through the double doors and begin to climb up the stairs. I can feel the tension change as he glances around, hesitating as he follows me in.

He wants to say something but decides against it as he shrugs. He clears his throat, not making a dent in the tension blooming in the air as he moves. He shakes the umbrella outside and closes it before pacing fast to catch up beside me.

"You live here?" Alarm filters his words.

"Yeah," I respond, trying not to flee at the worry morphing into his expression, attempting to think of every possible scenario this conversation may lead. He's so dramatic. Why does he look like he's in a movie? The way he's so tensed and how carefully he's selecting his words.

It's as if he's trying to unravel such a big plot twist. "For how long exactly?" he questions, trying to mask the concern in his voice.

"A while, a few years," I answer,

"Right."

"Right," I say.

I'm not sure where this is going, but he looks ready to scream for help. This is going better than I thought,

"Where are you going?" he warily questions. I don't know if I can carry on without him losing his shit. "Welcome to my other humble abode." I gesture to my door.

"You live *here*?"

"It would appear so…" I gesture to the door.

"No, seriously, are you fucking with me? You live here?" Maybe he isn't taking this as well as I thought.

"I live here," he says.

"I'm your neighbour." I didn't exactly rip the Band-Aid off nicely. I live at the end of the hall, three doors down from him.

"Wait, is this how you're able to follow me so easily?" His face drains of colour as my words sink in.

"Yes, because I peek out of my door every day to see if the light of my life has left his bed yet."

His face stills as he tenses. "I'm kidding, I'm kidding," I quickly backtrack.

"Oh, so you don't actually live here?" he eases, relief washing over him.

"Um, no, I do really live here." Suddenly, the vein that seems to be itching to rip out of his neck is back. "You really are a creep, huh? I was kidding when I said you were a stalker. I didn't think you'd make it your whole personality trait." And here we go with the insults.

"What's your name?" he questions.

"That's a bit random," I remark.

"You mean as random as finding out you coincidentally live three doors down from me this entire time? I'm going to need your name in case anything happens to me. You know, if I turn up dead one day or something."

"I don't know how you've never considered acting. You'd be amazing."

He ignores me. "Your name?" he demands.

"Alessia Summers."

"Alessia?"

"Yes?"

"No, I'm confirming that your name is Alessia? Dumbass." I grab my bundle of keys and try to unlock the door as swiftly as I can. I need to act casual. Otherwise, he will lose his mind and take me out with him, trying to pick apart my mind. It finally unlocks as I open the door and step inside.

"Yes, that is my name, and you're going to find out soon enough, so I might as well tell you. I kind of went to school with you, too. We've known each other a very long time." And with that, I close the door in his face. His eyes grow wide, and disbelief embraces his entire face.

He doesn't bother saying anything else or knocking. I look through the peephole. He begins circling as he talks to himself, trying to figure out whether I'm telling the truth or not. Slipping off my dress and pulling his hoodie over my head, I pick up the towel off the radiator and wrap my wet hair in it. He'll know when Nate confirms it. Maybe it will be easier for him to open up to me now that he knows I know Tyler. Or maybe I've messed this whole thing up. I could have done that better. I was panicking. He didn't exactly give me time to prepare.

We were friends once before. We could be once more, and I won't let him down this time. I'll help him find his purpose again.

I hope I haven't scared him off for good.

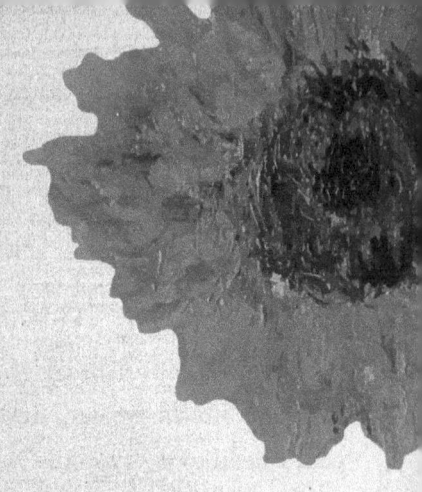

CHAPTER TEN
ASHER

Alessia. It's weird saying her name. I prefer Summers. It suits her better. I don't know why she didn't tell me, how I never noticed. No wonder she is on the ledge, why I always see her. Why do we keep having these long ass pauses every time something freakish happens? It's always her doing.

Except when I decided to be Mr Romantic and tell her how much I like her, that was my doing. This is why logic always overrules feelings; I had to be the sap and confess. Everything lately feels like a blur. On the outside, it looks like it's meant to make sense. But when you look closer, nothing about anything that's happening makes sense. I try to steer clear of my dad. I feel too guilty when I look at him.

When he's talking and laughing, I would've ruined him if I was dead. I don't know what to do anymore. I can't stick around for him and can't live like that anymore, but I can't be why he stops living. I can't make him feel how I feel.

"How did you not recognise her?" Tyler takes his place on my chair at the end of my bed.

"I keep asking myself the same thing, but I don't get why she pretended to not know me. But forget that for now. Why are you always here?" I'm tired of seeing him.

"Like I've said many times before, brother, I'm here because of you." I feel I should be embarrassed that my subconscious is growing tired of me. "Why are you whining? I'm practically the only company you have." He's got me there.

"Tyler?" I say, throwing a basketball at my ceiling and catching it, Repeating the motion.

"Hmm?" he says, spinning around on my desk chair.

"Do you think you'll ever go away? That I won't see you anymore or hear you? I won't look over my shoulder to check if you're there? That one day, I'll be the person I was again, that I'll be able to forget long enough to live properly?"

He stops spinning and faces me, his stare heavy. "I can't answer that for you. I'd like to think I won't be here one day and that you'll move on, but I can't decide that for you. I can't force you to see beyond the past. You're stuck, and I can't be the one to free you."

I run my hands through my hair and sit upright.

I can't just sit here and drive myself to insanity. I might as well seek that stalker out. Get some answers from her instead of assuming the worst. People forget faces all the time. I hadn't seen her for a while. I shouldn't feel bad about that. Nate laughed when I told him and said she must've not been that memorable.

But she would have been to me. I rummage through my wardrobe and find a hoodie, pulling it over my head and tying my shoelaces. I grab a pen marker, which is lying on the kitchen counter. I write 'I'll be back later' on the whiteboard attached to the fridge.

Dad and I have this system; if we're not home or going out, we write on it to let each other know where we are. He started doing it when Mum left. If it brings him comfort, I'm happy to do it. I open the door and walk towards the end of my corridor. The walls are as plain as they've always been, dull.

I glide slowly past each door until I reach Alessia's. I shouldn't have even told her I liked her. I don't know what came over me. I didn't contemplate how messy this could get. How telling her I can't stop thinking about her could lead to anything else, something more. Something I don't want. What am I doing?

Why am I chasing a life I can't have? Just because I don't have a future doesn't mean I have to fuck hers up. I like the version I imagine of my life where we're not just friends and we are something. But this isn't my imagination. It's real, with real feelings and people, and I can't pull her along like that.

She's just a *friend*. I keep saying it, trying to convince myself there's nothing wrong with any of this. I'm allowed to have her as a friend. It's not hurting anyone. I should have knocked ten minutes ago instead of wandering back and forth. Justifying every reason why I should talk to her again.

I lift my hand to knock, but she opens the door before I have the chance. Her hair is gathered up in a messy bun, her loose ends tucked behind her ears, and she wears an oversized purple floral and white jumper with baggy blue jeans. How is she always so vibrant? She looks surprised to see me.

"Hey," I say, unable to stay still as I begin rocking back and forth on the heel of my shoes ungracefully, unsure where to put my hands. I was aiming to slide them in my pockets by the waist, but it looks like I'm wiping something on myself because the pockets seem to have disappeared.

Alessia rests her head against the door, "Well, it took you long enough." She laughs, trying to stop herself from being so eager. Biting the inside of her cheek, she doesn't wait for me to move, pulling me inside.

"A simple 'come in' would suffice," I say, taking her hand off my sleeve.

"Come sit," she instructs me, gesturing towards her yellow bean bag on the floor, which fit nicely into the corner. Her place is everything I expected it to be. It resembles her perfectly. The chaotic mass of light bursting with colours. It's not one but a mix of everything. She has the centre wall covered in painted sunflowers.

It's not one colour but more of a splatter to fill in the outlines. The layout is the same as mine, except her place is bursting with colour, and mine reminds me of a very neutral-coloured prison.

"I'd offer you somewhere else, but as you can see…" She gestures to her sofa.

It's cluttered with her belongings. Alessia pulls a blue bean bag from across the room, dragging it beside me as she sinks into hers. Her aura is still as spirited as it was the moment she opened the door. "You like it?" Her hazel eyes follow my gaze around the room.

"Yeah, it's pretty cool."

It isn't normally my style, but she makes it work. "So you finally calmed down?" she asks hesitantly, nervous about why I'm here to begin with.

"Can you blame me? You didn't really explain yourself."

"I know, um… if it makes you feel better, we weren't friends like we hung out or anything. We just knew of each other, really. We had similar classes, that's all." Alessia begins sinking deep into her bag, rummaging through its contents. I feel relieved.

I admit I feel a little disappointed I didn't get to meet her sooner, but I knew I wouldn't forget her if I really knew her the way I thought I got to know her. "Good, I'm glad I didn't know you properly then. You had me worried for a second."

She stops searching and sits up. "What?"

"Not like that, I mean… I felt embarrassed that I could forget someone like you, so that means if I didn't know you properly, if I barely knew you, I didn't forget you. I could never forget someone like you" I laugh a little to break the tension a bit. She shouldn't feel embarrassed or hurt.

"I'm glad." This time, she doesn't meet my gaze, and she clears her throat. "Since when did you get so sappy?" Fidgeting with the strands that come loose in her bun, twirling the hair around with her fingers. "Why did you pretend not to know me?

"Well, you didn't recognise me, and I thought it's less embarrassing to say you knew me and have you try to figure out how. Or I could get to know you now without making you feel obligated to because we went to the same school or whatever."

"I get it." To be fair, I don't blame her. How we met… I'd be mortified if I knew then; it was someone who knew me from before. I lie down, looking up at her ceiling; she turns all her lights off.

"What are you doing?" I ask, sitting up, wondering if she really is a psychopath.

"Wait, I got this projector thing. It makes your room look like the galaxy or a gazillion stars."

"I think I get what you mean…"

"Oh, just wait," she says again, unbothered by my confusion. "Here." She flicks the switch on, and the whole room lights up as she says, a gazillion stars. I watch her as she beams proudly, staring up in awe.

I lay back down on the bean bag, this time really making myself comfortable, folding my arms behind my head and resting on them as she does the same. It's a comfortable silence I don't mind spending all my days in. I don't know how she does it, how she makes everything so *normal*.

"Asher?" Her voice is soft.

"Yes?" I reply, unsure of what she's going to say next.

"I have one more thing I should tell you about," she says nervously.

I still don't look at her. I don't want to make her uncomfortable. "Go on."

"I didn't first see you on the ledge. There's a reason I was there that night."

I don't move, and she continues, "I met you in school."

I clarify.

"No, well… yes, but I mean recently." I don't say anything this time, and I can feel her stealing a few glances in my direction, waiting for a reaction. Her tension eases as she sees I'm calm. "I, um… I saw you that night on the bridge." This time, I still.

I try to control my breathing so as not to show her a reaction. I don't want her to be afraid of talking to me. "I saw you… um…

fall, and I tried to run after you, but when I followed your steps." She gulps. She means the blood trail I so kindly left. "I saw you talking to someone, and that's when I realised who you were. I wanted to make sure you were okay, so I followed you back, and when you walked through your door, I knew it was you. It was really you," she says quietly and apologetically.

"So… how'd you end up on the ledge?" I ask.

"There's a reason you call me a stalker," she jokes, but I don't laugh. "I'm sorry," her voice breaks a little.

"I'm not mad, I'm just wondering, do you pity me?" abruptly breaking the ice she built.

"What? No," she blurts. "Never. I just… I know I don't… well, we don't know each other that well. But I know a lot about you, and I couldn't live with myself knowing I watched you fall."

I cough, and she shifts uncomfortably, "I'm sorry. It's a lot," she murmurs apologetically.

"Alessia, you can't keep chasing me. I'm sorry for making you worry, but you can't live your life around me. You're free. You get to do as you please. Don't waste it worrying about me." She gets to live, and I shouldn't be stopping her, making her wonder what crazy thing I'm planning on doing next. "If it's any consolation, I feel warm when I'm with you. It's the kind of warmth you never want to escape. You make me feel like I'm normal." It feels surreal saying that out loud.

She turns to face me. Leaning forward, she plants a kiss on my cheek, sending sparks everywhere inside me. "Thank you."

Still hypnotised by her sudden gratitude, I open my mouth to say something, but no words seem to come out. "Why are you thanking me?" I ask.

"Because, Asher, I like having you in my life."

Alessia throws her arms around me, her head resting against my chest. I instinctively wrap my arm around her before I can stop myself, stroking her arm. Letting her tenderness bury me, intoxicate me in all the best ways, not daring to take my eyes off her ceiling. "Alessia, this may sound like the dumbest thing you've heard in a while, but will you be my friend?" I expect her to laugh, at least a little. I would have.

But she doesn't. "I thought we already were."

"Good. Let's stay that way; we're just friends."

"Just friends."

If there's one memory that I want to treasure for eternity, it's painting with Alessia.

I breathe heavily as I finally catch my breath. I've never run so fast to end up in nowhere.

"About time." Alessia slaps my shoulder, her hair braided back, and she holds up her purple silk dress, just a little high above her ankle. Her anklet glistens in the light, and she wears a white blouse over her dress.

As she hurries along to the pebbles formed across the river, she urges, "Come on."

"How close do you want me? I'm practically right behind you. I'm almost touching you." I try to walk carefully without falling over.

"Oh shush, will you?"

I nudge her a little. "You're the one complaining." I laugh.

"I like your laugh." Is it weird that I can feel her smiling, if that's even a thing?

"Here we are." She gestures to the open space with a red picnic sheet spread across the grass. Instead of food, there are two cushions and a bunch of paint and brushes with two canvases. "You wanted me to teach you? Well, here we are."

She hurries forward and sinks to the floor. She pulls my arm down with her to join her as I fall face flat onto the ground, "I'm sorry," she says, trying to pull me upright. I sit up half-heartedly and brush myself off. At least she's not trying to kill me this time, although it doesn't bode well for my nerves being near a river with someone as clumsy as Alessia.

Sometimes, I'm glad she does this. It reminds me that she's still an idiot. I can't believe I'm sitting in the middle of nowhere with a paintbrush and a woman who looks like she belongs in a painting. "Thank you for actually wearing colour today. I happen to really like the colour blue." I wish I knew how to stop my face from flaring up.

"I suppose colour suits me well," I say, trying not to steal glances at her. I grab a brush and start dipping it in yellow. She peers over at what I'm doing, and I try not to lose focus, but I don't have the slightest clue what I'm doing. "Don't try so hard. Just start off simple, draw a flower. You can never go wrong with that." I guess she has a point there.

I want her to be proud of what I do. "I'm perfectly capable of painting without your input, thank you." I know exactly what I'm going to do.

"I believe you," she casually remarks, picking up her own paintbrush. "I still can't believe you're voluntarily doing this with me and the fact you even made an effort to wear colour," she says dumbfounded.

"I had to bless your eyes at some point, right? Everyone deserves to see how I look in colour. It's a crime to keep you oblivious for so long."

I can feel her eyes roll. "If you say so."

Why does she always need to get the last word? She's clipped the loose strands of her hair back and taken off her cardigan so she can paint more freely, and I try not to stare.

I wonder if she realises how beautiful she looks. How everything seems dull in comparison to her. Time passes by, but it feels no more than a minute later when we exchange canvases. "I don't know how you do this so effortlessly." She painted where we are, the tall trees and the light cutting through the gaps gleaming down, the autumn leaves falling so graciously, the illuminations of the river beside us, the way the water crashes against the stones.

"You painted me a sunflower?" Her voice cracks ever so slightly. I don't know whether she wants to laugh or cry.

"Yeah, they're your favourite," I say, casually shrugging, preparing to be embarrassed if she thinks it's lame.

I start to ease when I notice the tears gathering along the line of her eyes and try to ignore her desperate attempt at keeping them in, even if it means her eyes start to sting and she can't see a thing.

"I love it, really. It's the best gift ever," she says, peering down at it in awe. "Why yellow as your background choice?" She giggles as she wipes a tear that rolls down her cheek.

"I really like yellow," I admit.

"Is it your favourite colour?"

Holding my canvas so carefully. I say, "Recently it is." I fidget with the brush dipped in the paint. "Isn't it yours?"

"Yeah. Sunflowers are my favourite, and yellow makes me feel safe. It's silly, but it makes me happy."

Her eyes linger in admiration on the sunflower. Her hazel eyes seem to be absorbing the light around us with the sun's intensity. Does she realise how glorious her eyes glow in the sun? How it seeps rivers of honey and specks of gold?

"Why is it your favourite?" she questions warily as if to not get ahead of herself.

"Because it makes me feel a little less empty and a little more whole." Her smile grows wide, and it's still impossible to fathom I can make that happen.

Before I can protest, my words pour out. "You're my yellow, Alessia."

All I see is colour. All I see is yellow.

All I see is her.

CHAPTER ELEVEN
SUMMERS

I want to go on vacation. I've always wanted to see the northern lights. I don't mind trying to seek that out. Everything seems a bit chaotic lately, and I want to see something magical.

"Asher, huh?" Cyra questions, a huge grin curving on her lips, disturbing my thoughts.

"I'm happy he's back. Maybe this time it will work." She grabs the orange juice out of my hand as she gulps it down.

"No!" I grab the bottle back off her. "That was the last bit, thank you very much." I take a sip.

"Oh, here you go. I couldn't live with myself if you fainted from not having the beloved beverage."

"This is why I love you," she says, blowing me a kiss. "I was thinking…" mischief lingers in her voice.

"Don't even think about it." I shut her down before she has a chance to ponder on her schemes.

"What? Oh, come on, you can't be serious, can you?" she says, trying to figure me out.

"I don't get how you're being so normal. Aren't you a little bit curious?" she questions, leaning against the countertop.

"Curiosity isn't going to help me at the minute. I don't want to open Pandora's box."

Cyra finishes the glass and washes it up before taking her place next to me. "There's nothing wrong with wanting to know."

"I get that, but right now, I don't want to, and I'm okay with that." Not now, anyway. Things are going so well. Before, I wanted to know, but too much has happened since, and I can't be selfish and ruin that. "

What if I ask him?" She poses the obvious question.

"You already know the answer to that." She can't tell him.

I won't even know what to do with myself. How would I face him after that? I've finally got him to trust me. I'm not sabotaging that. This way, even if he seems to have forgotten me, it must be for a reason. I can't imagine how he would react knowing I lied and didn't tell him the whole truth.

I still see him, I still get to be by him, and that's more than enough for me. I've wanted this for a long time. Even if we did meet again, the way we did, I'd just woken up that night to grab a drink. It took everything I had not to approach him, and it worked for a short while, but then I heard him.

I knew it was him even though I couldn't see him, and it broke my heart. When I realised he didn't head back inside his door, I'd never run so fast. It haunts me to picture him there, ready to end it all to fall and in the worst way. I was trying to hold back my scream when I thought I wouldn't make it in time.

It took everything I had to hold myself together, and when he left and locked me out on the stupid roof, I cried. I was so relieved. He might not see a world worthy of living in, but he's worth everything in my life. What if because he likes me, he stays with me out of sympathy? Because he feels like he owes me?

I couldn't imagine anything worse than having him remember, but it doesn't mean anything to him. Because it's a past life he can't connect with. They're my memories, and I think that's all it's meant to be; it's just mine to relive. I think sometimes the memories are only meant to be just that.

Just a snippet of what you have to live, love and hold onto. They're mine to honour and keep alive, and that's what I intend to do.

"Aren't you worried if he ends up finally remembering you?" Cyra cautions. She means well, but I'm not like her.

In that way, she's braver than I am. She wouldn't hesitate. She'd flat-out make him remember, and if he didn't, she'd walk away even if it killed her. I want him to remember me, but not like this, not as someone he has to but as someone he wants to.

"I know what I'm doing. I get it. You're worried. If the shoe was on the other foot, I would be too. But you have to let me do this on my own. You don't need to hold my hand." I inhale in a breath and let it out as I fall onto the yellow bean bag. Contemplating every moment in my life right now.

"You didn't need to do this, you didn't need to put yourself here, but you are. This isn't going to end the way you want it to." Frustration seeps through her words as she slides down on the sofa in front of me.

"Why is that line so popular? Have you thought maybe it doesn't always have to end so badly? That hoping for something different isn't the end of the world, sometimes it's okay?"

"Alessia, if hope was enough, he would know who you are, really know who you are, but he doesn't. He remembers everyone else but you. Have you considered you aren't important to him the way he is to you?"

I have considered that. Gone over it endless times. "It's obvious that's the case, but this isn't about me. I'm fine, I'm living, aren't I?"

"Why are you doing this?" her voice is unsure and desperate, "Alessia, he's going to hurt you, and you're showing him exactly how to do it."

The silence is loud between us, and it feels, for the longest time, none of us say anything. She's right, but I want her to be wrong for once. "No one deserves to be alone, not like that."

"It's not your job to fix him," she says, cutting sharp like a knife.

"I didn't say it was. Don't talk about him like that. I don't want to fix him, but I can make my own decisions. I'm not with him because I have an ulterior motive or trying to implement myself back into his life as something else. I don't want that. I want him to be okay. I don't plan on ruining myself for his betterment. He deserves to be here as much as you and I. And nothing you do or say will change my mind." I want to be hopeful for once and see how that works out for a change.

"I won't tell," Cyra says as she kneels beside me. "I promise," she says, slicing through the tension. "If you want this, I won't tell him."

She leans in for a hug, throwing her arms around me, and I throw my arms around her. "I promise it'll be okay, I'll be okay."

"Thank you," I say, squeezing her tighter.

I love my den, but I need to figure out how to order food here. Walking with a pizza doesn't work when it's always cold. I decide to paint a little, then I'll try taking some photos after I'm done. I fish into my pocket for my key and immediately want to throw myself in the river.

How could I forget it? I guess eating pizza on the bench isn't too bad. I have my umbrella this time. I lean it upright against the bench and place my pizza box underneath it. There's nothing wrong with going back. I quickly finish up, hold the empty box in my hand, and start walking.

My daze is cut short when I see Cyra in the distance. These days, I see her taking strolls more than I see her in the flat. She normally never walks this route, but I guess things change. I was sure I left her asleep. I try to run, but she's already beat me to it, bumping into me so hard she almost sent me headfirst into the trash.

"You didn't need to start running, too. You just turned it into a Bollywood moment. It can't get any more romantic than that." She helps me up as we brush ourselves off.

"You didn't need to keep on running when we collided. You could have stopped," I growl.

"Yeah, but it's very slippery," she says defensively.

My walk seems longer today. The days seem kind of long in general, but I don't mind. We grab our coffee from our normal place, and as usual, it's pretty much empty with a few regular faces. I smell the fresh chocolate muffins that seem to be fresh out of the oven. I want to order a dozen. I turn back to ask Cyra if she wants anything else, and a familiar laugh floods my ears. It's Asher in his usual seat in the back.

Cyra sits across from him, both drinking coffee and lost in each other's conversation. How does she move so fast? Why is she talking to him? I trust her. She won't say anything, but why do I feel like someone has just punched me in the gut?

He hasn't seen me yet, I want to run, but my legs won't move. Instead, I seat myself away from them with my back turned. I don't know why the hell I'm doing this, but even Cyra seems to have forgotten she came with me. I instantly regret my decision and start planning my exit without being seen.

I need to grow up. This isn't me. I'm not shy, I don't get jealous, and I don't hide. The bell rings, and Nate steps in. He looks uneasy as he sets his gaze on Cyra and Asher. He hurries over, and the tension disappears from his face. You wouldn't think he had a problem to begin with.

I want to ask, but I know better than to make myself present now. Why did I sit here? I can't even hear them. Nate tries to hide his smile from Asher as he steals some of the muffins he has left. He picks it apart instead of taking a bite out of it.

I hurry out of my seat and out the door, praying nobody notices me, sighing heavily as I peer back and see Asher smiling so brightly. I should be glad she hasn't said anything and that he's happier, but why does my heart feel heavy? He doesn't even know her, and she makes him smile.

I couldn't do that at first.

Why can she?

I lean against the wall and take a breath. Why did I leave? I'm still hungry, and I can still smell the muffins from here. The bell rings, and they all walk out. I almost lose my balance and debate running. Cyra ignores Nate as she laughs, her hand brushing against Asher's arm.

Her laugh is different. It's a laugh I know all too well. She's flirting. I can't be mad; I have no right to be mad, and this is what I wanted. For him to be happy if he's laughing, genuinely laughing, who am I to be mad? Asher quickly runs inside. I think he's forgot something, so he leaves Cyra and Nate to spend a moment in their own company.

As soon as he heads in, Nate's face drops. He's trying not to raise his voice.

He whispers something, and they look like they're arguing as he steps closer, and she steps forward, unfazed by his intimidation. He sighs, running his hands through his hair, and says something else.

As Asher comes back, I can sense the same tension.

"Everything okay?" he questions, cautious of them both.

"Fine, as I was saying tomorrow, is it then?" she confirms. Their tension is erased as quickly as it came.

"Can I come?" Nate questions, unmoved by his lack of an invitation to join to begin with.

"Um, no. You can next time. I promise." She winks at him, and he couldn't look more displeased.

"I guess one day with you can't hurt." He shrugs.

"Great! Okay, now I'm going to be right back, and we can make it in time for that movie."

She glances over to Nate. "Yes, you can come." She rolls her eyes.

"I wasn't waiting for your permission," he remarks.

"That's why you're standing there like a lost puppy," she fires back. Cyra hurries past them. "Well, I'm going to quickly use the restroom. I'll be back."

She pats his shoulder as she rings the bell, making her way in. Asher doesn't seem so hopeless and confused anymore. I can't help but laugh as he mutters he's doing this for Tyler under his breath, but he's not as quiet as he thinks.

He seems to be coming out of his shell. I ponder what to do next, and a sudden realisation hits me: he's not wearing black or stupid grey. I thought he wore colour when we painted as a one-time thing. And the other time, he couldn't find anything to wear, which now sounds like a lie.

He's wearing green. He's really wearing *colour*. He's starting to make an effort. I knew he would! I hurry to him and tap him on the shoulder to get his attention.

"Hi." I try to be casual, like I wasn't just standing there for God knows how long.

"Alessia." I love the way he says my name; no one else says it with so much affection.

"Are you busy? I was wondering if you wanted to do something." Why am I pretending?

"Yeah, actually, I literally just made plans." He gestures behind him and realises no one is there. "I swear I did make actual plans,

I'm not brushing you off." He made plans. I don't know why I'm making him nervous.

"Good, I'm glad you're doing things." I am really proud, even if I don't seem like it right now. Before I can say bye, Nate comes out, and Cyra rushes back and starts to pull him along. "Come on, we don't want to be late. The queue will be long otherwise," she moans.

He doesn't hesitate and turns away, oblivious I was standing there to begin with. He doesn't say bye. He doesn't even notice me. My phone vibrates in my pocket as I pull out a message from Cyra. "Hey, sorry! Don't wait up for me. Thank you for the coffee, and I hope you finish your work. I love you!"

I slide it back into my pocket.

As long as she's not saying anything, I guess it's none of my business. I wonder if he remembers her, and that's why he's so comfortable. My aim is to make sure he's okay. Is Cyra right? I'm not a high school lovesick puppy. I'm a grown woman. I'm twenty-one years old. That should count for something.

I turn to walk away, but I turn back for a moment to see if he looks back, even if it is just for a second, but he doesn't. This isn't supposed to hurt. I shouldn't be jealous.

It's fine.

Everything's fine.

Did I imagine the way he started feeling towards me? I can't be having a meltdown now. I'm more composed than this. He hasn't said anything to me today, not even teased me in the slightest. He barely even noticed I was there. But I can't help but resent how Cyra makes him smile so easily—how genuine he seems to be around her. I'm contradicting myself, and I hate it, but I can't help it. I can't feel like this. I don't want to feel like this. It shouldn't bother me; I should be happy.

This was the aim, right?

But why do I feel I'm ready to fall apart? I should be better than this. For God's sake, he's laughing, really laughing, and I'm bitter that I'm not the one making him feel good, that it's someone else. What's wrong with me? I'm better than this. *Pull yourself together.* I continue repeating it until I get it through my skull.

This is a good thing. I don't need to twist it and make it about me. I'm meant to be his friend. Maybe that's all I ever was. Sometimes, feelings aren't meant to be reciprocated. Just because I may have feelings doesn't mean he needs to make the feelings mutual.

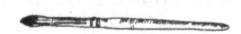

It's late. I should head back home now. I've basically spent my entire day in my studio. I'm not complaining. It's therapeutic. I head out and lock up behind me, this time making sure I don't lose the key. Laughter fills the silence surrounding me as I bump into Asher. Surely, this can't be a coincidence.

"Hey," this time, he says it.

At least he remembers how to say that.

"Hi," I say as I start walking again.

"Why so grim?" He nudges me as he follows beside me.

"I'm not grim. It's just a long day, that's all." I don't know what it is about today. I feel so tired.

"You need to make sure you're taking care of yourself," he warns.

"I know." I smile. I feel bad. I shouldn't be mad because he might like someone else. "Can I ask you a question?" I slow down my pace. "What do you see me as?"

"What do you mean?" He's confused by my wording. Sighing, I venture for words to make myself clearer.

"I mean... what do you see me as?" I repeat again, stopping as he turns to face me.

"My friend," he says softly. "That's what we said, right?" His eyes scan mine for confirmation. He didn't even hesitate. *His friend.*

"That's all?"

Hesitating, he says, "That's all. Just my friend."

"Nothing more?"

"Nothing more." His words are sharp yet delicate.

"Okay, um... I just realised I forgot something," I stammer as I try to come up with a decent excuse.

"That's fine, I'll catch you later then?" Turning, he waits for me to go ahead and for him to carry on. How do you stop your heart from sinking?

"Yes, I'll catch you later." I try not to let the tears burning my eyes escape.

Without another word, he turns around, leaving me alone again. I wait to see if he turns around, but he doesn't. Why am I the one always yearning for him? I feel drops on my hands as it starts to rain, becoming heavy so fast, and he doesn't seem to care. Instead, I turn the other way, and it seems I've been walking forever.

I take my shoes off. They're rubbing the backs of my feet, and they're sore and pain me every time they press against the skin. I don't even mind that it has started to pour with rain. This is what I need.

I reach the bench in my garden, my dress getting wet as I take my seat, the rain soaking through my clothes, breathing in the air.

I put my legs up and lay myself down, feeling the droplets trickle down my skin. I tuck my hands underneath my head and smile. Everything is ruined, including my dress and my shoes, but that's okay. I laugh to myself. I'm not as cut out for this as I thought. How could I ignore everything I feel? How am I supposed to forget?

I close my eyes as I remember the last time I saw him, the one who knew me. His heavenly blue eyes were warm and full, gazing into mine. I have so many questions I'm dying to ask, but I'll make a fool of myself if I even utter one. I remember when I met him again, he looked at me like he'd never seen me in his life.

Even now, his eyes don't recognise me. He seems to have forgotten it all. I wish I could erase it as easily as he did, just pretend I don't exist, and maybe it won't hurt as much as it does now. I was such a fool for pretending I didn't feel anything.

When he looks at me, that's who I am to him, nothing. I'm his friend, but above all else, nothing. Nobody worth falling for. I can't tell whether it's the rain burning my skin or my tears. It hurts. I promised myself I'd be better.

He said I was perfect, but he doesn't have a clue who I am. Nothing hurts more than how he looks at me so easily, so intensely, with no recollection of who I am or who I was. I thought he was being cruel, pretending not to know who I was. He looked straight past me. No guilt, nothing remorseful behind his ocean eyes.

I waited and waited, and he finally came back to walk past me as if I didn't mean anything. Sometimes, it feels as though nothing has come between us, and it feels surreal. But then I remember he's not laughing in the way I am; he's not thinking about me in the way I'm thinking about him.

When Tyler was here, Asher was so full of life; they were inseparable, and you couldn't tear them apart even if you tried. That's how we became. We liked it like that, being with each other. I wonder how he came to be the way he is now. Why has he changed so much?

We all change, but I guess this is what it means to grow up. I laugh and choke back the part of me wanting to scream. He's going to break my heart.

Whether he ends up choosing someone else, I have no choice but to be okay. There's nothing I can do. I guess my role is to make sure he's okay. I have to.

I won't stick around to watch someone else take my place. I should have enough pride to leave him, but I don't know how to when he's all I know. He once said I was the reason he believed in love. He once gave me his heart without realising it, and he never wanted it back as long as I always held it.

Who would've thought he would be the one to rip it out when

MARYAM A.H.

I made it a part of mine? I let myself fall asleep, letting the rain consume me wholeheartedly.

I guess he didn't find me this time.

I don't think he'll ever find me.

CHAPTER TWELVE
SUMMERS

I fidget with my necklace, careful not to accidentally break the chain. It's a silver chain with a butterfly attached at the end. It's my favourite thing in the entire world. Asher seems to be doing better, and I should be happier. I hate that I'm not. I have this feeling in the pit of my stomach, and nothing I do seems to get rid of it. Even my art seems darker, and it's not me.

I'm a cheerleader. I'm happy for people. I don't get jealous, especially over someone who has no attachment to me. So what if he seems happier without me? So what if we haven't spent much time together? I don't need to spend my every waking existence in his presence, and he doesn't need to spend it in mine.

So why am I acting like this? I can't stand it. What am I supposed to say to him? Pay attention to me? Why can't you see me? Why am I not good enough for you? It's exhausting. I feel like a high school girl. These feelings are so ridiculous, and I know that; that's what makes them so annoying.

Why did I think wearing a shirt would be the right fit today? I'm frozen. I stop in my tracks, watching as Asher fiddles with something in his hand. His smile is bright and alluring. If you didn't know him, you wouldn't think he had a single moody bone in his body.

My stomach swoons in somersaults, noticing the way his green sweater makes him appear so much more intense and handsome. His eyes light up the second that he sees me, and I try to ignore the buckling of my knees.

"Alessia." My name is like a song from his lips.

Why am I like this?

"Hey." I ignore the thundering of my heart, praying he can't hear it.

"I was hoping I'd run into you," he murmurs gently.

"It seems unlikely you wouldn't run into me here; it seems you're here as often as I am. I should make you a key for my den," I joke. I'm unsure why I'm laughing. I'm being completely serious. *Pace yourself*, I remind myself.

"Hold out your palm, please." He softly waits.

"You're not going to push me and run away, right?" My expression is tired and unimpressed.

"Don't make me wish I didn't see you in the first place." He rolls his eyes.

"Fine." I shrug.

"Close your eyes," he gently orders. Why are my cheeks turning red? I can feel my face burning, but nothing has happened yet. I don't understand what possessed me to turn into a lovestruck teenager. I reluctantly open my palm, and he eagerly places something in the middle of my hand.

I open my eyes, and my breath gets caught for a moment. My eyes fixate on the butterfly clip placed in the centre. Small and delicate, but the details are intricate and so beautiful. It's emerald and is easily a treasured piece I'm always going to cherish.

"It's beautiful..." the words come out as a fallen whisper.

"When I saw it, I thought of you." His words strike me so effortlessly.

"You can't just say things like that." I close my hand and hold it carefully.

"Why?" He doesn't realise how much power his words hold.

"Because we're friends, right? Nothing more? Nothing less? You call me beautiful; you buy me a gift, and then what? There's nothing more to it." Surely, he must know what he does. He must know how I feel, too, right?

"Just because I'm your friend doesn't mean I have to see you as anything less. I'm allowed to think you're beautiful. I'm allowed to be in awe of you. To think you're the most incredible, talented person. Just because I'm your friend doesn't mean I don't get to admire you or think of you. I'm allowed to think of you. Let things remind me of you."

What am I supposed to say to that? Why does he say things like this? I try to say something, anything, but words fail to escape my lips.

"I want to thank you." His eyes are tender and kind.

"Thank me?" My words sound breathless.

"I noticed before, but I was too scared to admit it, to realise what was happening. But I want to thank you because I forgot what it was like to feel safe and stable. For the longest time, I couldn't remember what it felt like for my heart to beat a little slower, for it not to be racing. Every time I'm around you, you make my heart beat the way it's supposed to. You make me feel the way I never thought I could. For that, I'm forever in your debt, always."

"Asher." My voice cracks. What is this man doing to me? My eyes move a little lower, and I watch my name escape his lips.

"Alessia." My name is a sweet whisper falling from his mouth. Awe cements in his gaze as adoration seeps through his irises, watching me intently, madly.

Does he know the way he's watching me? How heavy I can feel his gaze? How affectionate and soothing his words pour so effortlessly like they used to, before everything.

"You can't say things like that, okay?" I blurt, trying to tame the chaos unleashing in my mind.

"I don't understand," he says baffled.

I sigh deeply, not understanding how to even start. "Look… Friends don't think of friends like that. You can't say these things and expect me not to be confused. You say things, and then we're not meant to be anything more. Because you don't want to be anything more, and that's fine. But you can't expect me to not be confused. One second, you like me. The next, you want to be friends. Friends don't think of friends that way, okay?"

I hate how complicated this has become and how confusing and tiring everything is. I didn't want it to be like this, but he doesn't want anything more. He doesn't even know who I am, not really. Why am I expecting some sort of a miracle when it's clear it's not going to happen.

"I want to be honest. Am I not allowed to compliment you now?" he reaffirms in disbelief, not understanding what I'm trying to say.

"And stop looking at me like that." I laugh, uneasy.

"Like what?" His brows furrow. *Like I'm the one person who matters the most to you. Stop looking at me the way I look at you.*

"Just..." I let out a deep breath. "Go easy on the compliments, okay?" It sounds like I'm thinking too deeply into things. "Words carry power. I don't want either of us to get the wrong end of the stick."

"You worry too much." He ruffles my hair.

"I know," I whisper honestly.

I owe it to myself to not do this, whatever this thing is. I need to let things be, and so does he. But I don't think either of us understands what that is.

What things are supposed to be like.

I was a fool for thinking I could go into this *untouched*.

CHAPTER THIRTEEN
ASHER

I made pancakes for Dad today, and he was so surprised. You can tell it made his day. I stacked them on a plate with Nutella and strawberries. He took the plate off me so fast and dived in faster than I'd seen him eat his favourite takeaway. I was ready to throw up when I had a bite. How could I forget to put in sugar? You'd think I was trying to poison us both. How he ate that with a straight face, I'll never know.

I'm glad I got past the stage where I couldn't talk to Dad properly, for thinking how I still sometimes do. It's weird. My days are getting better, but I can't help but crave the familiarity of the emptiness that I knew.

I don't know how to move on from that properly, but I am getting better. I haven't heard from or seen Tyler lately. At night especially, it feels strange. I'd gotten used to him. I'd even tried calling him, but he didn't answer. It feels daunting to move on in some form, and he's getting left behind.

My heart aches for everything Tyler's missing, everything he could be doing. I'm not drowning like I used to anymore. I can breathe more than I could in a long time. But I'm scared that this is only momentary, and I'll forget how to breathe again. Trying to fight the same battle and win a war you don't know can be won is tiring.

I was thinking of seeing Alessia today, but she seems distant, and I don't really want to overwhelm her if she doesn't want to see me. I don't see myself as the one chasing her. I never thought I'd want to. I didn't think I would care if I hadn't seen her or if I'd upset her, but I do.

She makes me question everything; I can't remember how it began. When I'm around her, I can't think straight. When I look at her, I get lost in admiration. She consumes every thought I have. It's not right. We're just meant to be friends, and we can't be anything more.

She doesn't deserve anyone who isn't worthy of her. I get jealous at the thought of someone else getting to experience her affection, someone making her laugh who isn't me. To make that smile that I adore so much appear and know I don't get to keep it.

I don't blame her for getting mad. But doesn't she realise I like her enough to not want to ruin her? That I want better for her? Cyra wanted to hang out today, and normally, I would say no, but she isn't that bad. Well, having to make and keep relationships is kind of tiring, but it's for the better.

Now that Tyler isn't around much, I owe it to him to at least try not to stay cooped up all the time. Cyra wants me to meet her in what seems to be the middle of nowhere.

I'm wandering aimlessly, trying to follow where the hell these directions are. I think I'm here, but I can't see her anywhere. I slump down against the tree and regret saying yes to her in the first place. Either I'm lost, or she is. I'm probably in the wrong place, and this isn't as creepy as it seems.

I throw twigs I find on the ground the furthest I can possibly throw them into the distance. She doesn't even seem like the type of girl who likes to get her shoes dirty, so why am I standing in a field? The air feels strange around here, familiar almost. It reminds me of Alessia's garden, but not nearly as beautiful.

It still feels weird saying her name after calling her Summers for so long.

I wonder how she's doing and if she's well. I bet she's painting something, something amazing. I hear footsteps behind me, disturbing my train of thought as the leaves snap. I look up to see Cyra.

How is she managing to walk in this mud? Her heels are literally digging in the grass with every step she takes.

I must look concerned as she defends herself. "Oh please, don't look at me like that, I'm fine," she hisses.

"Tell that to the holes you're digging." She looks down as her heels puncture the mud.

"Okay, maybe you're right, but it's not harming anyone, so don't worry your pretty little head," she says. "Although I doubt much is in it," she whispers.

"I heard that," I snipe. "Are we going to be walking this slow the entire way? I'm kind of hungry and wondering how long it'll be the next time I'll be able to eat. At this rate, I don't think I'll see food ever again." I try to ignore the rumbles coming from my stomach.

"Oh, shut up," she mocks as she finally stands beside me. Her hair is braided and placed over her right shoulder. She's wearing a navy tank top and jeans with black heels.

"Oh, look at that, we're matching." She beams.

I look down and curse myself for not choosing literally any colour but navy.

"I realise that. I'm trying not to vomit," I say honestly. "Do you have a thing against coats? Do you enjoy freezing? You do realise it's winter, right?" I gesture my hands up and down at her to make my point.

"Are you going to moan the entire way?"

"I'm just saying, don't you know how to invest in things you actually need?"

She stops and looks at me up and down. "You do realise you look homeless, right?"

"You realise we're basically wearing the same thing, right?" I say sarcastically. I guess everyone I know is a little slow. "At least I'm not going to freeze to death."

Actually, why do I care? It's not like she's Alessia.

"Well, you know what they say. Body heat does the trick," she teases. "I don't know whose body you're going to get to heat you up, 'cause it's not going to be mine."

"Oh, relax," she says, pushing past me. She grabs my arm. "Well, follow me then." She pulls me forward. What did she think I was doing?

"So?"

"So...?" she questions.

"Where are we going?"

"You'll see, it's a surprise." She winks. "Don't worry, you'll like it." She laughs.

"What are you thinking about?" Her voice sounds curious.

"How long this is going to take."

"Yeah, I don't think so." She nudges me. "A woman, right?"

"I haven't seen my friend for a bit, and I miss her. I don't really understand what's going on with her. I think I've done something, but I'm not sure what," I say.

"Well, why don't you ask her?" she says, stating the obvious. "Because it's not that easy. I think I'm going to see her today." I've decided after this, I'm going straight to her.

Regardless of whether it's late or not, it depends on how long this is meant to be.

"You like her, huh?" she says softly.

"That's random, even for you," I say, taken aback, I don't even know how to respond. I hate my reaction.

"Well, you do, don't you?"

What's the use of denying it to her? It's not like she knows who she is. "I do."

She turns to look away. "Why?" she questions. "What's so great about her?" She finally looks at me, her tone frustrated and harsh.

"What's it to you? What do you mean what's so great about her?"

"I didn't mean it like that…"

"However you meant it, I'm not the person you want to insult her to." Whatever she expected me to say, that wasn't it.

"We're here." She stops, and I take everything in.

"We're still in the middle of nowhere."

She crosses her arms. "Look properly, will you?" Her tone

sounds fed up. "What do you think I'm doing? Was I meant to bring a pair of binoculars with me?"

"Do you always have to be so sarcastic?" she snipes.

"How else did you expect me to answer that?" She's telling me to look properly, but it's still trees. I don't even know if I'm being genuine or sarcastic anymore.

"Wait," I say, walking more forward. "Here we go."

Muttering under her breath, she says, "Took you long enough." She pats my shoulder as she strolls past me. "Well, come on then." She hurries me along.

She's not even fazed that she can barely walk. I don't know whether I should offer to pick her up or something. How has she completely switched? One second, she's near the point of crying, and now, looking at her, it's as if nothing has happened. "Are you high?" I ask.

"Do I look high?"

"I'm just wondering. I didn't think when you said you wanted to hang out, you meant we'd be standing in the middle of nowhere in awe at a bunch of trees." Perhaps I do need to lighten up.

"Okay, now." She comes to a halt. "Tell me, what do you see?" Her eyes search me for any kind of reaction.

"More trees and a really old house." I feel like I'm taking an exam I didn't prepare for, and I don't know any of the answers.

"Come on." She tugs me forward.

I stumble, losing my footing for a moment. "Are you mad?"
I try to balance myself,

"Oh, come on." She pulls harder.

"There's a thing called personal space. Try looking it up

sometime. Here, I'll demonstrate." I take her hand off me. "There we go."

"You're exhausting, you know that?" Cyra rolls her eyes.

"We have some issues, but we can work on them. You don't need to kill me." Why else would she be trying to drag me in there? My life is practically flashing before my eyes.

"Could you be any more dramatic? Shut up."

I decide against my urges telling me to leave her, and I finally listen to her. It might be the only thing that saves me. "I suppose it's not so bad."

Now that I'm actually looking at it, it's actually kind of beautiful. There's a fence around the house and a big porch you could have every meal on. A broken swing on the far-right corner looks so comfortable, overlooking everything so you can't miss a single thing.

Cyra locks her arm with mine and holds it. "So far so good?"

Before I can answer, she pulls me a little more forward, pulling me down to the far end of the porch where the swing is.

"Allow me." She takes my hand and places it on the wooden fence. "Look."

I reluctantly follow where my hand is placed. I sit down more comfortably, crossing my legs across the floor. "It looks like something is etched here, but you brought me all the way here to look at an etch in a fence?"

"Look harder, will you?"

"Alright." I wish I had glasses. "It's a carving. What's that got to do with me?" I ask.

She sucks in a breath and exhales as she punches my arm.

"Can you concentrate? Do you wear glasses or something, or are you genuinely blind?"

"I'm not the one pointing to a random house saying 'look'."

If she wanted to look at carvings, a shop around the corner from where we live could have done that for her.

"Asher."

My name is almost faint. I'm surprised I didn't see that before. "My name?" It's probably just a coincidence, but why is it there? "I don't get it," I admit.

"What's under it?" she hesitantly asks.

"Why are you nervous?" I question.

"You'll know once you see it."

"Whatever that means." My chest feels tight, and I'm afraid if it gets any tighter, I'll stop breathing.

I don't get it. Is this a joke?

"Why is Alessia's name there?"

Before I wait for an answer, my eyes catch a glimpse of a star. This looks like mine. I pull it out of my pocket and hold it against the carving. "This is mine. Is this a trick?"

"You really don't remember?"

"If I did, I wouldn't be asking why my name is there, or hers and why my star is there and a butterfly? Aren't those her favourite?" I stand up. "I don't really care for games. Either give me an answer or let me go." I demand some kind of answer to make sense of it.

"You know who Alessia is?"

"Yes, bu—" I cut in before she has a chance to give me an excuse. "So why the hell are you pretending you don't know her? Why are you bringing me here to see our names carved? Did she do this? Did you?"

Too many questions come spilling out, and I watch as she struggles to keep up. Contemplating which one she should answer first.

"How old must I have been to do this? I wouldn't write our names like that. Am I really that flawed that I can't remember a thing to do with her? Were we more than friends? Or maybe that's something we found funny. Why am I left in the dark?" My mind is spinning.

"Asher." She tries to reach for my hand.

"Don't." I pull back, trying to get as far as possible.

"Why are you doing this? Why are you pretending?" she says, accusation masking her tone.

I stop and turn. "Pretending?" What does that even mean? "How am I pretending?"

"Exactly the way you're acting now, the way you pretend not to know anything!" she yells.

"Because I don't know anything!" I yell louder than I meant to. "I don't know a thing about you, that stupid carving, anything." I run my hands through my hair.

"I met a woman I really like, and I mean really fucking like, and somehow, I keep fucking things up with her. I make her cry, I make her mad, I make her hurt, and I don't know how to make it stop. I don't know why she won't see me or suddenly gets quiet when she looks at me. When she looks at me, it feels like she's waiting for something I don't know I can give her."

A moment passes between us, and neither of us says anything, but she's the first to break the tension rippling through the air.

"Don't get mad," she pleads. "Maybe this isn't the best thing for you, that she isn't the best thing for you. This" —she gestures to the carving—"everything…" She exhales heavily. "None of it is good for you, and I'd do anything to make you see that, but I don't know how." Defeated, she takes a seat on the swing, taking off her heels and looking ahead.

"I'm selfish. I get you're trying to protect her, but I can't let her go. I want to so badly, but I can't, and I hate myself for it," I confess.

"Don't you hear yourself?" Cyra sighs as I take a seat beside her. "You must know she was more to you, right?"

"No. Well, not before this, but I figured now she must have been." I watch as the breeze blows the leaves ahead of us. "I take it you're not going to tell me who she was to me."

"I wish, but it's not my story to tell. It's yours alone to remember, and I can't make you feel what you're meant to. Remember what you're supposed to. It's not the same, but you know it's not going to end the way you want, don't you?" She heeds, her words carrying a silent plea to be cautious.

"I'm trying, I'm trying to be better, to change. I'm not going to hurt her if I can help it. I'm going to be the man she deserves. I'm not that person yet, but I will be, and when I am, I'll ask her to be mine. But right now, I can only be her friend." I can't hurt her or make promises when I know I might break.

"But you don't remember her?"

"No, I wish I did."

"Wow." She huffs.

"What?"

"Anyone would think you did. Don't you realise how you talk about her and how you feel? It's more than just liking her. You're wise enough to know that you're not a fool." Unexpected judgement fogs her words.

"I'm not in love with her," I say.

"I didn't say that you were." I shoot her a glare. She's not as smart as she thinks she is.

"You did once. Maybe you remember more than you think." Sympathy lingers in her tone.

"I was what?" I loved her? Why wouldn't she tell me that? How could I not remember that?

"I have a question." I'm ignoring that she told me I loved her in a past life. Her voice is uneasy.

"Even if I say no, you're going to ask anyway." I'm not going to pretend this entire thing isn't making my head want to explode, but something about sitting here.

The scenic view makes my heart beat a little slower. I don't know why I can't remember Summers and why she is the person I've chosen to forget. I really don't know a thing about her. She knows me, a me I don't even know. "Do me a favour?"

"What?" I say.

"Please don't say anything about this," she pleads. "Please?"

"What's the big deal anyway? You showed me. It can't be that big of a secret." I glance at her, her eyes suffocated by regret.

"Look, I wasn't supposed to say anything. I thought you were joking. Please don't say anything. Please?" I contemplate her plea, and her hand squeezes my arm.

Her eyes search mine for confirmation I won't say anything.

If I want the truth, I have to find out for myself. I need to find the right time to ask Alessia. I don't want to scare her off or give her another reason for disappearing from me. "Fine, I won't. Yet." I try to free my arm from her grip.

"Thank you." She lets out a sigh of relief.

"Can you please stop holding me? You're becoming too comfortable."

"Oh. Yes. My bad." She pulls away and plays with her braid. "Thank you."

She leans forward and kisses me on the cheek. My cheeks flush, and she giggles. It takes everything I have not to make a huge deal out of that. Surely, she can't be that gullible? Does she think giving me a peck on the cheek is going to make me forget about it?

I try to change the topic, but even the silence is screaming at the tension between us. Whatever I do, it's still awkward, and I can still feel her eyes on me, seeing if I've changed my approach to this or if I'll tell anyone. "You really change your tune fast, don't you?"

She flinches. "Let's not make this weird, okay?"

"Okay."

"Thanks." Relief washes over her. I smile to let her know it's okay. All I can think of now is Alessia and how tangled this whole thing has become. Asking questions doesn't seem to be getting me anywhere, so I have to try different ways to get my answers. When she's more comfortable, she'll tell me then.

Lately, I've been hanging out more with Cyra. I really think she and Nate would be perfect for each other, but they can't stand the sight of one another. I've tried asking why, but they start ranting about their days to avoid answering. They think I haven't noticed, but I've let it go. That's all I can do lately.

"Okay, I'm going to go. I'll be back later and try not to burn the apartment down when I'm gone, will you?" my dad says as he rushes out the door, not waiting for me to respond.

I guess burning the place down is off my agenda for today. I don't have anything planned anymore. I take a final bite out of my apple, throwing it in the bin as I rush out the door. I'm going to say hey. There's nothing wrong with saying hey. I pace back and forth outside her door. I need to knock.

I have so much pride; it's going to be the death of me one day, but if she wanted to see me, she would. I'm not the one who should be reluctant anyway. I'm not hiding anything. She is. I knock louder than I intended to, and just when I debate walking off, I hear rustling inside, and the door opens wide.

"Come in," she says, piling a stack of papers on the table. "Sorry it's such a mess." She laughs nervously, her hair tied back in a bun with loose strands dangling free.

"You're not wearing colour," I say, surprised. I've never seen her in anything but colour.

"Oh, yeah." She peers down at herself. "I've been busy. I can't always be so bright." She seems drained from her usual perkiness.

"I just… uh, I just wanted to see how you were doing." I don't know whether I should sit down or carry on standing. Her place is scattered with paintings and papers.

"I guess you can be sweet." She stops fidgeting with the papers and gestures to me to take a seat. "I've been good, really busy lately. It seems I've overbooked myself these days." I take her up on her offer and can't help but notice the tiredness that's consuming her skin.

"I hung out with Cyra a while ago, and she took me to this house. It was really weird."

She bites her lips, and her cheeks start to lose colour. "Oh yeah? How was it?" Her voice is careful.

"It was okay." I don't know how to begin to ask her the questions.

She doesn't even question how I know Cyra. "That's good." Her smile returns. "How are you?"

"I'm good, I'm really good." It doesn't feel like a lie, but something feels off.

"I'm really glad," she says genuinely.

"Have I done something to offend you?" I ask. I don't want her to avoid me anymore. If I've done anything, I would rather solve it. I don't want it to be like this.

"No, you haven't done a thing." She doesn't look at me this time; instead, she grabs a piece of paper and starts fidgeting with it.

"Are you sure? Because I would rather you tell me so I can fix it." Alessia stops fidgeting with her paper and places it down, sighing heavily.

"There's nothing you can do to fix it because there's nothing for you to fix. It's me, I just... I'm just really tired." She stands up and brushes herself. "I promise this isn't your doing, but um... if you don't mind, I really want to sleep, and I don't want to leave you sitting here by yourself... so..."

I immediately stand up. "No, I get it. Well... um, sleep well, I guess."

She smiles, and I close the door behind me. I haven't moved from her door yet. This doesn't feel right. She isn't her. It doesn't make sense, the house, her. Nate didn't even know who she was.

Were we a secret? But I can't think of a single reason why I would keep her a secret. Or were we really nothing, and she was the one who had all the feelings? I fight the urge to go back inside. I don't want to upset her, whatever this is. I don't know what I did, but I can't force her to like me. If she can't stand me, that's okay.

I have to be fine with that. I hope things work out for her and she finally gets some sleep.

I miss her.

She always has so many questions for me, any excuse to be in my face, but today, I can't shake the one question I have for her.

Who is she?

Who is she really?

CHAPTER FOURTEEN
CYRA

Why couldn't I have listened for once? I had the right intention. I just didn't realise it would backfire on me the way it did. He really doesn't know anything. Now I have to walk on eggshells around him in case he slips up, and it'll be because of me, and that's a fight I'm not ready to have.

I've created this whole mess, and the guy is practically a ticking time bomb itching to go off. I can't believe I did that; he hasn't said anything yet, but so far, so good, I guess.

"Are you fucking insane?" Nate storms in, slamming the door shut behind him. Asher lasted longer than I thought.

"Make yourself at home, I guess." I throw my hands up.

"Do I look like I'm in the mood for your sarcasm?" he says, pacing back and forth.

"Before I admit to anything, what are we angry about?" I'm sure if Nate had a gun, he would shoot me dead in an instant.

"Got it." I slowly walk backwards and take my seat on the sofa.

"Are you done talking shit yet?" he snaps.

"I really want to say no, but I'm afraid this might be a trick question." Now, he really wants to kill me, and honestly, I can't say that I blame him.

"Okay, look, I swear I didn't mean it. But even if I did, he can take care of himself." My words spill out fast. "He should know. He has every right to. I don't know why everyone is tip-toeing around him."

"You know why. For God's sake, Cyra, you've seen firsthand why we can't do this shit, and you go around pulling this crap."

"Well, why shouldn't he know? Alessia has to do with everything, and he's acting like he doesn't know anything. It's insane. You can't pretend to be okay with it and hope the problem will sort itself out."

"Don't give me that—"

I cut him off. "Don't come in here telling me what to do, telling me what I'm doing wrong. How about when he finds out about you, huh? What are you going to do then?" Guilt momentarily seizes his expression, his eyes distant and cold.

"Whatever, just do everyone a favour and leave. Why the fuck did you even come back? We were doing fine until you showed up. Just stay out of everyone's business, especially his." He doesn't wait for me to say anything as he leaves, shutting the door behind him.

I want to hurl every swear word I know under the sun at him but decide against it. I'm only going to cause more damage. I've been so focused on Asher that I forgot about Nate. If he starts whispering in Asher's ear about me, I'll kill him. I'm going to do this whether he likes it or not, and he can't stop me.

I'm freezing. I won't admit that, though. Nothing or no one is more bipolar than this weather. I didn't think it would be so cold. I tried hinting for Asher to give me his hoodie to wear earlier, but only for a little while. I thought he didn't realise what I was asking him, but no, he understood. He just didn't want to give it to me.

It was like nothing had happened. You wouldn't have guessed I showed him anything. He doesn't seem curious and hasn't mentioned a single word about it. It's too easy for him to move on, though. I need to find out what he's waiting for. If he is waiting for something.

I can't be too sure that he isn't going to say anything the moment I turn my back. That's why I need to stay. I can see why Alessia fell so hard for him. I'd be heartbroken if he forgot everything about me, about us. He really does love her.

He doesn't know it, and he won't admit it for the life of him, but he really is *her* Asher. Still, I can't shake a part of me that feels like he's pretending, that he's cruel and this entire thing is just a massive joke to him. I can't help but wish a little that it was. It would make it easier to accept.

Do his feelings not feel familiar? Surely, he must know deep down. It's obvious, and anyone and practically everyone can see it besides him.

How does this fool not know he's in love? In love with the same girl he has no memory of.

I don't trust him yet, not completely. That much is obvious.

"Truce?" I say, putting a blueberry muffin in front of Nate as he tries to ignore me. He can't run far from me. We practically run in the same circles. "I thought I told you to leave," he says bluntly.

"You're not very welcoming, are you?" I say, pulling a chair out as I slide down. I love how the warmth never fails to embrace me in this place. I don't know what I love the most about it here, the coffee or the food. "Come on, have it. I'm sorry, okay?"

He lifts his head, and he meets my eyes. "I guess a blueberry muffin won't hurt." He reluctantly reaches for it as he splits it in half. "Want some?" He holds half, waiting for me to take it.

"Sure." I take a bite. I've been dying to take a bite out of it ever since I bought it for him, although I really bought it for me.

He's nice enough to share, plus I can't eat the entire thing. I have calories I need to watch. He breaks another piece of it before he bites into it and hands it to me.

"I get it. You're sorry," I say as I take it out of his hand and swallow it before he has a chance to retract his offer. He isn't normally *this* generous.

So, I wasn't taking this for granted. "Yeah, well, I shouldn't have shouted at you like that."

"It's okay. So we agree we play nice from now on?"

"Agreed, I'm tired of trying to avoid you. It's draining, and you're basically everywhere. Do you ever stay home?"

"Only on the weekends." I try to make him laugh, but he doesn't look the slightest bit amused. "I wanted to ask; how did you find out anyway? What I did?"

Asher didn't say anything, judging by how casual he was. It didn't seem like he would have said anything. And I didn't want to ask and open up a can of worms that didn't need to be opened to begin with. He's too caught up in his lovestruck drama to remember anything. This is why it's more confusing to figure out how Nate knows.

"I happened to be passing by." *Of course.*

"Hmm, that sounds believable to you?" I scoff.

"Alright, I was walking, but I saw you heading there. I knew you couldn't be insane enough to take him there, but I was wrong, and you did so." He looks at me like a disappointed parent, all pouty and irritated about how I could mess up so bad.

"If it makes you feel better, he had no idea what I was talking about, and he still seems to remain oblivious." I don't mean to sound so disappointed, as if I expected all chaos to let loose. Perhaps deep down, I secretly hope it will. It's about time already. I'm tired of this whole chapter. We need to move on.

"I don't know why you look so grim. No one is telling you to get involved or be here," Nate says. He isn't trying to be rude, just truthful.

"I don't look grim. You're projecting your moodiness onto me. I'm fine, thank you."

"That doesn't make me feel better," he mumbles.

"Oh well, I tried." I take the last bite of my muffin. I don't want to hurt Asher. That was never my intention, but someone needs to open his eyes and decide. If this is the only way to do it, I'll gladly be the one to make it all come crashing down.

It's for the best, and no one seems to see it except me.

Asher deserves better. They *both* do.

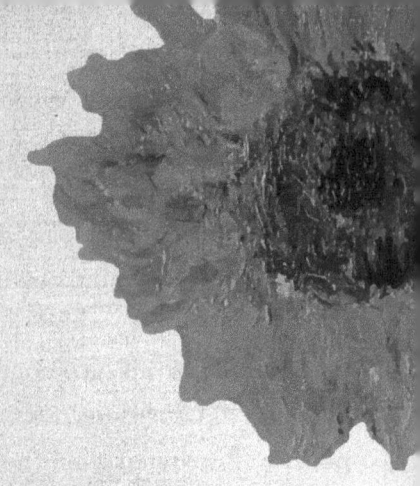

CHAPTER FIFTEEN
ASHER

I was going through my stuff earlier, hoping to find something to help me figure out Alessia. I haven't looked through my box of stuff for a while. I didn't feel any need for it. I'm glad I wasn't impulsive enough to throw it all out because then I wouldn't have any memories except the ones I remember left.

I opened the box to expect sentimental memories to overwhelm me. But I don't remember why I have half the stuff in there. It doesn't make any sense. Still, at least I remember some of it. Tyler always said to keep stuff. It's good because times constantly change, and the moment is forever cemented.

I kept it for his sake, and I carried on from there. I left it for Dad to know we had good memories, and he didn't lose me completely. It sounds morbid, but I wanted him to realise he didn't fail me. He had nothing to do with it. This box would remind him he's the reason why I had good times.

Even Nate, if he wanted something of mine. I doubt he would, and if he did, he would never tell me, not that I blame him. I'd make fun of him for the rest of his life.

I made a will a while ago and left everything for my dad. I even left Nate a few things. If Tyler had been here, I would have left things for him, too.

Although I don't think anything like this would happen if he was here. When I didn't know what to do, he did. Nate was more of our little brother; even though he's older than both of us, he's so childish. It's okay, though. He's doing fine. Even Tyler would be proud of him.

He's come a long way, and Tyler wouldn't let him forget it, even if he does have his moments. The box is all so random. There are bus tickets and pieces of random coloured paper. I'm sure it has something on it, but it must have gotten wet because the ink is too smudged to read anyway.

I used to have my star in here. I thought it belonged in the box as I got older. I didn't like the way it just sat there when it had so much purpose—to me, anyway. The star is old and rusty, but it's still in good condition, considering I've had it since I was six years old.

I remember the day I got it as if it were yesterday. I was going on an adventure. I was so excited about exploring the world that awaited me. So optimistic and hopeful. I was only allowed to explore across my road, in this park, but it was still something. The lust I had for life, everything was magical to me.

I was running, taking in the air. I loved the feel of the wind against my skin when I ran, the feeling of not knowing what to expect. I didn't mind if I fell or scraped my knee a couple of times. It was all a part of the journey. I thought I wouldn't mind if I got lost, that it would make me braver and wiser.

That was until I did end up getting lost. I remember the panic in the pit of my stomach, annoyed that I didn't listen to my parents when they told me not to go too far out.

When watching an adventure movie or cartoon, there's always a moment when the main character realises they have probably ventured too far. That they're up against something they didn't think they would have to overcome. But to become a true explorer, to say you did it, you have to complete your journey despite what you may be up against.

It sounds rather poetic for a child. I remember that was *my* journey. I didn't listen to my parents, and I went out to brave it alone. It makes me laugh how I built up this entire quest in my head and how invincible I thought it made me. The worst part? I didn't even wander far.

Like I said, I was *optimistic*.

I tried to find my way back, but I couldn't. I took this other route, which I didn't even know was there. Once I was done searching, I sat down and cried. I was too lost, and now it was getting dark. I was going to get in trouble once I got back. I realised I failed my quest, and it defeated me.

I was so distraught about failing my first big mission. I was sitting down, and I was crying. That excitement I had went, along with the curiosity to explore anything like that again. I knew I was going to get the scolding of my life. They would probably ground me from playing outside again.

They only let me out unless I was within their eyesight. I heard voices when I was wallowing, lost in thought, about how I was basically lost forever. I remember how much it startled me; I thought I was completely alone. They were laughing, and the girl I couldn't stop staring at was saying, "Again, please, please!"

I tried composing myself, but it wasn't working well. I didn't want to cry in front of a girl. I saw her tugging on the man's white shirt. His complexion was golden brown; his hair fell short. The chestnut colour was exactly the same as hers. I didn't really see his face. I knew he looked like her, though.

When he lifted the girl up, she covered his face, and he laughed. I started thinking how unfortunate it would be if he fell. I remember preparing myself to catch her because if he fell, he would launch that kid like a rocket. She was wearing a pink dress with sandals.

I remember thinking about how she had the type of hair you'd throw out of a tower and climb up on it. I remembered my dad's favourite story as a kid was Rapunzel, and I remember thinking if she might be her. I wanted my dad to be there so badly because he was going to miss her.

Obviously, it was much shorter, but all the girls I knew had kind of short hair, but hers wasn't. It was long enough to make me think about nothing else. Besides the fact that she looked like the kind of girl who belongs in a story, she seemed cold, and I wanted to give her the coat I should have been wearing.

Her tanned face was buried in her dad's hair, and her hands covered his eyes.

"Honey, for me to walk, I need to actually seem," he explained, laughing as he steadily balanced her on his shoulders. Her legs dangled down as she moved her hands to his hair. I can't begin to explain how ridiculously slow everything seemed.

It was as if someone was watching a movie and hitting pause

every two seconds. After what seemed like a lifetime of them walking in slow motion, they stopped when they saw me. Who wouldn't stop to see why a random kid was staring at you like he'd never come across another being in his life?

I was so relieved, but then it dawned on me that the girl had also stopped and was in front of me. I kind of forgot why I was crying in the first place.

"You okay, kid?" he asked, his voice deep, startling me. I thought he could make the trees cower. I had never heard someone's voice so deep before.

Before he could say anything, I burst out crying even more, choking between sobs. I suppose the girl temporarily made me forget why I was crying, but at least the man reminded me. He lifts his daughter off his shoulders and gently puts her on the ground.

I cleared my throat, and before I could say anything, the girl asked, "Can I sit, please?" I was still sitting on the floor. It was like my legs didn't want to move, and the last thing I needed was to fall again. I needed to reserve my energy for the hike home.

I coughed but didn't say anything, breathing more steadily now, wiping the tears trickling down my cheeks.

"Thank you." She beamed.

He smiled and reached down to kiss her forehead.

"Here," she said, holding out her hand. Her father curiously watched her; he didn't say anything. I looked at him, and he nodded, gesturing his head to her hand. I hesitated for a moment, but then I looked down and saw the star. My token. It was hers to begin with. "I'll tell you a secret." She leaned in, and this time, I stood up. I decided this was worth wasting my energy on. I was slightly taller than she was, but that's okay.

Her voice was gentle and soft, and something about her eyes wouldn't let me look away. "I made it myself. I decorated it so it could be like a rainbow," she proudly told me.

Now I realise she missed out on a lot of colours of the rainbow, but it's the thought that counts. I couldn't help but smile. "It's magic." Her eyes shone under the faded sun. The star did look magical. It felt like it at the time, only because I was convinced she wasn't a part of this world. If she made it, I'd keep it safe for the rest of the time. I was never shy; I was known for speaking my mind. For being cheeky. People liked that. It never occurred to me to ask her for her name. I was blown away by her.

I always thought I would see her again, I didn't think that time would be the last, but it was. She looked like something out of a fairy tale book. I felt so privileged, not knowing what that meant at the time, but I felt quite honoured.

I knew it was special.

"It'll help you get home. If you're ever sad, this will help you." I listened to every word, vowing never to forget it, and I believed it for the longest time. Her dad messed up her hair and put her back on his shoulders.

"That was nice of you," he said, holding onto her tight.

"He needs it more than I do," she said without hesitation, taking a lasting look at the token. See now, I would have found that sarcastic and probably would have thrown it back at her.

That day, I took Mum's butterfly off her bracelet. It was lying around, and I thought I could keep it. She wouldn't mind. I gave the girl the silver butterfly, which was small and delicate, and she looked as though I gave her my heart.

I remember she smiled, and for a moment, I couldn't move. I couldn't take my eyes off her and the smile that seemed to have me so starstruck.

After that, I found my way home, but I didn't go as far out as I thought I would. I followed her and her dad. It turned out that I had taken the wrong turn. I was small, and everything seemed like a maze to me. I never actually thanked her; I don't remember even saying anything. I smiled and hoped she understood how much it meant to me from that.

When I got home, I ran up to my mother and hugged her so tight she didn't even scold me. She knew I already learnt my lesson. I ran to Dad and told him I had to wait until I was older and bigger to go on any adventures. He didn't mind. He laughed and said it was okay.

I remember talking so fast, telling him how I met the girl from the story, the one with long hair, and how real she was. He said he wished he was there but that if it was true and I did see her, it was for a reason. Magical people don't turn up for anything. There was a reason.

I showed him the star, and he studied me and told me I should keep it safe because it was important to her, so it should be important to me, too.

It was.

It still is.

I remember the excitement I felt. I finally did what the other explorers did before me. I finished my quest. I found my treasure. The star was it, and I wasn't ever letting it go. I wonder if I saw the girl after that, but I just didn't recognise her. I wish I could meet her again so I could thank her.

I wouldn't be rude or sarcastic. I'm not a mean person. I would love to genuinely thank her for it. It's weird how such a small thing can make such a huge impact on you. Ever since then, I've always kept it by me. Obviously, that wasn't the case when I got older, but it still made me feel safe.

When I have it, I feel like I can overcome anything. I'm not a sentimental type of guy, but it's important. It seems pointless, but she guided me back home to being safe and sound that day. I can't throw it away even after all these years.

It's funny. I never usually keep many things and tend to break everything, but I haven't ruined this. Not in the slightest. I've been thinking about the story recently and whether the girl was right. I haven't felt at home in a long time, but I feel like I've finally found my way.

Ever since Alessia has barged into my life, as much as I've tried to force her out of it, I wonder if she realises she's kind of like it, the magic the star that was missing for a while. Now she's here, it might start working again. Perhaps the star will really guide me back this time.

CHAPTER SIXTEEN
ASHER

"Hey!" I shout, and Alessia almost trips over.

"Hi?" she says cautiously. "I wouldn't expect to see you here." She looks past me, wondering whether anyone else is here.

"It's just me for now," I say, handing her a coffee cup. "Don't worry, it's hot chocolate." Her smile grows wide, and she reluctantly takes the cup from my hand. "I know how you're not a fan of coffee. I don't blame you. I was coming to see you anyway, actually."

I try to ignore the jitters forming in my stomach. Nerves aren't a usual occurrence when I see Alessia. "Thank you, and I guess you found me then." She seems different. Alessia unlocks her door and gestures for me to follow.

"Don't worry about it." I try to ignore the strained tension threatening to suffocate us, but her smile is stiff. I swallow and try not to fidget, placing my hands in my pocket. I don't know what I'm missing here, but I don't like it. I try to reflect on what I could have done, but nothing comes to mind.

Is she busy? Perhaps I'm keeping her from something, and she's too polite to kick me out. But then again, she wasn't too shy last time.

"You brought two cups but didn't know I'd be here? Bit risky, if you ask me," she says, teasing, as she takes a sip.

"I took my chances," I lie. I knew she would be here. She's always here lately. If there's ever a time when you need to be sure where she is, it's always her den, without a doubt. But these days, she doesn't seem to leave her apartment; I don't see her outside as much as I used to.

"You're not around much these days." I cough. I don't know why I'm being awkward; it's as if she forced me to say that.

"I've got a lot of things to do, but you seem to be doing great, really great, actually," she says sincerely, but her smile seems dishonest.

"I miss you," I blurt out and immediately regret it when she looks as though she's about to cry.

"I have to admit I miss you, too." She nudges me. "Finally thinking about me, huh? I knew you would at some point."

Is she mad because I haven't been by?

It's been hard not to. I wanted to give her space. "You know I do." I don't want to overwhelm her, but I always think of her.

"You shouldn't say stuff like that," her voice says softly. "You'll give a girl the wrong idea. After all, it's not like we'll be anything else."

"What do you mean?" I don't say this to everyone or anyone, just her.

"Just... don't want you breaking anyone's heart." Her voice is playful. "Anyway," she quickly carries on before I can say anything, "you want to take a seat? I'm getting kind of tired of standing." She pulls my arm and pulls me down next to her.

"The likelihood of me saying no is next to nothing, so you don't need to pull me every time." Sometimes, I forget she doesn't really have any social skills. "I don't tell anyone else I'm thinking about them." I go back to the comment she made. "I haven't seen you around, and I really miss you. You don't seem like yourself lately. You got mad when I said that, but there's no harm in it. I was just checking in to see that you're alright. I'm allowed to do that. Right?"

"Nothing is wrong. I'm allowed to do my own thing. I don't always need to be by you." She sighs heavily. "I do have a life, I don't know why you think—"

I cut her off before she started ranting. "I didn't say you didn't." I bite my tongue. "Are you mad because I'm saying I miss you or that I've come to see you?"

She drops the glass of water she was drinking. "Just stop worrying." I grab a cloth to wipe the water. "Don't worry. I can do that," she says, taking it out of my hand.

"It's alright, I ca—"

"I said it's okay, don't worry. I can do it." Her voice is stern and cold. I debate whether to leave, but if she really wants me gone, she'll say. I clear my throat and try to think of something to say to ease the tension as I take her apartment in, noticing one colour that stands out, yellow.

It's like she can read my mind as she says, "You wore yellow for me?" Her eyes gesture to my shirt.

I didn't realise I was wearing it. "It reminds me of you, you know that. These days, I've been missing you a lot more lately," I answer honestly. Am I doing it again? Saying words that confuse her?

"How's your work?" I distract myself before I say anything else. Besides, she's been working hard on it.

I haven't met many artists, but I admire how much she puts into it. I've surprised her because she double-checks to see if she heard me right.

"It's good. I've been caught up in more pieces than I realised. I have this thing with thinking I can accomplish everything, and it won't wear me down. But I guess everything does in the end, you know? Anyway, I'm not complaining. It's how I can afford to make a living, so I can't be too reckless around it."

"Do you feel tired?" Now that I'm looking at her, she's still beautiful, but her eyes look tired, and her skin looks a little pale. She laughs, but it's vacant with her general bliss.

"No, I don't sleep that much anyway. I do my best work during the night and during the day. I feel guilty for wasting a day when I know I could be doing something," she admits. "I don't mind, though. I love painting. It's yours to do what you will. There's no pressure to be perfect. It's just you. Whatever you do has no right or wrong, but to you, it means everything. It's an escape I can't seem to find unless I paint. You capture what you feel in the moment, and you can keep it for the rest of your life." She fiddles with the strands undone in her bun. I can't fathom the life that ignites within her when she talks about how she paints.

I could listen to her for hours on end and not get bored. It's one of my favourite things. I'd let her talk for a lifetime if I could. You don't see it often; things are usually primarily money-driven, and people don't do anything unless they profit from it. No one seems to do anything that they genuinely enjoy anymore.

I miss that. That passion and genuine enthusiasm you have about something you love. It's refreshing to see the flame you used to have, knowing it still exists. Even if you don't have it anymore, it still exists somewhere. I remember being like her.

"I've seen you take a lot of photos. Do you like photography?" I ask. I didn't mean for that to sound as it did. It seemed more natural in my head.

It's funny. I've seen her trip up with every other step she takes sometimes while trying to get a good shot. She doesn't seem aware of her surroundings or what the word 'safety' means.

I don't know how she's still walking. I'm surprised she hasn't broken a leg. "Yeah, I get excited by everything, it seems. I just... I don't know why, but you know when you see things from a different angle, it changes your perspective on everything? It's kind of like that. There's beauty everywhere. You have to be willing to see it." There it is again, the flame. Her eyes are distant, but she carries on. "The world is always going to look colourless to you if you choose to walk through it blind," Alessia says, sipping her hot chocolate and scrunching her face as she burns her tongue a little.

"How is it still hot?" she says, blowing into her cup.

"When do you think is the perfect moment to take a photo?" I ask.

"Full of questions today, aren't you?"

"I'm curious," I say, shrugging. I seem random today, but I can't think of a better time to ask.

"Well, don't blame me if you get bored," she warns.

"Well, believe me, I'm anything but bored." Her cheeks flush a little. I like it when she blushes because of me. When she smiles, and I'm the reason for it.

"Anything can be a perfect moment. I don't wait for a time when I think things will look their best. There's not something that needs to happen for it to be that perfect. If you see something worthwhile in it, then that's the moment to capture. Right now, there are several things I can take a photo of."

She explains, fiddling with her cup. "Okay, look over there." She gestures with her eyes. I follow her gaze as she stands up by her window. She waits for me to stand beside her and points to the other end of the path in the far corner. "See that couple?"

I nod in agreement. "Yeah?"

"Look at the way they're laughing. Genuine laughter. They're not trying to be anything but themselves. That, to me, is a moment worth capturing."

Alessia gazes at the couple in wonder. It's a middle-aged couple. I'd say they're in their late forties. The guy is pale white, like the woman; she's ginger, and he's brunette.

"They may have stuff going on generally. I mean, everyone does. But the way they're laughing, it seems as though they're the only two people to exist right now. Nothing else matters at this moment because they're too busy living *right now*. They're not thinking about what stresses them out. Their worries. Right now, all that matters at this moment is they're happy."

I know what she's doing. She's also looking at me to see if

I realise it while she gulps down her cup, subtly licking her lips clean. I don't think anything could beat her flame, and I'll pray every day if it means it'll never burn out.

But lately, I haven't seen her flame or tried to get to her spots to take the best photos. I haven't seen her come alive doing what she loves. I didn't realise how much that scares me until now, the possibility that she could lose her light. I love the way she doesn't see fault and tries to look for the good in everything.

To be able to think the way she does and refuse to see anything bad is a blessing. In spite of everything, she would still find a way to survive and repair every broken piece she sees, still find the colours of the world and collect them one by one to make the universe whole again. I never want her to feel hopeless or lose *her colour*. Maybe that's why she's the way she is. She carries the light of the messes she's had to repair, the colours of the universe we take for granted.

I would never take that for granted. When I spend time with her, I feel like Tyler would be cursing me right now, making fun of how I'm sitting here and listening. I don't listen to anyone, but I listen to her. He would probably make fun of the way I notice everything about her.

I still notice, even if her eyes look a little lighter than usual. I remember things about her, and I don't remember anything. I remember her laugh, her smile. I know he wouldn't stop making fun of me. He would sit me down and try to understand why the fuck I haven't done anything about her.

I notice this, but I won't do anything. I won't make anything of us. Even if I know something could happen. I can't slip up, not more than I already have. I can't help myself though. Sometimes, I want to hold her and never let her go. I want to spend all my hours with her, all my days with her. I would never admit that. Even if I want to make something of us and tell her how I feel. Back when Tyler was alive, it was different. I'm not in the place I am now. I'd try to make something happen. Even if we didn't get off to a great start at first. I wouldn't stop until I gave her the world.

Even then, I'd find a way to give her more and never stop. Lately, I have seen potential and hope that I can make a go of things, but not until I'm certain. I can't do anything until then; I can't start something I have no intention of committing to. I planned to leave, which meant leaving her, too. I can't pretend that didn't happen.

I can't pretend I'm miraculously fixed, that I don't still have my lows. I can't be with her like this. I can't ask her to wait for me. I don't know when I can be the man she truly deserves. Even spending time with her is dangerous; it's dangerous to get close and feel things.

I don't want to hurt her. I would do anything to keep her safe, to be whole. I already noticed things about her. Her smile slowly fades, and her appearance isn't as vibrant as it used to be. How she's not wearing colour anymore or as bubbly as she normally is. It's killing me to think I could be the reason for that. I can't ruin her.

Whoever she is, whatever story she may have to me, that doesn't matter. It can't. I don't want her to question why she wasn't enough for me. Perhaps Cyra is right; there is something here. I can feel it when she's with me. All I want is to be free, and I'm slowly starting to be, but at what cost?

How can I be free knowing the cost of my freedom is potentially hers if I choose to give up mine and keep hers? I wouldn't hesitate to pick hers if that's what this ultimately leads to. I'll choose her an infinite number of times and continue to do so if it means keeping her whole.

CHAPTER SEVENTEEN
SUMMERS

The air feels suffocating lately. This whole thing gives me déjà vu, except I'm the only one who knows. He has no idea who I am, not truly. I hate the way I'm beginning to snap at him. It's not me. All this, this isn't me. I tried staying away, and I tried to avoid him. I no longer know how to be in the same place as him.

I didn't think it would be this hard. I thought our past wouldn't matter. It wouldn't bother me. When I look at him, I feel a lump in my throat, and the air in my lungs begins to get trapped, and I can't breathe. I try to remind myself he doesn't mean it. It's not as if he's doing it on purpose.

But it's getting harder to be around him. I miss him. That doesn't make sense, but I miss him so much. Recently, he's more himself than he has been in a long time. It reminds me of us, of how we used to be. I should be happy, and I am, but I don't know how to love him silently.

If he wants me, he would do something about it. He wouldn't constantly flirt. He would make something of us. Does he know the way he's talking to me? The way he looks at me, does he remember me? I hate how familiar it feels when I'm with him. But then I remember when I look at him, he's not looking at me in the same way.

When he says he misses me, he doesn't mean it like I do. I forget sometimes this isn't the man I know; this isn't my Asher, and I'm not his. I'm trying to think of anything but that. My hopes are going to drive me insane. Right now, he's in front of me. He's listening intently to every word I'm saying.

He's not focused on anything else but me. I know because it's the way he used to light up whenever I'd talk. He could sit for hours and listen to me talk about anything and everything. I knew him from the beginning, but he's getting to know me. When he's here, when we're together, it's as though he never left.

In such a short time, he's become so comfortable around me. It's kind of unreal how quickly he's grown to trust me. At least, I think he does. I waited for him. One day, he picked up and left, not a single word to me. I thought I'd never see him again.

When he returned, I remember having one of the worst days I had in a while. I lost my buyers because I couldn't cope with everything. I kept screwing everything up. I remember thinking he would be the one I'd run to if I had any kind of news, if I was happy, sad, or just everything, but I didn't have anyone,

Honestly, I forgot how to deal with things myself. I didn't have to go through my bad days alone; I always had him, and he was my greatest comfort. How he used to make everything okay. As cliché as it sounds, if I had him, I was okay; he'd catch me if I started to sink, and without him, I drowned without knowing.

I was outside the apartment building to drop some stuff off.

I had a bunch of papers that I dropped. They started to rip apart when they reached the wet concrete. It was autumn, and the leaves were rustling over my ripped drawings. I was so exhausted and tired that I collapsed and started crying. I was so frustrated, so angry.

I didn't know what I did so wrong that he left me without a word. Angry because he promised me he'd never leave my side, but he left me without a second thought. I remember a hand handed me one of my drawings that didn't get ruined. It was a broken sunflower like the one I was painting in my apartment.

I looked up and saw him, I froze. I had thought of so many things I had been so desperate to say. I wanted to scream and yell at him, but nothing came out. I was just so hurt I didn't realise how much he broke me until he was in front of me. He placed it in my hand and walked off.

He looked right at me and walked away as if I was nothing. Everything was bottling up, and I didn't know how to let it go. It took me a second to realise what happened. I got up and shouted his name between choked sobs. *He must not recognise me*, I thought. I was so angry, I cried.

He ignored me and walked away, pretending not to notice me. He paused and looked at me, those serene, deep blue eyes gazing obliviously into mine. I bared open my soul, and he ripped it apart, leaving my heart barely holding on. He looked at me, saw a stranger, and walked away.

He isn't pretending now, but then I didn't know any better. It broke me. He came back and left me again like it was second nature to him. He built me up so high to knock me down, like I gave him the power to. I gave him the power to destroy me, and I let him.

Cyra said not to get my hopes up, but I'm not. He's starting to remember me. He doesn't realise it yet, but he will. I'm thinking too much about it. I miss being so simple-minded. This is all so tiring. Does he love me, or does he not love me? This isn't me. I'm not this girl, but I don't know how to ignore every sign telling me not to go down this road again.

"Enough about me," I say, tugging my sleeve forward

"What about you?" After the other day, I didn't think he would come again; it was so awkward, and he was trying so hard to break it.

Instead of staying in my flat, I decide we'll go for a walk, but we don't wander far. His leg seems to be hurting him today, so we take a seat inside the café. I may as well start paying rent here.

I need to start going somewhere else, but I'm running out of places to go.

"Me? What about me? You need to learn to finish your sentences." He laughs. Did I mention how much I like his laugh? I've never seen him laugh so much. When I try to be funny, he doesn't laugh.

He'll have this look of disgust smeared across his face; he makes no attempt to hide it.

"Well, you ask me a lot of stuff, so what about you? What makes you happy?" I ask. His expression changes, and he seems distant.

"I'm not sure," he says bluntly. "I want to say a few little things, but what makes me completely happy? I'm not sure yet."

"Surely there must be something; you're always smiling these days." Probably not the wisest choice of words, but surely there is.

"Honestly, in comparison to before, my days have been better. For a long while, I didn't see any worth in anything. But you helped me prove myself wrong. I smile so much these days because I witness things and feel things I thought I was incapable of ever experiencing. I'm not going to pretend. You obviously saw what you did. I can't change that no matter how much I want to, but I'm kind of glad you did see it," he confesses.

"You're glad I pulled you back?"

"I wasn't at first. Believe me, I wasn't your biggest fan."

I scoff. "I wasn't hard to figure out."

"Yeah," he says, embarrassment highlighting his tone, "but I am now, sort of. I still have my days, but you somehow make it bearable. I can't stop the way I feel. I can't pretend it doesn't tempt me. I don't know about tomorrow or what the future has in store for me, but at this moment, I'm glad."

I try to hold the tears that begin welling up in my eyes. I don't want him to see me cry. "Why are you glad?" I am hesitant about bringing it up, but his change of heart and vulnerability make everything easier. Maybe now is the right time to finally clear the air. To finally know where he is at.

He sucks in a breath and lets it out as he sighs, running his fingers through his hair. "Because you're the only person I don't have to lie to. Pretend to be something I'm not." He used to say that to me all the time. I didn't know I could make him feel like that again.

I can't get wrapped up in this. I need boundaries. I can't overstep them. I'm literally handing him the knife to pierce through me. I can't melt at the sight of him. I can't swoon over his words, not this time. I'm not changing anything; he still feels the same.

Perhaps not entirely, but a part of it is still there. I should be happy with the days we get right, when things seem to be looking up. Even if I'm not changing anything completely, I'm bringing him comfort, and I'm grateful.

We sit silently and let the laughs and voices around us fill the space between us. I'm the only person he doesn't have to lie to. That keeps playing in my head.

How am I meant to save him?

"I should probably head off. I have things I have to do, but this was nice," he admits, getting up.

I don't want to leave it like this. I don't really have a choice, though. He's leaving. I need to clear the air. This is my chance to find out where I stand.

"Have you always felt like this?"

What kind of response am I expecting? He looks surprised but shifts a little and stands up.

"Wait, I'm sorry! You don't need to run."

"Alessia, I'm not going to run." He laughs. "I was stretching my legs. Relax." He places his hand behind my head and leans forward as he plants a kiss on my forehead. "Okay?" He studies me. "I'm sitting back down, happy?"

No words seem to escape me. All I manage is a little nod.

I shrug and say, "I was just saying," pretending as if my body isn't on fire.

"Tyler..." He begins fidgeting with his hands.

"I'm sorry?" I know who Tyler is, but mentioning his name has caught me off guard a little. "He was my best friend, well is. We were practically inseparable."

He continues, "We guided each other on everything. He was never out of line or had to be grounded. It was always me. He was always there." He doesn't wait for a response and carries on, "I don't have any siblings. He was basically my brother, and people believed he was too. You couldn't have one of us without the other."

He's right. They were inseparable. I don't think I ever saw them apart. "Anyway, he was my brother, and he died. When he was alive, I was kind of wild, I guess, but not in a law-breaking, ending-up-in-jail kind of way. When he was alive, I guess that was the only time I can truly recall the time I was happy. So, to answer your question, no, I haven't always felt like this."

He studies me for a reaction and appreciates the calm expression I have. No judgement, just someone to listen. "He didn't deserve what happened, nor did he deserve to go the way he did. He had so much potential and so many plans. He was kind of like you. He'd have really liked you," he softly says.

"How did he die? If you don't mind me asking," I ask. I don't think I've ever found out how he died.

"I do, sorry. I can't tell you that just yet," he says. He quickly carries on, "Don't think I'm being rude. I'm not. I don't think I've said it out loud yet, and I guess I don't want to do so for now. Is that okay?"

He gazes at me, waiting for some sort of confirmation. "You don't need to ask if something is okay for you or not. Everything happens in its own time. I'm not going to rush you. I'll still be here when you want to talk."

He nods in agreement.

"I am curious, though."

"Hmm?"

"Why do you never talk about him?"

He never mentions him, maybe once or twice, but so rarely. Even when Nate is talking sometimes, and he stumbles upon his name, there's always a pause, and he quickly brushes it off. Asher always looks kind of unsettled; you can never really say it without him looking like he is getting ready to beat you up.

"I don't talk about him, except now, obviously. He's not a topic I like to bring up." His voice is serious, as he avoids making eye contact, shifting uncomfortably.

"It must be hard to be without him," I say, not sure how else to respond.

"It is." He stares at his palms and breathes steadily. Of course, it is. Cyra was crazy about him; he was always flirting, but he never really had any interest in her. That's her turn-on, wanting a guy who wants absolutely nothing to do with her. She sees this as a challenge since she's used to getting her way. It's very unlike her not to get what she wants. When Tyler died, she was gutted for a little while, but she moved on. If it bothered her for longer, she never showed it. My mind begins to wander, and curiosity stirs inside of me, and I wonder whether he felt okay with me. If I made him okay.

It was a long time ago, and back then, he was fine, but I'm curious to know if he was happy with me the way I was with him. I decide against my better judgement and ask the question that's been bugging me for a while.

"Was there another time you knew that you felt okay besides Tyler?" I ask.

I'm not even sure if I'm ready to hear the answer. "Not that I recall, no. It all kind of ended when he passed. It went downhill from there."

"You can't remember a time without him?"

"He was my brother. My life went with him," he says coldly, as if the answer is as clear as day.

"He deserved to live. He should have lived." He clears his throat. His words begin to fade as my own thoughts take over. I didn't make him happy or do anything for him. I was just there. Did I interpret the whole thing wrong? Were we actually not anything? He would have remembered me if I was important, but he doesn't.

He's practically forgotten my entire existence, and I don't know how that's possible. Am I so meaningless he couldn't make room for one more memory? *He couldn't make room for me?* Why is it when you already know the answer, and it will hurt, you ask anyway?

Why do we desire to shred what's left to protect our sanity? To satisfy the urge of being right at the cost of ripping ourselves apart? I don't know why I do this, why I always do this. I guess it's like closure in a way; you need to be hurt to heal and move on.

"This is kind of off-topic, but have you ever been in love?" I ask.

I know better than to ask this.

I hate the way I need to hurt to confirm what I feel is real. If it doesn't hurt, then it doesn't make sense. He looks at me, his blue eyes peering right into mine.

"No, I haven't."

He didn't even hesitate. How could he not hesitate? It takes everything I have not to break in front of him and keep myself together.

I can feel him staring, and I look down, trying to hold back the tears. I take a deep breath as a black card captures my eye. It's attached to my shoe. I lean down and pull it off, seeing my face. A shiver washes over me, and I become still, my heart breaking by the second.

My Polaroid.

My hand trembles when flashes of the moment warp my mind, seizing whatever reasoning to paint him another way and take over.

I catch a glimpse of Asher patting his pockets, becoming uneasy as he stands, patting himself down. He took this. He always wanted to carry me. At least, that was what he said. I didn't think he was being serious. Cyra was right.

"Have you lost something?" trying to stop the tears from pouring, I can't let him see me break.

How could he? Was he pretending this entire time? Had he been playing me? Too many thoughts are racing at once to make sense of; he had this the whole time, and he played me like a puppet.

"Yeah, I... uh... Okay, don't jud—" he cuts off as he spots the Polaroid in my grasp. "You have it?" A hesitant grin appears, unsure of its place, as he tries to keep himself steady.

I laugh loudly. I've been a joke to him the entire time. My insecurities burn a permanent stain in my mind.

God, I'm pathetic.

I asked for this.

"What, you think this is funny?" My demeanour is fragile, threatening to shatter any second.

"I don't know what you mean." Letting a nervous laugh fall, his expression softens, and he watches me, puzzled, waiting for something, anything to tell him how to act next.

It really must have been one-sided. Maybe he said all the things he did because I'm so fucking gullible and naïve. I feel so stupid. He used me. It wasn't love, not in the way I thought it was. *He used me.* I try to collect myself, but I can't help going numb, my body paralysing. God, I didn't think I could hurt like this.

All this time, I thought we were something more, but I was nothing. Did I imagine this whole thing? Did I misread the signs? Did he do this to other people?

How could he be so cruel?

He can't break my heart a second time. I won't allow him to. I can't believe I let myself fall for this; I can't believe I played his stupid game for so long. Was he laughing at me the entire time? I shouldn't be surprised. I should have guessed with the way he is.

Deep down, I knew he was playing this game, yet I played right into his hands. I've never felt so humiliated, but I can't just up and leave. I frown, forcing my lips to do me justice and pretend I'm okay.

"Are you okay?" he asks as he studies me.

"I'm fine," I say, trying my hardest to not let my voice betray me.

He doesn't even care. He looks right into my eyes. He made my worst fear come true.

I scrunch the Polaroid in my hand. "Hey, hey, what are you doing?" he utters frantically, opening my fist as he takes the Polaroid out and tries to straighten the crinkles.

I watch as he attempts to salvage what's left of what was once unruined.

"Do you realise how this photo has saved me? I found this and was going to throw this away before I knew who you were," he begins, unaware of how my heart is breaking. "I saw your smile and decided to keep it. I thought if there was a chance I could one day live to experience it, see it in person, then I'd know I'd won in life. Then I met you, and everything changed."

I don't understand.

I have to stop myself from asking what I did so bad to hurt him. How can he sit there and pretend so easily? All this time, he knew.

I'm okay.

I need to be okay.

I did this to myself. It's not his fault.

He never felt anything, and I was the fool who fell too hard.

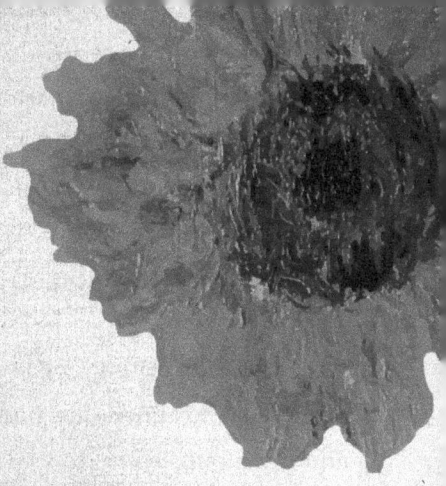

CHAPTER EIGHTEEN
ASHER

I'm glad I'm seeing Alessia more than I was before. I was worried that she didn't want to know me anymore. Today feels different. I feel more at ease. It's refreshing to admit stuff out loud. Being able to open up to someone and have them accept you exactly as you are. I'm glad it's her. I'm glad I met her.

I let the minutes pass us by, and at first, I think perhaps this is a comfortable silence, but neither of us says a word. Clearing my throat, I begin fidgeting with the strand of cotton on my shirt. I can't recall anything that I might've said to hurt her. My thoughts begin getting the best of me.

She doesn't deserve to deal with this, with me. I can't burden this crap on her.

"I'm going to catch you later, Summers."

I think she needs space. She sniffles, wiping her face, laughing to herself in disbelief. "Of course you will," she mutters. "I'm sorry I'm such a mess." Her voice is cracking in between her sobs.

I didn't realise she was even crying. I've been so wrapped up in myself.

"What happened? Did I say someth—" Alessia cuts me off

before I can finish my sentence.

"Just stop." Her voice is sharp. She doesn't let the softness of her sobs enter her voice.

"Stop what?"

"Stop, for crying out loud, just fucking stop!" she yells, and I can't seem to move, my body still. My palms start to get sweaty, and my mouth starts to dry.

"Tell me what happened." I don't know how to make her okay. I start to feel panic, is she hurt?

"Just tell me one thing. I understand everything else. Well, no, in truth, I don't. But why?" She's trying everything in her power to not break.

"I don't understand. I—"

She cuts me off. "Of course, you fucking don't. Why would you? It's not like we planned anything or we spoke about our life together. It's not as if I was your everything." The betrayal in her voice illuminates her tears like a waterfall streaming down her skin. Alessia stands up and tries to pass me. I don't let her. I can't let her leave like this.

"I don't want to hurt you, b—" she breaks off my sentence.

"Alessia, can you let me talk? I'm trying to understand."

I try to console her, but nothing is working. Her voice is hollow and cold. "I don't understand. What did I do?" Her tears let loose and run down her cheeks. I move my hand to her face, stepping closer, but she pushes me aside and heads outside.

I want to make it stop, her hurt. I never want to be the reason for her tears. Why is she doing this?

Why is she falling apart?

"Did you ever mean anything you said?" her voice is a broken whisper.

"I've meant everything I've said to you. Everything about you I adore endlessly." I sincerely mean every word. "You've been distant recently, why? The real reason this time."

"Why me?" Her eyes are red and hurt, pleading for me to confess what I don't know.

"I know about the carvings, that maybe we were something more, but I don't remember it. I don't know why, and I know that's the most pathetic excuse to come from me. You won't probably believe me, but it's the truth. But I've been nothing but honest with you, but you haven't been honest with me."

I didn't mean for everything to blow up like this. I wanted to know when the time is right. It's as much to do with her as it is to do with me.

"So you knew something? But you still led me on anyway?" I feel like I'm digging my grave deeper.

"What do you mean? No, I didn't know anything to begin with. You're the one who knows everything, but you won't tell me a thing. I never intended to lead you on. I didn't plan on meeting you or getting to know you. None of it, I didn't want any of it, but it happened, and I can't help myself when I'm around you."

I can feel the panic rising, and it's taking everything to breathe. "I don't understand any of this but you. I understand you and want to get to know you and learn new things about you, but I don't want to make anything yet."

I'm making this worse. God, I don't know how to fix this. She sucks in a deep breath and lets out a heavy sigh, wiping her tears, wiping her nose with her sleeve.

"I thought I meant more to you. I don't understand how you can be someone's everything one minute and the next you're nothing. How do you become nothing?" she questions. Her breathing is heavy from her ragged breathing between her sobs.

"Alessia," I say softly. "I-I don't remember saying those words to you. And if I did, I'm so sorry to have abandoned you like that, but from what I know now, I never said you were my everything. I'm sorry if that sounds harsh, but I have never said anything like that."

I don't want to hurt her, but I never said anything of the sort, ever. I know better than to admit that. "I wouldn't lead you on like that, Alessia. I'm starting to get to know you, and believe me, I'm loving every second, but I barely know you. The you that you're so convinced I know of..." My words try to come out in one piece. "Let alone be in love with you."

Her body stills, her face turning pale, the soft smile that warms up the entire room. Gone. "I can't be the man you deserve, but I'm trying to be and won't stop trying. But I need to be the best version of me to become even a piece of the man you deserve."

The air grows thicker, and the sounds of everything else fade. Nothing exists but us right now. "I thought I knew you." She's trying to mask her pain. She smiles, not the one that makes time stop but somehow pierces your heart.

"I never thought you could be so cruel to me, ever. Out of all people, I didn't think it would be you." Her voice is broken; she's broken.

I did this.

"You wanted to hurt me? You warned me, didn't you? Well, guess what? Congratulations"—her voice is barely even a whisper—"you did it. You really did it, and I let you do it."

"You're not understanding me. I'm not trying to hurt you. I never wanted t—"

"You want me to understand you, but you're not understanding me. You don't get what I'm saying because you're too clouded by your own judgement," she cuts in.

"I'm trying to be honest. Alessia, can't you see how much I'm trying for you? I don't care about the past. I know you knew me once, but I don't remember that. I'm not the same man I was then. I've changed. I swear to you I'm really trying for you, but this can't work if you remember me as someone else. I don't know how to be that person for you, and I'm sorry. If I could, I would."

"You want to leave me?"

I don't know how to hold her together. I can't stop her from falling. "No, but if it means you'll be happier and gives you some kind of closure, I will. I'd do anything for you." I step back, widening the gap between us.

I need to do this. She needs this. I didn't think about what everything was doing to her. *I can't be selfish anymore.*

"The one thing I could bet with my life you couldn't do, you did." She wipes her tears staining her skin, her lifeless eyes tirelessly searching mine for any recognition.

A slight glimpse of hope resurfaces for a moment, and I'm me again, the me she knows. My chest feels heavy, and when she's gazing into me, I see something familiar, a darkness I know all too well, and instead of me, it's found home within her eyes. It's like I sucked everything out of them, everything that made them hers, the hope, the happiness.

I shattered it.

"Alessia, I'm s—"

Alessia steps forward, pushing me. "You're sorry? Is that all you have to say?" Her frustration seeps through her words. "I didn't know by trying to heal you, I was mending you with the pieces of me. Or perhaps I did, but I was okay knowing you were going to be okay. I didn't think to fix you that I had to lose me."

Reality dawns on her. "I had to break me, and now I'm the one that's drowning." She runs her fingers through her hair, breathing heavily.

I broke her.

I ruined her.

I did the one thing I feared most.

"Tell me what I need to do to fix this. Do you want my true feelings? Fine. Alessia, I adore you more than you realise. I think about every single moment of the day. I don't know what this is, Alessia, I—" I stumble on my words. Why can't I say it? I'm not ready yet.

"Does it really pain you that much to tell me you love me?"

"I'm sorry."

"You're always sorry."

"Alessia, please—"

"I'm tired of always being so fucking understanding that people think they can use me. Am I that repulsive you can't bring yourself to tell me you love me?"

"You know why I can't say it. I'm not trying to hurt you. Please believe me." I desperately plead for her to listen to me.

"Asher."

I know this tone.

"You want the truth? I'm in love with you, and I have been for years. Only you loved me, too. At least I thought you did, but you can't even bring yourself to say it."

Her composure is ruined. Her voice tries not to crack. "I'm sorry." She starts to turn, and I close the gap between us, taking hold of her arm and pulling her into my chest. The light rain begins to turn heavy and drenches us before we have a chance to think about what's happening.

Her strands of hair are wet, laminating against her skin as the rain falls heavier. I don't want to lose her. Everything is happening too fast. I don't want to let her go. I didn't want to confess like this, but if it means she knows I'm not playing her, I'll bare my soul for her. Her cries stop, and she sighs, letting out a deep breath.

I hold her hand tighter, moving my hand to her face, gently caressing her cheek as I wipe her last drops rolling down her cheek. I lean in closer and softly brush my lips against her forehead and cheek, and finally, where I've been yearning to touch—her lips.

"I love you, Alessia." I kiss her lips again. "Don't apologise again. You don't need to apologise to me."

I'll be the man I have to be for her. I can't run anymore. I need her, and I can't deny I don't love her because I do. I really do. "You're okay. I got you, Summers," I softly whisper in her ear, my breath against her skin.

"I'm sorry," she says again, realisation settling into her features.

"Why are you saying that?"

She breaks free of my grasp, places her lips against mine, and kisses me, lingering for what could have felt like a lifetime.

"I love you more," she confesses, her voice an apologetic whisper as she turns away and runs.

"Alessia!" I scream after her. The rain is heavy, and I can barely make her out. A bright light blinds me, a loud blare echoing through the rain. I look up and run towards her. The horn getting louder.

"Alessia, move!"

I try to run as fast as I can, and suddenly, time stops. I wish my eyes were fooling me.

My world stops, and I only see red.

Blood, blood everywhere.

I only see her.

Alessia.

CHAPTER NINETEEN
ASHER

I bared my soul open for her, and she stole my heart, breaking it until it was impossible to fix. January flew by, and somehow, we're in December. Time hasn't stopped, even if I have. The world won't stop to comfort me, and yet time is meant to be my healer.

I thought I knew grief. I swam in it, but this... this, I can't begin to fathom. I'm losing my mind; everything seems to be falling apart. I feel like the universe is mocking me. I decided to give the world a chance, and this is what I got. I thought I was finally getting somewhere, only for everything to slip through my grasp. I'm tired of trying to dodge what comes my way. I'm so fucking tired of fighting. What am I even fighting for anymore? It's been almost twelve months since I've seen her. I can't stop replaying the moment she got hit. The memory of her blood all around her.

Her lifeless body, pale and wounded. It haunts me, replaying endlessly, never pausing the scene but rejoicing in my torment. Having to relive it until my body finally gives up on me. And I can finally escape the *enjoyment* my mind has crafted for me.

My Alessia, lying there, and I couldn't do a single thing to help her.

"There was nothing you could have done, you know that." I don't need to open my eyes to know who the voice belongs to.

"I hate that you're back. And stop talking about her like she's dead. She's in hospital, and she just doesn't want to see me anymore." I didn't think I'd be talking to myself so soon again.

"I finally thought you moved on, that I did. But you show up as if you never left. Just leave me alone, you being back means I'm a fucking insane again. Just go!"

I smash my lamp against the wall.

"That doesn't do anything," Tyler says, his voice soft and empathetic.

"I need to know how she is. They won't let me in. The hospital won't give me any details about her, whether she's alive or not." I cough, my throat tight. "I mean, I know she's alive, but I need something to go on. How soon ago did she leave? Did she leave any messages? Did she tell them to keep sending me away?" My words pour out faster than I can stop them, rambling as self-consciousness creeps in about how much of a madman I am.

I message Cyra, but she avoids the entire thing. I keep begging for her just to tell me something, anything, but she won't. She won't tell me a single thing. No matter how much I try to fight, nothing works. You can't find a person who doesn't want to be found. The fact she's not telling me a single thing tells me a lot. Perhaps she came out soon after the accident, and it wasn't as bad as I thought.

I miss her.

I miss her and don't know what to do or how to be. How did

she become such an important part of my life, of me? I see her in my dreams, and I hate the part when I wake up because at least I get to spend time with her a little longer.

"Asher," Tyler interrupts my chaos of thoughts surging all at once. "You can't keep going around in circles like this."

I try to believe that she'll show herself to me when ready. I'm sure of it. But how long can I withstand this? The endless days of not knowing where she is, trying to grasp onto anything and everything that will keep me long enough to see her until I can hold her again.

I told her that I poison everything I touch. Alessia didn't believe me. She was adamant I was misunderstood and worth living despite everything telling me I was not. I laugh quietly. I outdid myself. I broke the girl who claimed she couldn't be broken. I took away her joy and gave her the darkness to swallow, to drown and become the one thing I feared her to become.

I turned her into me.

"Asher, you're spiralling. You can't keep doing this to yourself."

The last thing I intended was to *destroy her*. Why did it turn out this way? For once, I thought it might be different, that my story might change.

"You didn't do this." Tyler kneels beside me. Trying his best to console me.

"Then who did? She was fine before she met me again. I took her life slowly, and I didn't even realise what I was doing to her. I still haven't been to her apartment." I couldn't bring myself to after what happened.

I couldn't go in, knowing she wouldn't be there. I throw on a black hoodie and head out to do what I should have done at the start. I head down the hall to her door.

"Is this the brightest idea? I don't think you're ready," Tyler utters.

"She's not dead!" I snap.

The anxiety's building and I can't slow my heart down. I wipe my palms along my side. I need to pull myself together. I knock and slide my hands in my jeans, waiting for a response, but no one answers. I look back to my door to see any sign of my dad. I sigh in relief when I don't see him coming out after me.

No one answers. I haven't seen anyone go in since the accident. I'm kidding myself if I believed Alessia would open the door. I don't want this to be real. She is here. She hasn't heard me. *She's here. She has to be.*

She can't give up. She wouldn't give up.

"I don't think it's a good idea." Tyler stands beside me, his voice heeding warning.

"I don't need your advice," I bite.

I knock again, this time louder. I battle the impulsive thoughts to barge in, slam the door open and face reality. But what if she is there and she really doesn't want to see me? That she regrets telling me she loves me, and none of it is real? A woman like her wouldn't love me. How could she?

"This is exactly why caring fucking ruins you. I was right, but I decided against myself for the first time in my life. It backfired on me in the worst way it could," I say.

"Caring is part of life; you don't choose who you get to love or care for, but it's how you can truly say you lived." Tyler rests his hand on my shoulder. I bite my tongue and kick the door as the door becomes unhinged and slides open. The realisation hits me. It's one thing after another.

I stare in disbelief into the apartment and can't comprehend anything. Nothing is here. It's an empty space, nothing but a light blaring in through the glass.

Everything's gone.

She's gone.

Her colours have disappeared. Everything is white. It's like she never even lived here. Her walls, her random burst of colours; it's all gone. How could nothing be here?

"We can leave now," Tyler says, trying to discourage me from going forward any more.

Alessia, you can't do this to me. "Tyler, how can she do this?" My voice begins to break. "What do I do?"

My whole world is falling apart, and I can't stop it. *It's okay.* I'll hold her hand and make fun of how clumsy she is. How she can't seem to match anything, and then she'll punch me and laugh into my arms.

I hadn't realised how much I wanted her to laugh in my arms. I'm not giving up. I can't. *You haven't lost. Not yet,* I repeat to myself. Alessia must be somewhere. She couldn't have just disappeared. There's a logical explanation for everything. I'm not thinking hard enough. I'm looking at this wrong somehow.

Nothing adds up. I pull out my phone and call her number desperately. I wait anxiously for something, anything.

"Hello?" a woman answers. My heart stops for a moment, a wave of relief washing down my panic, but it's not her.

"Where is Alessia?" I say, trying to get my words out fast enough.

"I'm sorry you seem to have the wrong number. I don't know Alessia."

My heart sinks, and I can't do anything to stop it. This is her number. I've called her so many times. "Look, I'm sorry, okay? If she can hear me, I'm so sorry. I didn't mean to hurt her. I would never do it intentionally. Just tell me what I need to do, and I'll fix it." The lump forming in my throat threatens to get bigger. Taking a deep breath, I try to steady my voice. "I need her. Tell her I'll do anything to fix it. Please come back."

It seems like a lifetime before she responds, "I'm sorry, I really wish I could help you, but I really don't know Alessia. This has always been my number." Annoyance reflects in her voice, and she sounds so fed up.

"Stop playing games. How else would you have gotten her phone?" I question her and try to keep my temper in check. *Don't scare her*, I remind myself.

"I've always had this phone. Don't get mad at me for something I'm not even aware of. I hope you find your friend, but she's not with me."

She hangs up before I can say anything; I try calling back, but my number is blocked. I try to calm down.

I try calling the hospital, but nothing.

Try Cyra, and nothing.

Why is everything collapsing?

Is she trying to hurt me like I hurt her? That's not her. She's not cruel. I wasn't honest about my feelings for her. I didn't let her in the way she wanted me to. This isn't her. She wouldn't run. I can't find a trace of her anywhere. Why is she fucking with my head? I have two options here, find her or give up.

I don't even understand myself anymore. I hardly ever did, but now more than ever. This is different, I'm scared. I'm scared I'll never see her again. I'm scared I'll never hear her voice again.

"Doesn't she understand how much I need her? I told her I loved her. Why did she leave me? I thought she loved me too."

I frantically look around, searching for anything that could lead me to her. Never in a million years did I imagine this would be what I would do for a girl.

"Asher, enough. Come on, buddy, let's go home." His hand is on my shoulder.

"Why did she come into my life if she was going to leave? Why do people do that? Don't they understand how it breaks you?"

My heart is breaking. I begin searching for everything and discovering nothing. Nothing is left of her. I accept defeat and sink to the floor.

"Asher, buddy, please, come on. She's not here." Tyler tries to pull me up.

"Get off!" My throat is closing up.

"It's okay." Tyler kneels beside me. "We'll find a way past this," he reassures me.

"What if we don't?" I break, my tears burning my eyes.

"We will."

What has become of me? I was on the verge of death, and now my thoughts consist of this *one person*.

Alessia.

CHAPTER TWENTY
ASHER

If this is what my father felt when my mother left him, I don't know how it didn't kill him. I thought maybe she was hiding in her spot in that garden of hers. I thought if I wandered around aimlessly thinking, I'd see her because I'm not properly looking for her.

It sounds stupid, but sometimes, when you're not desperately searching for something, it shows up when you least expect it. It's terrifying how a single person can change your existence. If you let them, they have the power to destroy you by doing something as simple as leaving.

A corner of a box catches my eye, hidden underneath the slab. I wouldn't have even seen it if I hadn't crouched down on the floor; it's perfectly hidden, as if it was never intended to be found. I kneel down and pull apart the slab, lifting it up to reveal a small blue box. It has a red ribbon with bits of glitter on it.

It has Alessia written all over it. I can't help but laugh. Of course she would do something like this. I cross my legs and lift open the lid, placing it on the floor. This is probably the last thing I should be doing. I mean, searching someone else's belongings doesn't exactly scream sane. I need my sanity, though. I need to find her.

"Asher," Tyler calls, "is there any point in telling you that you shouldn't do this?"

"No." I look down to see bits of paper and old movie tickets. "I thought it was you who made me keep a box like this. Was it her?" I can't help but notice the similarities as I rifle through it more, and I can't help but feel like I've seen this before. I recognise this. I run my fingers gently over the token. It's old and rusty. She must've had this for years. A butterfly token, silver.

I remember having one like this, my mother's favourite. She had attached it to a bracelet, but it fell off, and I remember asking her if I could keep it. *Wait. No. It can't be.* I let the token slip through my fingertips as my memories pour from a deserted part I'm still unaware of.

Realisation hits like a tonne of bricks as I remember giving this to the little girl in exchange for giving me her star. I wanted to thank her by giving her something as important to me. Alessia was that girl. She was the one who guided me home when I got lost. I've met her before.

The void I thought couldn't get deeper descended into a bottomless pit, and it's getting harder to crawl out from. That's why she wanted to know how I found it. The way she was holding it so delicately, grinning to herself. A rusty envelope, it's white and torn. I knew I was right to class her as the sentimental type.

Alessia wouldn't cope if she threw away anything with meaning. It'd eat her up. I take out the envelope and place the box on the floor. Undoing the flap, I accidentally tear the corners and drop it. I try to catch it, but it hits the floor, and a series of photos spiral out on her floor.

"This is why I told you to stop," Tyler warns, "you're only hurting yourself."

I try to steady my trembling hands. I start to pick up the photo and turn it over. I begin turning all the photos over and see myself in every single one. I see us. "How can this be? I don't understand."

I run my hands on the side of my neck, trying to steady my breathing. I don't remember these. The void deepens, and I find myself grieving for the person this was. For me, a me I'll never remember. "Is this who she saw when she looked at me? Is this who she loved?"

"She grew to love the you that she got to know now," Tyler chimes. "You can't start thinking like that. You're only going to drive yourself mad," he says.

How could this be me? I don't like photos I never have; I hate being in the centre; it makes me feel all awkward and weird.

I have so many questions, but there is nothing to give me the answers I crave. If I have any sanity left, I'm sure every ounce has been drained out of me. Why would she hide this from me? I spread out the photos, analysing each one of them. At least one has got to point me in her direction.

I can't understand how a photo tells a thousand stories. Right now, it's like everything is screaming at me. It's trying to search for the part of me that recognises me and remembers this ever happening. I'm looking at every photo, but my eyes can't understand what it's trying to tell me.

I don't know the story I'm meant to understand. I'm kissing

her, holding her. We're laughing, our smiles are too real to have been fake, we look so happy. I rummage through the box and try to look for anything to try and make sense. I stumble upon a folded piece of paper. The edges are wrinkled.

I open it up and find the words:

> Alessia,
> I didn't think love was an actual thing. I always thought it was something that happened in movies or a myth you read about in books. It turns out you, you, my love, are living proof it exists. As long as I have you, I have everything.
> Love, Asher

What?

How is this even possible? How is any of this possible? I wrote this? This is me? Was I a game to her? I really knew her, but she didn't tell me a single thing. Yes, she loved me, but what else? Who was she? Who was I? Cyra, she knew all along. But she never told me, but I didn't think she would leave me in the dark. I never imagined they both would.

Nate must have known her, too. Why hasn't he told me anything? Alessia would rather disappear than admit any of this, but why leave this? If she wasn't going to tell me anything, why wouldn't she throw this away? I never gave her a real reason to stay; I always hurt her somehow.

I admit, at first, it was intentional, but she wouldn't leave, and the moment I acknowledged that I wanted her, that was the time she chose to leave. I guess loving her wasn't enough. Ironic. I need to find her. Now more than ever, I need answers. Is she punishing me for forgetting?

Was she trying to save me or keep me alive so she could watch me suffer? If this is real, I would remember. How could I forget the love of my life? I can't deny I love the familiarity I feel when I'm around her, but don't you get that feeling when you're falling?

"You know that's not her," Tyler says, I forgot he was still here.

"She asked if anything else made me happy, and I said no. She asked if I had ever been in love, and I said no. I didn't even hesitate. I broke her heart so effortlessly. She wanted me to say her, didn't she?"

"You can't confess what you don't remember. Why are you beating yourself up? We've been through this," his voice is tired.

"Do you think I want this? I hate being like this. But I deserve to know. It's my life."

"But—"

I cut him off. "They're my memories, too. This is me. I can't imagine how hard it must have been for her. But imagine not having any idea of who you were? I had this whole life, and I don't remember a single bit of it. But still, I can't help but feel bad. Alessia thought I finally remembered her."

She may have hidden my past from me, but I'm the one who broke her. I'm the one who left her. How does she expect me to know anything if she doesn't tell me anything? I want to hate her, but I can't. Despite my thoughts trying to turn me against her, I know she didn't mean it.

She doesn't hate me. I need to prove myself. I need her to

understand how sorry I am. Hating her would be much easier, but how can I hate the girl who helped me find my second chance?

How do I find the girl who doesn't want to be found?

CHAPTER TWENTY-ONE
ASHER

It's day 487, and I can't find her. I count every day, hoping this day will be different. If you ask me how I see myself in the future, I would say dead. But somehow, this seems worse. I feel like I'm constantly drowning. I only come up to the surface for a moment to sink again.

I don't understand how I'm surviving, how I'm coping. I thought I couldn't hurt like this. The irony of desperately trying to feel human again, to feel anything but the emptiness I had, and this is how I finally filled the void I once bore.

I'm not angry. I'm not hurt. I'm unsure what I feel anymore. I'm breathing, but I don't know how. I've lost so much weight because I can't seem to stomach anything. I throw everything back up. I never saw myself becoming like this. I once saw a future, but that got thrown out the window when a woman saved me one day.

Along the line, I somehow saw another one when I thought I had given up all hope. Never did I imagine this was what my future had in store for me. I don't know how it's possible to hurt even more as time goes on. I can't *give up* no matter how it seems like it's the only sane thing to do.

For the first time, I think, in my existence, I haven't given up. For the first time, I'm finishing something.

"Nah, you're not a quitter," Tyler says quietly in my mind.

"Can you stop reading my thoughts?" I can't keep anything to myself. The universe must really want me to cave into my reason for wanting to stay.

It made the person who gave me the faintest bit of fresh air in my lungs disappear. Life never fails to teach me just how cruel it can be. I'm not going to let it win. I'll find her. Nate is hovering around my bed and won't leave. I've been trying to get rid of him for a while now. Consistent pestering won't even do the trick.

He keeps pacing back and forth, and it's driving me insane. If it isn't my dad, it's him. It's like they're on a shift pattern. I'm dying for one of them to clock out already. I've never seen Nate so much in my life. I'd kick him out, but Dad keeps letting him back in.

I practically threw him out before, more times than I can count, but he turns up every time. So, in that sense, I've given up. I can't get rid of him.

"Don't you get hungry if you haven't eaten anything? At least drink something." He hands me a glass of water and waits for me to take it. I've never seen him so patient.

"I'm fine, thanks." My voice is barely even a whisper. I feel like I'm losing my voice. Maybe a little water wouldn't hurt. Perhaps I should start talking out loud rather than inside my head. He sees the change of reaction and waits a little longer as I take it out of his hand and gulp it down.

I place the glass beside me on the floor. "You going to stand there all day and watch me? It's beginning to get creepy."

I glance aside at him, and Tyler is there, too. I would swear at him, too, but Nate already thinks I've lost my mind. I'd rather not convince him I've finally descended into insanity.

"Can you just tell me what's up?" he nags, yanking on my arm like a child.

"Can't you drop it? I told you. It's nothing." I don't know how many times I can drill it into his head. This is my problem and my problem alone.

"And you wonder why nothing is working? You're practically your own worst enemy," Tyler chimes in.

"What's up with you?"

"Go on, tell him it's not as if I can help you. I'm dead," Tyler obviously states.

"Yeah, I hadn't figured," I mutter.

"What?" Nate says, confused.

"Nothing, just leave it for the millionth time. Just leave it." I ignore the daggers from Tyler as he sits on the bed, refusing to break eye contact.

"Not until you tell me exactly what the fuck's wrong with you." His patience begins to fade.

"You. Stop gawking at me."

"I'm not joking. Can't you see what you're doing? You're a state." I watch as his eyes scan me over, and I follow his gaze, taking in everything about me. I really am in a state.

"He isn't wrong there," Tyler agrees, nodding at Nate's remark.

"If you want me to make shit up, I can do that. Will you be satisfied then?"

"What?" he says, his temper rising.

"Well, clearly, you've got something to say, so what is it? You obviously have an idea of what you want me to confess, so why don't you just say it?"

His face flares, and the vein in his forehead struggles against his skin. "You wonder why things go shit for you? I'll tell you why. It's this." He gestures from head to toe.

"Why are you even here anyway? I told you I'm fine. I want to sleep."

"Do you do this on purpose? It's been a year. You need to let go and fucking move on. You won't tell me what happened, but you're not doing anything to help yourself either." He grips my shirt, slamming me into the wall.

"What the fu—" I try to get out of his grip.

"No, you shut the fuck up and listen for once in your life." He tightens the grip around the neck of my shirt. "I'm trying to help you. You never fucking listen. Why do you think I'm here? To entertain you? Dumb fucker, I'm trying to help you. Just as I have been for the past few years."

I push him back, connecting my fist to his cheek. He doesn't deserve this, but I'm tired of being a burden. "Past few years? I've never asked for your help, and I don't need it, especially now. I didn't ask you to be here," I say coldly.

"You never fucking ask for anything, do you?"

He punches my face, and blood starts dripping from my nose. I know he can do more damage. His breathing ragged, he watches the blood drip, and he tenses. Why am I like this? He's holding back. He is. He lunges forward, slamming me harder into the wall as he tightens his hands around the neck of my shirt.

"You want to die, huh? You bastard! Can't you see how much we need you?"

"Careful, I might stop breathing." Our breathing is ragged as I taste the blood dripping from my nose. His eyes widen.

"Do you care for no one besides yourself? Look at what you're doing to your dad. Do you not care how you're killing him? You saved him, asshole, he lost everything, but he stayed for you. I fucking stayed for you. I lost Tyler, my family and I stayed for you." His voice cracks. "Look at what you've become. You're not eating, you're not sleeping. You took more care of yourself when you were trying to kill yourself all the time." I don't know what to say.

"Every morning, I check my phone, scared to see if I've got a message someone has found you dead." He lets go, and the air fills my lungs again. He grabs the lamp that Dad decided to dig out on the side of my bed and smashes it against the opposite side of the wall.

"You idiot, why can't you let me help you? Don't you think I know you want to die?" I watch as the lamp shatters into pieces, wondering where Dad will pull a new one out since that's the second one that can't seem to stay intact.

This time, he lets his tears fall, and he lowers himself to the floor, looking anywhere but at me. "Do you think it's easy? Watching you all the time, knowing nothing we do is worthy enough of keeping you here, pretending not to see why you come back bloody and bruised all the time."

I still. "Dad knows?"

"How could he not? He watches his son trying to kill himself, and he knows there's nothing he can do or say that will ever be good enough."

I don't want to hurt anyone anymore. I'm struggling to keep my tears at bay. "I'm not trying to be the bad guy here." I try to avoid looking at him.

"You seem to be doing one hell of a job trying to prove us wrong," he mocks.

"I don't want to be selfish. I don't want to do this to him or to you."

"Then why do you?" Nate sits down beside me and leans against the wall.

"Because I don't know what else to do" The guilt is burning me alive. I don't know how to escape this hurt.

I really am *poison*.

"I understand what I'm doing. I hate every minute of it, but I don't want to burden you," I say honestly, rubbing my neck. "It's been so long. I don't know how else to be other than broken. This is all I know how to be."

"You're the only family I have. I can't lose you. You're my brother." His eyes turn red.

"Look, I'm sorry. It's a shitty reason, but it's the way I am. I try to fight it, but I can't. I can't stop. I did, but it's so hard. Living shouldn't be this hard."

I pause and debate whether to carry on, but Nate doesn't say anything, waiting for me to finish. "You think I want to be like this? I don't even want to die anymore. That's the hilarious part about the whole thing." Humour doesn't invade his expression, and he stills, his skin turning slightly pale.

"I can help," Nate says, his voice hopeful, "you've tried this for too long on your own, and you're not getting anywhere. Let me help for real this time; no games, nothing. Be honest with me, and we can go from there."

He's exhausted, I can see; he can't stand this any more than I can, but he's sincere. He means it.

My mind is only thinking of Alessia. I know if I tell him, he'll tell me what it means to heal without her, but I can't yet.

"You aren't meant to do everything alone. Just like I have you, you have me, and nothing will change that," Nate says genuinely, hoping it sticks in my thick skull.

I couldn't cope when Tyler died, but Alessia isn't dead. She's alive, and I'll find her. He wants to help? He can help me by starting to find her. He looks up at me, trying to hide the enthusiasm in his eyes, I don't know how to react. He's never been like this. The tension eases, and he breaks the long silence.

"Sorry about your lamp, but you wanted to die anyway, so you were going to leave it behind regardless. It is what it is." He shrugs, wiping his face with his arm.

"I think you're getting too comfortable with tipping me over the edge," I joke, clearing my throat. "If that's your version of an apology, I accept." I slouch down next to him.

"Idiot, you stretched out my shirt." He shakes the neck of it.

"I probably should throw this away." I wipe my blurred eyes.

"Or you could give it to me, and I can fill it up like a real man. Let's face it, you haven't got a lot of meat on you," he sneers.

"You mean fat?" I snap back. He rolls his eyes and nudges me.

"Also, that was actually a new lamp, so you actually owe me." I look at the shattered pieces.

"Just tell me, what is it?"

Where am I meant to begin if I don't even know where I went wrong?

"What is it already?" he pesters.

"Alessia," I say.

I didn't mean for her name to come out as flat as it did. Silence fills the air for a moment, and I ponder whether I should repeat myself or if he misheard me.

"Her. What about her?" he questions, his arms wrapped around his knees, his head against the wall.

"I can't find her."

"You mean to tell me you've been searching for her all this time?" He scowls. "I thought I told you to give up?"

He did many times. I can't blame him. The state of me is showing every reason why being fixated on this isn't a good idea.

"I don't get it. What's so special about her that you're ruining yourself because of it? Can you not see what it's doing to you?"

He's trying not to yell at me but can't help but snap. "I was on the verge of death, and she gave me a second chance at life."

I don't know if that's the reason, but it's one, and it's the only one I'm willing to admit right now.

He bites his tongue. "This?" He gestures to me. "This is what you call life? Take a look in the mirror. There's nothing left of you."

"You want to help? Don't throw the 'I told you so' at me." I get why he's angry. To be honest, if the roles were reversed, I'd be yelling at him. I wouldn't be able to comprehend how one person, one girl, can do this to him. I'd be so angry about how she did this to him.

Just like the way I was mad at my mother for what she did to my father. The irony is that I swore to never let a woman destroy me the way my mother ruined my father after she left him. I didn't think love was meant to do this to you, but I always knew it had the power to destroy you. I just didn't think it could happen to me.

But here we are.

"Fine," he agrees, just barely. He sits upright, positioning himself with his legs crossed towards me. "What do you mean you can't find her? I thought we knew that to begin with."

"She's nowhere. It's not something I can drop. I just want to make things right. I want answers."

Once I finally get the answers I've been longing for, once I finally see her, I'll be sane again. It's wishful thinking, but I need something to keep me sane. I need some kind of hope to carry on.

"Alessia, right?"

Why does he seem so confused?

"Yes, her," I answer anyway, trying to hold back any sarcasm. He's trying. "How did it happen?"

"What do you mean?"

"I mean, how did she disappear? What happened?" he questions. "Don't lie, just be honest. I won't judge you."

"I don't know, she seemed angry, and when I tried to calm her down, she left. I tried to chase her, and she got hit by a car, and she just disappeared," I say, trying to be as honest as I can.

"No one can just disappear, Asher." He's right.

"No, but you don't understand, she did. She went in the ambulance, and that was it. I couldn't find her after that."

I scan his face for some sort of reaction, but his face is a blank canvas. "It sounds insane, but it's true. I've been searching for her since then." My words are coming out easier than I thought.

"I think I can help with that. I know someone who may know what happened. Just leave it to me, and I'll get back to you tonight, hang tight."

Is he stupid? "If it was that easy, I would have found her." I shoot him a glare so he realises how stupid he sounds.

"Yes, yes, I know. Just trust me." His last words linger in the room as he takes his leave. Trust him?

I have nothing to lose, and with that, I pick myself up off the floor, throw myself on the bed, and wait. That's all I can do. I try not to get my hopes up that I can finally find her.

All I need to do is wait.

CHAPTER TWENTY-TWO
NATE

This is my chance to do something and not sit around making jokes all day long like a pitiful waste of space. I'm surprised. I didn't think he would expose his vulnerability like that. It's a rare thing for Asher to do. He hides, he always hides, and for him to expose himself like that, it's not something I'm used to.

I have to admit, it threw me off a bit. Now, I'm in a place where I can actually help, and I'm trying to think of the first place to begin. I didn't want to lose my temper with him. It's the last thing I wanted. I didn't want to make him bleed, but sometimes he's so God damn difficult it's hard.

I've never met a stubborn person more than he is. I'm not stupid. I obviously know that isn't his whole truth, but it's a start. I'm not going to screw things up. I need to begin setting things right. I wasn't lying when I said I could find her. I can. He can even do it if he tries hard enough. He just doesn't want to.

I finally arrive, and it takes everything I have not to walk away. If there's one moment I've dreaded most, it's this. This place hasn't changed a bit since I've left. The familiarity is comforting but daunting at the same time. I was expecting something to be done with all this empty space.

It's open and green, and the house is basically hidden in the middle of nowhere. It's an old house, a white Victorian kind of house. It used to be done up nice, but my brother has a temper that ruins everything. There's no point in trying to redo anything; he'll wreck everything again. What's that saying? Beggars can't be choosers?

I need to suck up my pride if I want to do the right thing.

If Asher knew I was here, he would freak out. Even if he knew this was his only shot at finding Alessia, he still wouldn't put me in this position.

"Why are you always trying to do things alone?"

Cyra steps out in front of me, startling me. I lose my balance for a second.

"What the hell are you doing here?" How did she even know I was going to be here?

"I... uh... came here for the same reason you did. I didn't expect to see you here. This is the last place I would've expected to see you."

"That makes the both of us."

"You think you're doing the right thing, but even Asher wouldn't want you to do this."

"How can I not? I need to give Asher a peace of mind. He's not doing well, and I promised him I would help him find her. So that's what I'm going to do." Asher will understand. Even if he doesn't in the beginning, he will. The only way to find the information I need is through this, and this is the only way I'm going to get it. I know that, and so does she.

"This is going to blow up in your face." Her tone is weary and pleading.

"As reassuring as you are, I'll take my chances. I need my brother back, and this is the way to get him back. He deserves happiness, too." Not letting her words sway me. I know this isn't the cleanest route to take, but sometimes, you need to go down the dark path to appreciate the light.

"Let me come in with you," she tries to plead her case, but she knows I won't let her.

"You already know the answer. Why bother asking?" I say, walking past her.

"I was being polite," she snipes, catching up next to me, tucking her red hair behind her ears. "I'm obviously coming with you." Authority is cemented in her tone.

I don't know why I bother arguing. She doesn't listen to anything I say. I wouldn't expect today to be any different.

"Cyra." I stop for a moment. "Why are you really here?"

I can't deal with her if she's here on some bucket list quest.

"Because I can't leave you this time. I have before, and that was really shitty of me. I can't do it this time, but don't worry, Asher won't know. I'll just be here if you need me."

For the first time, I think she's sincere. She has a track record for flaking when shit gets hard, but seeing her here, today, out of all places...

I don't want to let my guard down, but she must mean it this time. I nod, and she tries to hide the smirk on her face. I walk along the cracked pavement that leads up to the house. Pushing my key into the lock and unlocking it, I open the porch's wooden door. It looks like it's about to fall off.

I suck in a breath and mentally prepare myself. I turn the other key into the lock to open the main door, which is white and delicate. My stomach begins to sink, and the air seems to become suffocating, but I don't let it show.

The voice I dreaded most.

"Nathaniel, you finally decided to drag your ass back home."

I finally come back, and it's his ass I'm greeted with.

"But"—he pauses—"you dragged some of the trash in with you."

If there was a sign to run, this would be it. It takes everything I have not to smash his face. Cyra softly wraps her hand against mine and smiles to let me know it's okay.

If she's hurt, she doesn't show it.

"Still here? I'm surprised. The last I heard, you were abroad."

I push past him. He looks like he's put on weight, but unfortunately, he's not fat. Lucky for me, it's muscle and now his punches will hurt more. "Why are you pretending you didn't know I was back?"

I can imagine he knew the second I stepped off the plane.

"What's wrong with you? Don't you talk?" His voice is husky and deep. He's trying to be sarcastic. To my surprise, Cyra doesn't say anything, just shrugs, and I don't know whether to laugh or not.

"Aren't you tired of being used? Poor girl, does anyone want you?" His laugh is loud, almost sympathetic. He wants to see if I slip up. His expression is fixed; you never know what he's going to do.

"Is that the best you got for me? You're just bitter I won't let you fuck me," Cyra muses.

His expression grows bitter; he almost looks amused. His brown hair is tucked back. His white sleeves are rolled up with his signature completion, black trousers, and shoes. I think he must've just got back from a meeting.

"Still a goth, huh?" I thought he would have developed a taste for attire at some point, but his personality still makes you nauseous.

"What?" he says, confused, "do I look like a goth?" He must be hurt if he's asking me to clarify. I kind of wish Asher was here for this.

"Well, I just asked if you were still one, so yes, you do." He frowns.

"Aw, is this that brotherly banter you've been missing in your life?" he says.

I'm only trying to start a conversation, so it makes it easier to ask him something. I can't just be straight up. He doesn't work like that; he enjoys watching you squirm.

Plus, I don't know when Cyra's going to snap. This is the quietest I've ever seen her, and it's terrifying. If I had known she could stay this quiet, I would've hung out with her more. It's kind of nice when she isn't talking. It's almost peaceful.

"As much as I love this family reunion, I need something."

That pained me to ask as much as it did to think about it. Safe to say my pride is down the drain. "What is it? I'll think about it." He lifts the glass of red wine off the coffee table placed beside the chair and lowers himself into it. I knew he wasn't going to let me go so easily.

I take in the house's interior to distract myself; I can't think of how humiliating this is. The place looks like it's in dire need of a touch-up. I bet Cyra is itching to paint this whole thing herself. I can't imagine what this house would be like if she had the chance. I think the house is better off like this.

The paint's now green on the inside wall, and he has a lit fireplace in the centre of the room. There's one sofa that goes along the back wall and fits into the corner as it takes up the entire back space. He really doesn't know how to decorate for the life of him.

"The place looks... interesting."

"Yes, I know it needs to be done. I'm going to hire someone to fix this place since I'm the only person here now. I don't need to give a fuck about you anymore."

"Agreed," I say.

"Are you enjoying yourself now? You were desperate to leave. Now that you have, how is life? Was it everything you dreamt?" His tone is mocking.

"Do you want to hear about how it's falling apart? Because it isn't. I'm happy."

He laughs. "Yes, so happy you're here, aren't you?"

He's still waiting for me to lose it.

"I'm not here for me." My voice is flat. This is going on longer than I thought. I swear this place sucks the life out of you.

"You never are, are you? Saint Nate picking up everyone's shit, how's that working out for you?"

I can feel the rage slowly consuming me. I can't let him win.

"You were always everyone's lap dog, weren't you?"

My blood begins to boil, but my expression remains unchanged, "You're not going to get under my skin. I'm different now."

"We always claim to change, but do we really?" He twirls the red wine in his glass. "I don't think we do. To be honest, I still think you're the same. The same hot-tempered fucking pest who ruins everyone's lives. What do you think?"

"I didn't tell you to take care of me." It's getting harder not to fight back, harder not to smash his head against the fucking wall. "Oh, but you see, I had to. You didn't have anyone else who wanted you. I couldn't leave your pathetic ass, could I?"

"I left you, didn't I? If your life is so pathetic, don't blame me."

He smashes the glass against the wall, the red wine staining the green walls. It takes everything I have not to flinch. "You ungrateful bastard, you ruined my life. I couldn't do anything because of you," he slurs.

"I'm not here to discuss us. I need something," I say again, this time boldly.

He can't see that he intimidates me. He'll use it to his advantage. "Go on, what does sweet Nathaniel want?" He sluggishly gets up to get another wine glass, his whole demeanour changing. "Spit it out. I don't have all fucking day," he demands. He never was one to have any patience.

"I just want to know if you know where he is." I try to end this conversation as quickly as possible.

"Oh." Delight consumes his tone. "I see," he says.

"If you're not going to tell me, tell me now." I'm not wasting more time than I already have.

"You're kidding me, right?" He ridicules. "Let me guess, Asher? Come on, you can't be that absurd. "I knew this was a mistake."

"I don't need a speech. I need to find him," I snap.

"Oh, don't worry, I'll help you find him. Ironically, he's here for a while."

Relief washes over me.

"Are you sure you want to do this again? I've never known you to be a pathetic softie, Nathaniel. It's embarrassing."

He swirls the red wine in the glass, his smile so evidently clear I wish I could smash his teeth right now. "Careful now, we wouldn't want anyone to assume you actually give a shit about me."

Sarcasm is evident in my tone; he ignores me and carries on. "It's quite a painful story, wouldn't you agree? Trapped in an endless torment that doesn't seem to end. That poor lad," he sneers. "His best friend is after his girl. What do you think he's going to do when he finds out you're in love with her?"

He's laughing hysterically, his tears escaping his crazed eyes. "Fuck, I can't breathe." He falls back into his seat. "Fucking waste of space. You could have anyone. I've seen what a player you can be, but no, you decided to go for the woman you know you can't have. I don't blame you; your own parents didn't want you. Can you blame them? Look at you."

His words don't burn like they used to. I can finally listen to them without feeling like I'm about to fall apart. I'm so glad. Yes, I'm in love with her, but I didn't do anything about it. I don't even have the right to think of her like that. I can see why he's so obsessed with her.

She gave me a second chance without meaning to, I wasn't on

the verge of death, but I was on fire, and I couldn't be tamed. I was screwing my life up before I even got a chance to live it. The person I am today is because of her, everything that I am, my success, my life, everything I owe to her.

I love her enough to let her go. I couldn't make her choose. Alessia loves Asher. I need to do this for her. If not for him, then definitely for her.

"He's going to be at The Plaza at 3 p.m. sharp tomorrow," he interrupts my thoughts and is helpful for once in his life.

"Don't let Asher go in front of him. You already know what's going to happen," he warns.

"Why do you care what happens?" He doesn't give a fuck about nobody.

"Unlike you, I'm not setting him up to kill himself again."

"He's not going to die." My voice is raspy, betraying my facade.

"You were always naïve. If there's one thing I know for sure, it's him. He's not far from meeting his end. If I'm lucky, this will push him over the edge, and then I can finally watch you suffer." He delivers his final blow.

I turn around and clench my fists. I can't burst. He'll win. I've got this far; it's killing him. I'm not losing my temper. I don't care what he says. Or how he even knows about Asher and what state he's in. I'm not going to let him die. He's made it this far; he deserves a chance to live. With that being said, I don't hesitate and waste another second, I open the door and head out.

"If you don't come back, I'm going to come for you, don't make me come find you. Don't think I'm letting you off so easily. You've got a lot of amends you ought to start getting to."

With his last threat hanging in the air, he slams the door shut behind me. He wishes I'd gone back. I'm not a kid anymore. He can't hurt me.

"You're silent," I try to start the conversation. It's too quiet, and it's making me nervous. I don't like that Cyra heard that. She's the last person I wanted to hear that shit.

"You still love her?" she whispers as I open my car door, and she lingers behind.

"I'll have any conversation with you but that."

"I mean, I don't blame you." Her voice is tired. "It is what it is, I guess."

"Cyra." I hate it when she talks like this. I hate it when she pretends to be okay with everything.

"Please, Nate, don't make me seem like a pity case, I don't need your sympathy. I'm okay," she reassures me, but I don't quite believe her.

"You know it's okay not to be, right?"

"I do. I was just wondering if you did. You can't save everyone, Nate." Her voice is soft.

"I can try," I say, kissing Cyra's cheek softly and wishing her goodbye when I close the door behind me. My mind wandered, and I hadn't realised how long it had been.

It's been five hours, and I'm finally back. I reach Asher's door, and before I can knock, Mr Scott steps outside. He really hasn't aged a day.

"Tell me, how is he?" His voice comes out as soft as a whisper.

"I'm working on it. He'll be okay." I don't know what else I can say.

"Please, Nathaniel. I can't do this again."

Before I can say anything, his breathing turns into choked sobs. "What more can I do? He's my son. I thought he would be better. Did he tell you he tried to kill himself a couple months ago? How do you think that makes me feel? I'm his father, and I can see he's suffering. I can't do anything to ease his pain."

I feel guilty, but I hate how they're both suffering and how much this is killing them both. It's not Asher's fault.

"Mr Scott, this time, it's different. This time, it will work. I promise you, you won't lose him."

"Alessia." He exhales slowly. "She brought back my son. But I can't help but wonder if he would be better off not knowing she existed. He wouldn't hurt nearly this much if he knew nothing of her." I don't know how I'm meant to respond to that. "She's killing him, but it's not her fault. You can't help who you fall for. You don't always get to choose the ending you want."

Instead, all I can think about is she really is the warmest soul I have ever met. I miss her. "Mr Scott, can I see him? I promise you I'm going to do all I can." How else can I reassure him?

"Nate, don't make promises you can't keep. I'm his father, and I can't promise to keep him safe." He's right, but sometimes it sounds more like wishful thinking than actual reality. But this time is different, and I'll prove it. He'll prove it.

"Mr Scott, can I?" I ask once again.

He probably thought he avoided it the first time. Does it have to be now? It's almost midnight." Hesitancy lingers in his words.

"Yes, sir, it does."

"Fine. Just bring my son back." His eyes plead, and he takes his leave and fades out of sight, where he heads down. I push open the door and let myself into Asher's room.

He isn't where I left him, so that's a bright side. He immediately sits upright and stands up.

"Did you find her?" The desperation in his voice fills the room.

"Yeah, I did. I told you I would."

I need to stay alert; tomorrow is the day things change. However it plays out, it'll be for the best.

"How did you do it?"

Curiosity settles on the end of his words. "I know someone who knows where she is."

I have to be careful; I can't afford to make any mistakes.

"You have to give me more than that. I searched for her everywhere, and you miraculously found her within a few hours. How's that? It doesn't make sense?" His voice is raspy and hopeless.

He punches the wall. "Why does nothing make sense?" he screams in frustration, smashing everything he can grab within his reach. "You're playing me. Why? There's something you're not telling me; I'm meant to be your brother. Why are you hiding it?"

Did he hear? He couldn't have been here the entire time.

"How are you mad? I just told you I found her." This is what he wanted.

"Yes, this is what I wanted, but the lies, the lies I didn't ask for..." His voice is steady despite his clenched fists. Why has he suddenly gotten suspicious? He was fine when I left him.

I would have heard him if he had listened. He wouldn't stretch out his curiosity longer than he needed to. He's always been blunt like that. One thing I admire about him is his ability not to sugarcoat the truth.

"I'm telling you, I know someone."

"Wait... your brother? That bastard hates you. Why would he help you? He's the only person I know."

He's not as clueless as I thought. "You're not wrong there." I shrug. "He isn't helping me; he's doing it for you." Whether he's doing it because it's the most fucked up thing he could do by far. Or maybe he has a genuine concern, which is unlikely. It's probably one of his mind games. Nonetheless, it's the truth; he wouldn't lie if he knew it would benefit him in the slightest. "You expect us to follow what he says?" He's right, but it's the only option we have.

"No, but we have to. You want to find her. This is it," I admit. I am slightly terrified.

"Where is she?" he questions. How am I supposed to get myself out of this? He won't go if he knows she's not the one we're seeing, or he might. Either way, I'm not willing to risk it. He's doing this whether he wants to or not.

"Get some sleep. We need to be up early."

After the conversation, I make my way out of his room and launch myself on the sofa. Placing my arm under my head, hoping if I close my eyes, it will make things slightly okay. I hope he forgives me for setting him up.

CHAPTER TWENTY-THREE
ASHER

It seems like sleep is the last thing that wants to embrace me. You know when you're so exhausted, but your body is so against the idea of it? I can't shut my mind off long enough to have a decent sleep. I can't remember the last time I had a good one.

I've been tossing and turning for hours.

"Ash," Tyler whispers.

"You don't need to whisper. It's not like anyone can hear you," I murmur groggily. I finally give up and turn on the light, rubbing my eyes.

I lay back, my hand tucked under my head. I gaze at the empty ceiling.

"You need to sleep. Trust me, you'll need the energy." I sit upright.

"Yeah? Meaning what?" I question.

"You're tired. When you go tomorrow, you need something about you that doesn't scream you're so broken and weak," he says.

"Thanks for that pick me up. Really, that was much needed."

If I could strangle him, I would. "Why do you think he's lying to me?"

"Why does anyone lie? To protect you." His words carry a heavy weight.

"I didn't ask for protection. I want the truth." I sound like a broken record, but somehow, this feels familiar.

I wish it wasn't real, that I don't love her, but I do, and I'd give anything not to. "I thought my days would get easier, but I remember everything that happened too clearly. I feel it too deeply to have been almost a year ago. It still hurts the same, if not more. I thought when you died, time would eventually heal me, but it didn't, and that was you. Now I have to grieve for her? Someone who is alive? I don't know how to deal with losing her too."

Tyler doesn't say anything; he lies down on the bed. "Ash, you never lost me, I'm still here. You don't need to feel guilty or grieve for me. I never wanted that for you. I never wanted you to stop living. Especially because of me," Tyler says softly, remorse illuminating his tone. "Plus, don't you think I would kick your ass in the afterlife?" He chuckles.

"I started to feel different when she was here, like somehow things got better. I never understood how a person could heal someone. I have always found that baffling. How is a person meant to mend you? It's unfair to expect a person to fix someone so broken. But I was slowly becoming me again. When she was here, I found myself enjoying the little things I couldn't care less about before. I started to see a different side to things, to life. She convinced me without even trying to try again. When I was on the verge of death, she saved me only to destroy me." My heart hurts, and I can't stop it.

"You don't need someone to remind you how to live, to be your reason for being. You live life meeting different people, but never once are they meant to become your purpose. They only mean to add to it." Tyler nudges me, careful enough not to push me off the bed.

Nate won't tell me the full details; he's being so vague with his answers. He thought I hadn't heard, but I could see he had returned. I heard the sound of the car. I was thirsty, so I thought I'd grab a drink, but I heard him talking as if he knew exactly what my problem was, promising my dad it would all be okay. I had no idea he knew. Nate said he knew, but it's different actually hearing him say it. But why does he think Alessia will be the one to save me? Why is she brought up like that? She isn't my salvation.

Did they know her before? They talk about her as if they've known her for years. "Why is it when her name is mentioned that his eyes get lost for a moment, and he loses himself for a minute? It's like he has to pull himself to reality to maintain his composure," I ask Tyler.

One pro about him being whatever he is, he doesn't tire of me. "Does he know her? Why is he so eager to help me find her? I thought this was for me, but I'm beginning to wonder if it's even for me."

Tyler doesn't say anything, just looks at me carefully, watching a puzzle become complete.

Standing up, I kneel and pull the box out from beneath my bed. Her box. I take the photos out and scan them carefully, but so far, they're just the ones I've already seen. I lift the photo of us to make sure my eyes aren't playing tricks on me. Staring in disbelief at the memory of me, Nate and Alessia. She's in the middle, and he has her arm around her while I'm glaring at him. It looks like they're laughing. I carry on rummaging through the photos, trying to find something, anything, pissed at myself how I missed this in the first place.

"How did I miss this?" I throw them on the floor, spreading them apart.

It takes everything not to rip these photos to shreds. I'm getting played, and they all know it. They don't care. It's been almost a year, and now I find this? All this time, I could have confronted him. He could've made my life so much fucking easier. He's lucky I don't kill him now.

"There's more. This can't be it."

There's got to be more. I missed this all this time. There's got to be something else. I begin kicking the desk, tearing it apart until I grow tired. This time, I can't stop the tears from falling. Instead of wiping them away, I let them fall, and Nate slams open the door, startled as he takes a moment to take in the scene. He starts picking up the wooden bits on the floor. Lifting the desk up to see if it's fixable. He sighs and lifts it up, turning it on its side flat and pushing it against the wall. He looks so fed up.

"What happened?"

I try to steady myself, control my breathing from ripping him apart now. "What do you think?" I wonder what lie he'll conjure up this time.

"Asher, I don't know what's wrong."

"Asher, talk to him," Tyler urges.

"You enjoy watching me lose my mind, don't you? Devious bastard." I angrily throw the slab of wood at him, and he moves out of the way as it hits the wall.

"Listen, I don't know what you think you know to set you off, but I—"

I cut him off. "Do you want to see this?" I hand him the photo. "Turn it over, and you tell me what happened." I try to control my voice, so he can see what a fucking mess I am.

He wants to clean it up? Fine.

I'll let him. It's the least he can do. He turns it over, and his face is pale. He doesn't look up at me; instead, he stands up after a lifetime of silence. He takes a deep breath and tightens his grip on the photo. I follow his gaze, and it's fixated on Alessia.

"Some things you need to know for yourself. I can't tell you this. I've tried before many times and failed many times."

He begins to stutter. "H-How did you even find this? You aren't meant to even know these exist." He's treading carefully.

"How am I meant to react to that? What kind of a fucking answer is that? Why are you all acting so oblivious? Don't I have the right to know? This is me." I hate the person this obsession is turning me into.

"Look, I can't tell you who she is or what she did. I can't do that, you already know. Yes, I know right now you fucking hate me, but believe me, this is what's best. I can't break you anymore. I refuse to do that to you," Nate says, his voice adamant.

"Break me?" I scoff. "You didn't do anything to me, this"—I gesture to myself—"this is me." I pause. "You wanted to know what you did? I was already broken, so don't worry; you had no helping hand with that. What you did was watch me lose myself for almost a fucking year, going out of my mind trying to find this woman when you knew who she was all along. Does this mean you knew where she was, too? You knew where Cyra was, too?"

How could he do this to me?

"I know you think I've betrayed you, but I haven't." His voice is careful.

"You've kept the woman I've been searching for a secret. You begged me to tell you, and I did, and you carried on hiding her from me? You and Dad talk about her as if you've known her for years. You talk to me like I'm a fragile mess who's going to explode any moment. Granted, a part of that is true, but why are you deciding my life for me?"

"It hurts now, but you'll understand why I can't tell you," he says pitifully.

"You're not making sense; you think this has to do with you? It has nothing to do with you or her. It's my own fucked up mess. This is my problem and my problem alone. I don't want your sympathy, your pity. This is why I don't share shit. I'm not your fucking charity case, why don't you get that? Stop treating me like you're doing me a favour. This is my life, and you both don't get to hide that from me." What more am I meant to say for him to hear me? There's a familiarity to his words. They hurt more than I thought they would.

I never imposed myself on him. I'm not his responsibility. I'm not anyone's. I don't care what they think. They can't just control me. "You have every right to feel the way you do." A lump begins forming in my throat, and I feel like if my blood pressure rises any more, I may pass out. "I hadn't realised I needed your permission to feel anything."

"I didn't mean it like that. Look, let's get tomorrow over and done with. Well, today even. It's late. Well, early, and now isn't the right time," he says softly.

"No. I've listened to you; you and Dad clearly know something I don't. Quite obviously you do." I gesture towards him. "There's a photo of you." I snatch the photo out of his hand.

"What happened to me?" I sigh in defeat, and he sits down at the end of the bed.

"She's the reason we're in this mess. She didn't do it on purpose, but you fell for her. You fell for her hard. Alessia saved you only to break you again. I'm not letting it happen this time," his tone is stern.

"Was I in love with her?"

"Yes. Deeply," he admits, "you never failed to show how in love with her you were. You always said that you never felt empty around her. You had this sense of familiarity and warmth you craved from her. No one could make you feel like that besides her." I wish I could remember everything.

It's so frustrating finding missing pieces to your past but not being able to link anything together. "So, what happened?" I ask again.

"That's not for me to say. I know that's a mind fuck of an answer, but it's the only one I have."

"Why are you helping me then?" I question.

"Because you need to realise you need to live for yourself, not her." He coughs, clearing his throat. "Now I'm sorry, but that's all I can say. I gave you part of what you wanted. Now, for heaven's sake, if you're not going to sleep, at least close your eyes or something."

"Until we find her, I'll pretend nothing's happened." I close my eyes, and minutes later, I hear his footsteps lead out.

As he turns off the light, I'm left in the darkness with my thoughts. Today might be the day I find her. I pray I do.

I need to.

I've been left in the dark for so long. I don't want this anymore. I thought I was used to it. It was all I knew, but she shed a light I never knew existed, and now I want it. I want her. For so long, I've felt so lost, so empty, but now things are starting to come together.

Wherever she is, I'm going to find her.

I won't stop until I do.

CHAPTER TWENTY-FOUR
NATE

Days like this are becoming too common. What are we doing here? I'm starting to get used to this feeling, and I never want it to end. I never really know what's going on half the time, especially when it's with Alessia. She always has me running around. She knows she has me wrapped around her finger, but I don't care.

Asher gets annoyed when I spend time with her, but he never says anything. He trusts her. I'm not sure about me. I'm not even sure I trust me. I'm always getting roped into doing things that make me question myself more. You wouldn't catch me doing any of the things I do for Alessia for anyone else.

It doesn't help that I can't see anything; she wrapped a piece of fabric around my eyes and expected me to get up and trust her.

"We're almost there." She's holding onto me, guiding me carefully.

"Do I always have to be blindfolded half the time?"

"Yes, when you get surprised as easily as you do." Her voice is soft and melodic. I mean, she's not wrong there.

"Don't you have a painting you need to finish?" I question while trying not to trip, I trust her, but she has guided me to fall on my ass a couple of times.

"You whine too much, you know that?" she says, her voice not bearing the slightest hint of irritation.

"So I've been told." I try to take my blindfold off, and she slaps my hand away.

"Not yet."

"Then when?" I frown.

"You are the most impatient guy I've ever met."

I pull her into a hug and don't let her go. "Let's stay like this."

She wrestles out of my arms and kicks me. "Do you have to kick me every time?" I groan.

"Yes, besides, I feel bad for kicking Asher all the time. Someone else has got to take some kicks, too," she teases.

"Yeah, yeah." I scoff as she pulls me back up.

It's not even morning yet. The sun still needs to come up. I know that I may have my eyes shut because everything's dark, but you can still tell. I never understand how she is so energised. It's like she's consumed every caffeine drink she could find and finished it to the very last drop.

She's always so secretive and happy to be doing shit, sometimes it's tiring just watching her. The ache in my legs is forcing me to go slower, but she won't let me. She senses my lethargic temptation and pulls me along harder. "Easy, I'm not on a leash."

"Oh, stop your whining." She laughs. "Now stop!"

Coming to a halt, she lifts my head up to face the trees. I lose my balance, stumbling as I fall over. "You were meant to stop."

"A warning we were going to stop would've been nice."

"I thought you knew." Her voice is flat.

"I'm wearing a blindfold," I say, stating the obvious. I'm not even trying to be sarcastic. I stand up and dust myself off, forgetting I'm still blinded. Her hands unwrap the knot, letting the cloth fall. My eyes begin to adjust, and it truly is stunning.

"You said you wanted to see the autumn leaves at sunrise, see all the colours come alive."

I can't think of any words except how much I want to kiss her. I gulp as I try to look at the sunrise and not at how beautiful she looks, so effortlessly beautiful. I pull her into my arms and hold her against my chest. It's the only thing I can do, the only thing I can do that isn't pushing any limits. Even Asher can't be mad about this.

"I take it you like it?" She beams.

Of course I do. How could I not? "I love it." I plant a kiss on her cheek.

It hurts that I can't be anything more to her. She will never truly accept me. She will never love me, not the way she loves Asher. I longingly gaze at her. I don't want to resent him for having what I can't.

I can't be mad because it's not him who chose this, but I can't help but resent him ever so slightly. The fact that it'll always be him and not me. What am I doing wrong that it can't be me? I've always been so open; from the start, I've been open, I've never tried to hide the way I feel. But even knowing how I feel towards her, Asher is still the one she wanted.

Not me.

It's never going to be me, and it breaks my heart every second knowing it'll never be me.

"Alessia?" This is going to hurt, but I need her to break my heart. I need her to break it so much. "Will you ever love me?"

The words escape easier than I thought, and my heart starts pounding so loud I'm sure she can hear it.

Alessia sighs deeply and hesitates. I watch as her smile fades, and she turns towards me, raising her hand against my face and softly stroking my cheek. She breathes deeply.

"I do love you, I always will, but not like that." *She pauses for a moment.* "Never like that. I would say I'm sorry, but I'm not sorry for who has my heart," *she says boldly.*

Her hand lowers from my skin. She knows she's breaking me, but it doesn't faze her. I don't know what I expected her to say. I knew better, but I still asked her. Asher would kill me. The only reason he hasn't gone for me yet is because of her. I've never seen him so protective of anyone the way he is of her.

I think I could love her the way he does, as much as he does. But deep down, I couldn't love her that intensely. I do love her, but I don't know if my feelings would be the same as mine. Anyone can see how much he loves her and how he would do anything for her.

I would do the same, but the feelings wouldn't seem to compare to his.

"Don't look so down. I know how you feel about me. I've thought about backing off from you, but I can't do that to you." *She pauses.* "It seems like I'm the only person right now, but I promise I'm not. You'll see that eventually. But regardless of who my feelings belong to, I will never stop taking care of you."

I laugh and take her falling hand within my grasp. The pieces of my heart falling apart so effortlessly. "Why couldn't it be me?"

I don't know what I expect her to say. "Nate, you know how people say there's someone for everyone? I didn't believe that for the longest time." *She laughs softly.*

I don't need to ask what she's thinking. I know that smile, and that smile only belongs to Asher. I sigh in defeat, and she gazes at me apologetically, "I thought that was complete bullshit, but then Asher came into my life, as did you." *She holds my hand tighter,* "I don't know how to really put it into words, but we weren't meant to be. You don't complete me in the way that he does. Yes, you are important to me, but you're not him. I don't love him because he saved me or because he was all I knew. I love him because life doesn't make sense without him. I always had a missing piece. A void I couldn't really fill, and he filled it. He's it. He is the other half that I cannot be without. Even if you came first, you wouldn't be the one for me."

Her words sting more than she intended. She meant to hurt me partly. She had to. Her phone buzzes, and she pulls it out, her expression tired.

"What's wrong?"

Brushing past me, she picks up a bike lying down on the path, sliding her leg over, and positioning herself comfortably.

"Um... Alessia?" *I wonder if she realises she's basically stealing a bike.*

"Yes. I promise I'll give it back. I'm just... um... borrowing it." *She never fails to surprise me.*

"Oh, one more thing!" *she shouts.* "You're my best friend, and that will never change. I'll see you later. Tell Cyra to get her ass up on time for once in her life, and maybe you should take a closer look at her. You might find what you're looking for."

Taking off down the path, she soon fades into the distance, and I contemplate how the fuck I'm meant to find my way back.

Why does she do this to me?

I hadn't realised I had fallen asleep. I can hear him, his footsteps echoing through the corridor. I would go check on him, but I'm sure he will find something to smash in my face. I'd rather not get my face broken today, not that I can't see it happening. I do see it happening, one way or another. It's pretty much unavoidable.

"You ready?" he asks.

"I've been ready for a while," I lie.

"Get your ass up then. I don't even know where we're going." He slips into his black sweater. I really need to get him a wardrobe. The man doesn't know any other colour than black. Although he did start wearing colour for a bit.

He had only ever worn colour before for Alessia because it would make her smile. He always did it for her. He'd wear some colour but not nearly as much as her. He always described her as an exploded colour palette. Where everything is mixed up, and nothing makes sense, yet somehow it works.

I lean forward, placing my feet on the floor. I could always go back to hiding. It was nice for a while. I push aside the temptation and suck up the reality. This is happening whether I like it or not. We both get into Mr Scott's car. I was just as surprised as Asher was when he agreed to let me drive it after the last time.

Awkward doesn't even come close to describing the tension right now. He's ready to explode, and he's nervous. I'm practically leading him to his final push, the final nudge to let everything go. I'd be glad if it was any other time. Sometimes, they say you need to vent to go back to normality. It's healthy, but not with him.

He's bottled up too much anger, and I don't know how it will turn out. He feels everything too deeply, and I don't know how he will cope with his feelings, if he can even control them. I'm afraid that if he loses it, he really will be gone, and this time, it'll be all my fault. I can't lose him, not this time.

Not again.

Some say the silence can be comforting, but this isn't one of those times. I do appreciate it, in a sense, that he's not hounding me with questions. Should I ask how he's feeling? No, that's asking to set him off. I wouldn't want him to swerve me into a ditch. He wouldn't mind killing us both.

He clears his throat. "Oh God, please don't start cursing at me."

"What are you doing?" he questions. I didn't realise I was pleading out loud. That's awkward.

"Driving?" I answer, trying to play it cool. Now this is really fucking awkward.

He slaps the back of my head. "I'm aware of that, dipshit."

"Do you have to slap me?"

"If I don't, no one else will," he says as if it's obvious.

"Do you ever think about Tyler and what happened?"

This is the first time he's mentioned him without making it sound like a disease. Every time he mentions him, he usually loses his shit. He hates to be reminded of the past; he hates to be reminded of him.

I try to keep my expression neutral and blank. He's trying to be open. The last thing I want him to do is go silent. I try not to get my hopes up that the conversation will continue. If anything, I'm surprised it's even taking place. "All the time. I don't think there's a time that I don't." He looks surprised.

"What?" I question. "Why don't you ever say anything?" I try not to sound hurt.

"The same reason you don't." A moment of acknowledgement illuminates the silence. "What do you think about?" I question.

He needs to say what happened out loud, just once. I don't think he ever has, even when he died.

"How I was too late. I wish I had gone straight after him but didn't get to him in time. He needed to let off steam, and I thought that was best. He always did that, but this time felt different, so I followed anyway, just in case." He stops and clears his throat, his voice trying not to crack.

"You don't need to carry on if you don't want to."

I don't want to make him feel like I don't want to listen, but this is the furthest he has gotten with talking about it, and I don't know if he can handle it.

"Don't do that, it's alright," he insists. "You can't always be trying to protect me. I'm not going to lash out if that's what you think." His smile fades and becomes burdened.

He's right. I can't keep trying to fight his fight. I nod, and he carries on. "He was so happy; you wouldn't have thought that he had anything going on. I know that's such a stereotypical assumption, but sometimes you can't help but make it. It's alarming how someone can fake being happy so easily. It makes you wonder if they have any demons at all. How do they manage to tame them? I've never understood. I knew he had shit going on, but he never let it show, ever." I don't interrupt and let him continue. "That night, I heard them arguing, him and his dad. See, the thing is, I knew he was an ass. But we all fight with our parents. I didn't think he was capable of that; I didn't think he would kill his own son." I want to question him further but don't want to throw him off. I've never heard him say this out loud. He's never come this far.

"You saw him kill him?" I calmly ask.

"I saw everything, well, partly. He was shouting, and he was trying to leave, but his dad grabbed him by the arm and bent it behind his back, slamming him into the car face front." He starts breathing heavily. "I was right to follow, and that's when I started going towards him, but then he lifted him back up and slammed him back down harder, and I ran. I didn't know someone could hate their child as much as he did. I panicked, and all I could see was blood. He threw him on the floor, and I was almost there, but I slipped," he says regretfully. He doesn't make eye contact, and I look ahead of me. "It was wet, and there was mud, and the pavement was broken."

He tries to control his voice, steady and strong, not letting the cracks win.

"His dad got back into the car, and as soon as Tyler managed to stand up, he shot him." His voice breaks and turns into choked sobs. "I tried to run to him, but I don't—I can't remember anything after that," he stammers.

"Why can't you remember?" I don't know what I expect him to say.

"I don't know what happened, if it's the guilt or if I blacked out if I got there in time. I'm not sure. All I know is I was there, and I let him die." This time, he takes a deep breath and wipes his eyes with his palms. He doesn't cry, instead he smiles.

"I don't deserve to talk about him, to see him. I wish I was fast enough; I wish I got there in time," he says, full of remorse. "There was nothing you could have done," I plead silently that he believes me.

"I let him die."

"No, you didn't." He can't let himself believe that he did.

"You weren't there."

I try to blink away the tears forming in my eyes. "I was," I confess. "I saw the blood too."

He looks at me wide-eyed, like I just stabbed him in the chest. "You were there?" he questions.

"Yes, and that's why I know nothing could have been done. You weren't meant to make it there in time. It didn't happen slow. Everything happened so fast. So believe me when I say you were on the ground for less than a moment, but you ran towards him with no hesitation." I hope he believes me because it's the truth.

"Why didn't you tell me?" His voice is hurt. He looks up and locks his eyes in the centre mirror. His eyes are sorrowful and dull.

"Do you see something? What are you looking at?" I say, following his gaze in the mirror, but nothing is there.

"Nothing." His voice is cold and flat. "Do you ever see him?" His gaze is still locked.

"Tyler? No. Do you?" Is that who he's seeing?

"No," he says, breaking his gaze and slouches back further in his seat.

"What else aren't you telling me?" he says, refusing to look towards me.

"I know you want the whole truth, and you will get it, but I can't be the one to tell you. You can't carry the guilt alone because there was nothing you could have done. I promise."

One thing I know for sure is this time is truly different. Maybe this time, he will finally break the cycle.

CHAPTER TWENTY-FIVE
ASHER

This is new for me. I didn't think I could tell the story out loud to someone else, not muttering to myself. I know he's hiding stuff from me, but he would tell me if he could. Tyler would be proud, really proud. I thought a weight would be lifted off me, but I guess that's a myth to con you into revealing your burdens.

I didn't know it wouldn't hurt any less to say it out loud; in a way, it really does make your demons real. I always thought he wouldn't be gone if I didn't talk about it and refused to say his name. He would be away somewhere I can't talk to or see him—well, the real him.

I hate that I can't remember what happened, if I did run to him in time to save him, if I was comforting him in his last moments, if he was in pain. Maybe that's a good thing, not remembering the look he embraced moments before he passed. It's okay not knowing whether he was content or afraid.

Tyler didn't have the best relationship with his dad; it was always rocky, but that's not to say he never tried to fix it. He always tried. It just made his dad angrier. I knew they had issues, but I never knew to what extent. Tyler's dad despised the both of us, but we still showed our faces.

He even tried to ban us from seeing each other altogether. It made us laugh, making it out like some type of Romeo and Juliet crap. He said I was a bad influence on Tyler. I can partly agree, but I wasn't. Obviously, Tyler didn't agree, but that didn't make a difference to him.

That night, he was supposed to be out of town for a while. He said there was business he needed to tend to, and he didn't need a 'piece of shit' like Tyler distracting him. I didn't realise how much shit Tyler had to endure daily. He was always happy. Smiles and laughs can conceal so much. They are part of a facade you can't tear through unless you look deeply. Even then, it seems impossible. I have known Tyler since I was a kid. We were always causing trouble together and getting caught up in shit, doing things we weren't supposed to.

We balanced each other out when needed. If I was the one doing dumb shit, he was the one to hold me back. If it was him, I would pull him back, and well, when we were both idiots, we had Nate. I keep having the same dream as before.

It's not a nightmare, but I've always wondered who is beneath the mask. Sometimes, I wonder if it's Tyler. After a long while, he finally pulls up on a side street.

"Now, we wait." He turns off the car.

"Why are we outside a hotel? Is she staying here?"

Now isn't a time to be vague. "Something like that," he answers.

"Then what are we waiting for?" I try to open the door, but he locks it and pulls me back.

"What are you doing? What if she leaves?"

Why does he have to make everything so complicated? Can't he just get straight to it for once in his life? "You want me to wait? If I do, what if she leaves regardless?" Panic tries to settle in.

"Then we'll get her, won't we? You need to have some faith." I try to crush the hope rising. I can't be hopeful because I don't know what I'll do if this doesn't end up with finally finding her.

"You don't need to child lock the car." I forgot this car has a child lock.

"It's more fun this way."

He nudges me as I slowly take my hand off the lock. His phone won't stop going off. "Aren't you going to answer the phone?" I reach for the phone on the driver's side. He snatches my wrist. "No, I got it."

"Easy, Edward." I pull my wrist out of his tightened grasp.

"I'm going to pretend you didn't just quote *Twilight* to me. It's been ringing for ages. At least put it on silent," I groaned. Now I know he's definitely hiding more shit. He frowns and hesitantly picks up his phone, "Well, answer it then. Why are you looking at me?"

"Alright, man, jeez, why are you always so aggressive?" He sneers.

He reluctantly answers his phone. Nate tenses, and his vein begins bulging in his neck. "You look like an angry toddler," I jokingly whisper, and he shoots me a deathly glare.

I shift more towards the window. It doesn't help that I'm right next to him.

It doesn't really leave much room for me to defend myself if he decides to strangle me to death. Right now, he looks like he's debating whether to strangle someone. "I told you not now. I'm busy. Don't pester me, I told you, I've got this." He throws the phone across the dashboard and slams the steering wheel.

"Just wait, for once in your life, have some patience. I brought you here, didn't I?" he says, punching the dashboard.

"Do I look like your girlfriend that you're throwing a tantrum with me? I didn't say anything dipshit." I start cracking my knuckles. Tyler hated it when I did this. "Who was it?"

"No one, don't worry about it," he casually says.

This is turning out to be a great conversation. "What are we waiting for?" I should at least know that since he refuses to reveal anything else.

"I can't have you go in yet; I don't want to say, 'trust me', but you should because I wouldn't keep you unless it was absolutely necessary. You can't make a scene, but you'll understand. Just wait." He scans my face for reassurance.

"Why am I going to make a scene?"

"Nothing, never mind." He coughs.

I gaze onwards to the hotel. I've been here before. I can't recall when. It's fancy as hell. The Plaza seems to be more of a business venue than anything else. The colour around here seems so dull. I can't explain it. Everything seems so lifeless.

The hotel is huge, with massive, double-glazed windows and a marble interior. You can't quite see the inside. It seems tinted; otherwise, I would have gone in already. For hours, we wait, Nate looks tired and rigid, but he doesn't take his gaze off the hotel. Saying I'm tired is an understatement. I'm more mentally exhausted.

Nate unlocks the door, quickly jumping out before I have a chance to process anything.

"Get out. What are you waiting for?" Nate looks at me like I'm an idiot.

"I've literally been asking you that," I snap as I shut the car door and watch Nate. He runs up to him and stands in his path.

He looks no older than fifty years old, wearing a navy suit, his grey hair slicked back and carrying a brown briefcase. Judging by his stance, he's trying not to hit Nate with it. I kind of wish he did. It would be pretty entertaining watching him get beat up by a random man.

Why is he bothering the poor guy? Tyler stands beside me, waiting as eagerly as I am to get some answers. But I don't see Alessia anywhere.

I don't allow myself to get occupied with my thoughts, and I make my way to join them.

"Tell him," Nate pleads.

"I'm sorry for your friend, but I can't do this anymore. Just let me be."

I don't waste my chance. "Do you know where Alessia is? Is that why we were waiting for you?"

He must; otherwise, I can't imagine why we would be waiting for him. "You were waiting for me?" he asks Nate, ignoring that I said anything in the first place.

Apparently, I'm invisible.

"I need you to, please. He needs this," he pleads. Do either of them remember I'm standing here?

"Do you never listen? You kids these days don't have any respect. No regard for anyone else's feelings besides your goddamn own," he spits.

"I understand why you think that, but just this once, please. Just one last time."

"What, like all the other times were just this once?"

"You thought of us like yours once. Why can't you do that again?" Nate searches for a part of the man that can resonate with him for a moment.

"Why? You really are brave. You have the audacity to follow me and do this to me, and you're asking me why? You're asking me to do what you can't? Because you're too scared?" He laughs at the audacity. "Do it yourself. I'm done." His words are final.

"Please," Nate pleads again. I don't understand why I'm a part of this conversation; it's intense. I don't even know why he's insulting me. I haven't even done anything.

"Nate, what are you doing?" He doesn't respond to me. I tap myself to make sure I'm still here. I'm not sure why I am still getting ignored.

"Sir, I don't know exactly who you are, but if you're going to Alessia, can you pass on a message for me? Please tell her I'm sorry. I didn't mean to hurt her. I'm starting to understand now, but I'm not mad. I just want to know the truth."

She must be here somewhere, right? I look towards Tyler for reassurance, anything, but he remains still and unflinching as he stares at the man.

I came here to find her, not for whatever show they've put on.

I don't recognise him, but Nate seems to think I know who he is. To be honest, I'm not even surprised anymore. My life seems to be one big joke that I can't remember.

"See? I had to bring him," Nate whispers. Why is he talking like that?

"Son," his voice is strained, trying to maintain the remorse that makes him feel some sympathy. "Why are you doing this to me?"

"Doing what?" I look between the two, and neither tells me what I want to know. "I'm not sure I understand. I haven't met you before, sir."

He places his hand on my shoulder. "I get that it hurts. Believe me, if there is anyone who can relate to you, it is me, but please, son. Enough is enough."

"Enough is enough of what? I haven't done anything," I begin to lose composure.

"Son, please," he begs.

"No." I take his hand off my shoulder. "Is this a joke? You brought me here to see her, and instead, you brought me to this guy?"

I grab Nate's shirt. "Why are you playing games with me? Don't you know how much this means to me? How much she does? Do I need to say every thought aloud for you to understand what I feel is real? Why are you taking this away from me?"

He doesn't try to fight back, so I let go. It takes everything I have not to prove Nate right, that I can't control my anger and let my rage get the better of me.

If games are all he knows how to play, why does he expect anything different from me? "I'm not playing mind games with you. If you try to understand—"

My fist connects with his cheek, blood dripping slowly from his mouth.

"I can't keep doing this." The man grabs my shirt and slams me into the car behind him. "I can't keep doing this," he repeats, tears pouring down his skin.

"Leave him!" Nate tries to get him off me, but he tightens his grip instead.

"You want him to understand, don't you?!" he shouts.

"Not like this, for fuck's sake. Why does everything need to be so dramatic?"

He continues to try to loosen his grip. His eyes meet mine, and I feel like I can see everything. "You can't keep coming each time you forget, each time you hurt. You think you're the only one hurting? How do you think it feels when you keep bringing up my daughter? Each time you come when you've lost your way and expect me to keep pretending for you? I'm done." His voice is a broken whisper.

"Your daughter? I didn't—" I stammer.

"No, you did. You've always known. She may not have been mine biologically, but she was mine." He lets go. "Son, accept it and let go. She's not coming back."

She's not coming back?

Nate finally manages to pull him off me and pushes him. "Why are you talking about her like that? As if she is—"

I get cut off as Nate grabs my arm. "As if she's dead?" He says remorsefully. "Because she is."

"You say you want to help me, but you do this to me instead?

How is this helping? How is any of this helping?" I let my anger get the best of me, my rage no longer being contained. I lunge for him as I tackle him on the ground, my fist connecting with his face as he lies there helplessly. Knuckles puncture his skin. He can't play me like this. I won't let him. This can't be real. He must be lying. There's no way she's dead.

"Twisted fucking bastard," I spit. Alessia's father grabs hold of me as he tightens his arm beneath my neck, closing in on me slowly so I can't breathe.

"Listen to him." He strengthens his hold as I try to break free, my knuckles cut from the force of the punches upon Nate's skin. He steadily stands up and holds the silver car beside him, trying to balance himself, wiping the blood from his mouth with his sleeve. I watch as he stumbles towards me, regret washed all over him.

"Listen to me," he pleads, his breathing heavy in sync with mine.

"How can she be dead?" My chest feels tight, and I feel like I'm suffocating. I can't breathe.

"He's telling the truth," he whispers. "I'm sorry."

No, this can't be real. "How would you know?" I ask, I'm done fighting.

Her father lets go of me, and I no longer bother trying to fight. I'm tired of being so angry. I want closure. Is that so hard?

"We've all known," he responds.

"Who's we?" My mind is spinning, and talking and seeing anything is getting harder. My vision isn't clear, and I can't comprehend anything.

"Me, your dad, everyone."

My knees are unsteady. I don't know if I have the strength anymore. "You've all been lying to me?" A knife pierces straight through what was left of my heart, of my hope. "We didn't want to, but we had to," he says defensively.

"You should really stop trying to sugarcoat the truth and play out his fantasies," the man says.

"Fantasies? That's what you're calling this? The only reason I'm not going to hurt you is because you're her father. Don't you dare refer to her as some fantasy. Have some fucking respect," I say harshly.

She had an accident, but she was fine. She must've been fine. How could she possibly be dead? She can't be. "When did she die?"

"Stop pretending," his voice low and grave.

"I'm not fucking pretending, for the thousandth time. I'm not pretending. I would never. I'm not some sick freak," I snap. I'm not cruel enough to do this. Do they think I want to be like this? Pretend? Never once have I pretended.

"No matter how many times you imagine her, she's never coming back. I'm not going along with you this time. I'm not playing out the story in your head until you find her again. Alessia was never here. She was never real," he says frustratedly.

"What? Can you even hear yourself?" Do they not realise how insane they sound?

"You're lying. How can you say she wasn't real? I have photos… letters… I have proof she exists. Stop making me out to be insane. Stop writing her off. She's not dead." I can't think straight. Why isn't Nate saying anything? He met her; he has seen her. Why are they doing this to me?

"Tell him she is real. Why are you just standing there?" I grip his shirt and shake him, trying to make him see sense and trying to make him see I'm not crazy. I'm not going to hit him. I've already hurt him enough.

"Stop!" He grips my hands and takes them off his shirt, lowering them and letting go.

"He's telling the truth, not in the clearest way, but he's right. She wasn't real these past times you have seen her. She was very real, just not this time." I back away slowly. "I'm sorry, but she's been dead for years." His sympathetic gaze follows me as my knees finally cave. I sink to the floor.

I really have lost everything. Why do I still remember nothing? I held her. I saw her. I remember her so clearly. How could she just be in my imagination? I fell in love with a ghost. How the hell can I fall in love with a ghost?

He kneels to the ground and places his arms around me. "I'm sorry."

My Alessia... she's dead.

CHAPTER TWENTY-SIX
ASHER

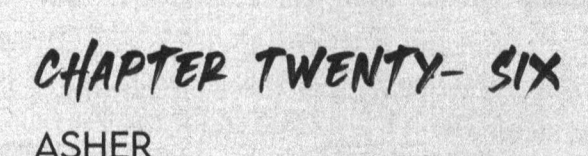

It's getting claustrophobic; the air feels like it's doing everything it can to give me life, but my body is refusing to accept it. My stomach is growling, and the ache is beginning to become unbearable. This is really my life, huh? It's becoming a joke, even by my standards. I knew I had issues, but never did I dream it would be to this extent.

I thought I finally had it. I found my chance to live the life I've always yearned for, and the second I thought I could be something more. I played myself in the worst possible way. I took my chance, built my hopes and crushed them as quickly as they came along with the remaining fragments of my soul.

I've been my own demon, I knew that, but I didn't know I hated myself to this extent. I wish Tyler was here. He'd never let me make a fool of myself like this. He wouldn't let me do this to myself. Everything feels so rehearsed. How many times have I kept on opening his wound?

No wonder he snapped. If I'm honest, I'm surprised he didn't do worse. Not that I blame him; if you've got a fool begging you to see your dead daughter, I would have had a hard time not snapping my neck. He would've snapped my neck if it wasn't for Nate wailing like a fucking banshee. I don't want to believe him, but I don't think I have a choice anymore.

"You okay?" Tyler whispers in the back. I can't say anything. I can't prove what they think I am. "It's okay if you're not, you know?"

"Stop, please stop," I beg quietly.

"Asher?" Nate says.

"Just stop, both of you, just stop!" I yell, pleading for the world to still for just a moment. "Asher, it's just me." He desperately looks for somewhere to pull over, trying to maintain the panic in his voice.

I start laughing because it's the only thing that seems to befit this chaos in my life. How pathetic everything is. I can't control my laughter; it aches, and my eyes burn. My vision isn't clear anymore, but that's okay. What do I have left to see anyway?

I hold my stomach and try to breathe, but I seem to have forgotten how to.

I didn't realise I started to cry, but the tears fell faster than I could catch them.

Nate pulls up and stops the car. He says my name again, trying to ground me. "Asher?"

I carry on, and it's starting to become suffocating.

Tyler resting his hand on my shoulder, his words getting lost in the echo of my strained laugh. I really can't breathe. No air seems to want to occupy my lungs.

"Stop." He begins shaking me. "Asher, come on, man, stop," he begs. I can't seem to control it, and it feels like I'm being punched in the ribs over and over again.

"I know this hurts, but come on, it doesn't have to be like this." He tries to hold me, trying to stop me from shaking. I hadn't realised I was shaking. "I'm sorry," he tells me repeatedly. "You're turning fucking blue. Stop, for God's sake," he painfully pleads. *I don't know how to.*

He places his hands on my shoulder and grips them tight. "Listen to me, we got this, okay?" I weakly peer at his hopeful face.

"Make it stop," I whisper low as if I'm making a prayer,

"Make it stop?" he says, confused. "Everything. Just make it stop. It hurts too much," I say, my voice refusing to steady.

"I promise you this time, this time, you'll get through this. This time, I'm not going to let you break." His hands pull my hair, masked in sweat, away from my forehead. Wiping my face with his arm, I weakly smile. It's a nice thought. Only if he knew how broken I really am.

I've been searching endlessly for her, and I thought this was it. I really thought once their games were done, she would finally walk back into my arms, and I could apologise for everything. I don't remember the time so long ago, but it didn't matter because we could make new memories.

Tell her the feelings I have for her now. Those are the ones that count. Her father told me letting her go doesn't mean the love I have for her dies. It's okay to let go and move on because the universe forces us to at one point or another, but it doesn't mean she is meaningless.

Am I so insanely in love with this woman she even haunts me after death? That the thought of letting her go, being without her, *destroys me*? I don't remember her enough to be so in love with her. Maybe deep down, I do, and that's why I'm chasing her. Maybe that's why I can't give up on her.

I need to remember. I need her.

I refuse to believe she is gone. But how long can I keep denying it? How long am I meant to stay this crazed fool?

My heart has been ripped to pieces, and I have no idea how to fix it.

To fix me.

Everything hurts, and I don't know how to make it stop.

I remember the day I saw her, the day I held her. She wouldn't leave me alone, and I was so annoyed, I wish it could go back to that. If I knew it would end up like this, I wouldn't ever confess my feelings. I wouldn't chase her. If I knew I got to keep her, to watch her from a distance, I'd live a lie until I die.

It seems impossible to have imagined her the entire time. I feel like someone is draining my life. My chest feels like it's tightening by the second, and there's nothing I can do to stop it. Nate sighs deeply.

"This is something I couldn't tell you. None of us could. Once we think we have you, you break and repeat the same cycle. Normally, we go along; we let you get it out, but you never do. You still don't believe me now, do you?" he questions.

"No," I confess. "I don't." To be honest, I don't believe a single word. How can it be true? I'm not insane, I'm not. There must be a reason. There's always a logical explanation, so there should be one for this. I'm not letting him destroy my sanity.

"I can't do this for you. I can't keep trying to pull you back and make you understand what is real and what isn't. You need to see for yourself. Surely, you must know she isn't here anymore; you remember she died," he tries to reason, but nothing he says will make me believe him.

I don't know the reasons for him wanting to make me believe. I can't distinguish between reality and what I hope to see. I understand the difference. I would know if I had somehow dreamt of her. "Why did you say you found her if you seem to already know the truth? Why did you lie to me? Have I done something to you to make you despise me so much?"

He looks defeated and worn out. "If I hated you so much, why would I try to help you? You're my brother. Whether you see me as one or not, you are."

I have always seen him like my brother. Just because I may not express my feelings very well doesn't mean I don't value him. Obviously, I see him as a brother. I always will, even if he doesn't make sense and drives me insane. I wouldn't leave him, despite what he may think.

"You are my brother," my voice is raspy. I don't know why I sound so weak.

"I'm tired of seeing you hurt, constantly searching for some sort of happiness, trying to find a way out. How do you think it makes us feel? I'm in no way revolving your feelings around us, but regardless of what you may think, how you view us, whatever we do is in your best interest."

His eyes focus on the road, his breathing slow and steady. The car is off, but his hands remain on the wheel, tight and trembling. "We don't understand how to help you anymore. You can't help a person who doesn't want to be helped. No matter how many times we reveal the truth to you, even when you realise it for yourself. You refuse to believe it. None of us realised just how in love you were with her; we thought it might pass and that you would be okay, but we never imagined you would fall apart the way you did and have."

How can he say all this so casually?

"Right now, everything is cloudy," I begin. "My judgement is off. I can't say exactly I'm in love. Sometimes, I think I am openly embracing it, but I can't say it out loud because it makes it true. She deserves more than a half-assed judgement. I might be. I felt like I was. Like I am. But then I change my mind and don't know how to comprehend how I can be in love with her, not the way you say," I say and catch my breath.

"You really don't remember her, do you?" Worry masks his tone.

"No, I wish I did." I wish for nothing more. Only she has the answers for me.

"I've never known a person like you before." Is he trying to compliment me or insult me? "You miss her so much that you can't imagine a life without her. So you make her come back as a new person, and you fall for her each time. You really did love her, and I am sorry you lost her." Am I really this tragic?

"Tell me about her. How did I meet her?" I have no idea how I met Alessia. I might remember her if I knew how I met her in the first place.

"I know you don't remember anything, but she was in the same school as us. She didn't really hang out with anyone. But she wasn't an outcast or anything, or maybe she was, but she chose to stay by herself. Alessia was always getting into fights, and she was a good fighter. I'm surprised she wasn't expelled," he tells me.

That's a hard thought to imagine. I sneer. Alessia? A fighter? This already sounds unrealistic as hell. I don't think she knows how to throw a punch, but then again, her strength makes sense. My face seems to have my confusion plastered all over it.

"I know, right? I wouldn't believe it either if someone told me that first. She was so ditsy."

We both laugh in agreement.

She was so clumsy. The number of times she fell over and banged her head because she wasn't looking where she was supposed to be was too many to count. "So, how did I meet her?"

He clears his throat. "I don't actually know how you two met. I know you kept running off every day and ended up with random bits of paint on you sometimes. We didn't really question it, but then it became a routine, and well, I got suspicious and followed you," he admits. That sounds about right.

"I followed you through this gate, and you went there quite a lot."

"That forest where she likes to go and claims that it's hers?" I ask, waiting for confirmation.

He laughs. "Well, I wouldn't know about claiming it as hers, but yes, there. You looked so happy when I saw you sitting next to her on the bench. I hadn't seen you smile like that before. Even when she stood up and pushed you off the bench."

I think he has our roles reversed.

"I remember I was pissing myself laughing. You looked so

shocked, but you tried to brush it off and play it cool, and when you tried to stand up, she pushed you into a bush again." Why is she so aggressive?

He continues, "I remember thinking to myself that she must have something on you for you to be letting her do that. I was expecting you to lose your shit, but you didn't. Instead, you smiled, got up and brushed yourself off. You patted her on the head and wished her better luck next time. Even she looked confused, not nearly as confused as I was. You grabbed her hand, and she was reluctant, but you pulled her along. That was the first time I thought I saw her smile, and when you turned to look at her, I remember she wiped the smile off her face, so you didn't know you had won."

Here I was, thinking she was the master of romantics. Clearly, I was mistaken.

"I was going to tease you about it, but I waited until you told me you had a girlfriend or a girl you liked," he finishes.

"Did Tyler meet her?" I question.

His expression changes, and he is hesitant to answer. "They actually knew each other pretty well," he confirms.

"Did I ever date anyone else? I mean, I don't remember if I had or not, but I'm wondering if I don't remember her, was there ever anyone else?"

I wonder how much of my past I don't recall and if there was much more to my life than I know. I scan his face, and he ponders whether I have ever been with anyone else.

"No, you haven't," he finally says.

So, it seems she is my first and my last. I have always wondered about those types of men. Those who stay devoted to the one woman they have known throughout their entire lifetime and still seem so in love in their old age. Had she still been here, would I have been one of those people? Would I have grown old and loved her till my last breath?

"When did she die? If she did?" That seems like a stupid question to him, but he must have a date.

"You are sick and tired of the same damn shit." He presses his foot down hard to pick up the pace and drives faster, "But you need to find out for yourself. It's shitty, but I can't reveal everything to you. As hard as it is, I would tell you everything and anything, but I have learnt from past experiences that's not the route I'm willing to take," he says.

"Believe me, if I have learnt anything, it is to let you find out for yourself. As much as I want to do this for you, I can't. It never sticks, and you never believe it."

The tension lingers in the air, and we do nothing to escape it. All we can do is embrace it.

"It's too long of a drive back. Do you mind if we crash someplace? I've got a friend who lives here. He said he wouldn't mind letting us stay the night," he tells me.

As much as I hate it, I wouldn't mind some different scenery, even if it's just for the night. Anything is better than going back home and being left to deal with myself.

I can't go back yet. I don't want to face reality, not yet.

CHAPTER TWENTY-SEVEN
NATE

Out of all places, this friend of mine decided to live in the middle of nowhere. Why does everyone like living where they're likely to get murdered? In all honesty, I'd shit myself if I lived out here and knew there was no one for miles. I want to say Asher handled it surprisingly well, but I know that would be a lie.

I know better than to expect him to not have an ulterior motive. He is too willing, too calm. There is no way he's not planning something. Yes, he's had his moments, but I was expecting more. It's making me uneasy because I don't know whether he is going to pull out a knife on me the moment I close my eyes.

The way I'm behaving must be driving him insane. No, it definitely is, and he isn't afraid to let me know. It's literally displayed all over my face. The vague answers I give him and how nothing makes sense, I am fully aware of how it must be frustrating for him.

He does this thing where he will stare into the distance. Or remain fixated on something, as if he's lost in a trance. Sometimes, he whispers to himself, never loud enough for me to hear what he's saying. I don't want to overwhelm him and drive him to the edge, but he's not leaving me any options for an alternative.

I have no choice but to drive him to the deep end. He needs to discover it for himself. I promised his dad I would help him, and that's what I plan to do. There might be a chance he will forgive me for not telling him.

Asher flings open the door and heads to the front door without any hesitation as soon as I stop. He doesn't even give me a chance to turn off the engine. He starts to walk, but then he pauses, realising he doesn't actually know the guy.

"You're a bit eager," I say, trying to figure out his game.

"I have to be. I've been stuck in a car with you for hours." He rolls his eyes as if he's tired of stating the obvious.

"It wasn't that bad." It could have been worse.

"Yeah, tell that to my pounding head." He's cracking jokes too soon. It's getting harder not to suspect him.

"Wait for me at least. Do you even know where you're going?" I jump into a little jog to match his pace.

"No," he says flatly.

"Then why the fuck are you running off like a hyperactive child?" Sometimes I forget I'm his friend, not his dad.

"You're making this really long," he says, growing bored.

"You really are a child, aren't you?"

"Yeah, because I'm the problem here, aren't I?" Asher shrugs.

"Yeah, I don't know what to say to that." Sometimes, I wish for a peek into his head.

"Are you done standing there dawdling like an idiot? I'm frozen," Asher says blankly. He winces as he takes in the altered appearance of my features. "Your lip looks like botched Botox."

It feels like it, too. "Well, it wouldn't if you didn't decide to use my face as a punching bag."

"Yeah, well, you deserved it." Asher tries to mutter under his breath. His face scrunches up into a sour expression.

"I heard that," I bite. It's hard not to be offended when he looks like he's trying not to retch.

"Oh, I know, but still, it looks gross."

This is too normal even for me. "Why are you looking at me like that?" He stopped and stood, his gaze pinned on me.

"I really can't get over how ugly you look." Distaste resides in his expression. "I don't know where you want me to go. I literally don't know the way." His voice loses the last bit of patience he has.

I stare at him for a moment, waiting until he realises he's standing beside the door. "The door's right there, you thick shit." I don't have the patience to let him get there by himself.

"I wear glasses," he murmurs.

"That excuse was valid the first time you used it, not the hundredth time since."

"You walk like a bride. Hurry up, man." His impatience is evident.

"Does your sarcasm ever have a day off?"

"Took you long enough," an unfamiliar voice says, making Asher jump.

"Did you get scared?" I sneer at him. I hold my tongue because it looks like he's deciding to give me another black eye.

"You good there, bro?"

Asher nods, his expression mortified.

"Thanks for letting us stay," I say as I go to shake Reece's hand. He's grown his hair out. Now, it's an afro. "Your hair." I gesture towards it. "It looks good."

He laughs. "I should hope so. It took me ages to grow it."

He's a couple of years older than Asher and me. I stayed here for a while when things were rough at home. I owe this guy a lot.

He doesn't look as if he's aged in the slightest. If only we could all age so elegantly. Instead, I am ageing as if I am on a life supply of drugs.

"You must be Asher," he says with his hand out towards him, waiting for him to shake it. He reluctantly shakes it and nods to confirm his assumption. You wouldn't think he's almost twenty-four years old. He makes me laugh at how awkward he is. You can tell he hasn't had much human interaction. He's a mess in social situations. This is just one person. I find it hard to imagine him with more.

"Well, why are you just standing there? Come on. He's been waiting for you to follow him inside, idiot."

He looks towards Reece, who motions in agreement. "Well, it would help if you actually said that out loud," he groans, tired.

Reece tries not to laugh, letting us inside as Asher mutters under his breath. No doubt he is presumably swearing at him or me in every language he knows.

Hours have gone by, and I wonder if he's finally asleep and not just pretending so he can eavesdrop. My thoughts linger on the possibilities of how this could have gone wrong in so many ways. I resist my urge to go and check up on him and see if he is okay. I know better than that.

"You want something to drink?" Reece questions as he fiddles with his empty glass while we are both sitting in the kitchen. The night could not be dragging more than it already is. "Did it go the way you planned?"

He's been desperate to ask me that since we arrived.

It's probably why he was so adamant about getting him to sleep as soon as he stepped through the door. Asher's like a resistant toddler, not wanting to get told when his bedtime is. Until he gave up and took a stash of Cheetos with him. "Yes and no. He's handling it better than I thought, but I don't think that's real. He's taken it too well—"

He interrupts me, "And that's a bad thing?" he questions.

"Well... yeah." This isn't him, and I don't believe his facade one bit.

"You're moaning because he took the news of his dead girlfriend better than you thought?"

If he knew him properly, he would understand. "Yeah, it sounds dumb, but you don't know him."

He doesn't disagree as he takes a sip from his glass. "You're right." I move onto his red leather sofa and sink. "Alessia's dad lashed out at him. I didn't think he would explode like that. He's never done it before," I admit.

"Can you blame him?" Reece sinks in the chair in front of me, shifting until he finds his comfort spot.

"No, but I didn't expect it to be that bad." He's a man of

patience, but I think we took the last shred of his.

"Take it that's the reason for your face?" He winces.

"This?" I gesture to the bruised skin. "No, this was Asher, not her dad." I try to think of whether it's worth applying ice to it or not.

"He's got a temper, hasn't he?" His voice is curious.

"I suppose, but he hasn't—I mean, he isn't like this normally. He lost it, has been so desperate to find her and thinks we're all playing games with him." That's the last thing I want him to think we're doing. "I didn't want him to find out like that. It wasn't right."

"What did you think was right?" His tone is tinted with slight accusation.

"I don't know." I sigh. "It's cruel, but I was hoping her dad would go along with him, just keep him somewhat sane a little longer."

Reece seems to be shifting uncomfortably. "Is there something you would like to say?" He won't stop moving.

"It isn't my place to say, but why are you telling him half-truths? Should he not at least know the whole truth? You are fucking with his memory, with his life—"

Guilt starts to pave its way through my consciousness. "Now wait a minute," I cut in, "that's the last thing I'm doing."

"Is that really what you're telling yourself?" He ridicules.

"I know what I'm doing, I'm not deciding anything for him?" He means well, but he's starting to piss me off.

"If this was you, how would you be?" I can't let him get to me. I'm doing the right thing, and I stand by that.

"Saner than he is," I blurt out before thinking.

"Now there's the dickhead I love." I try to ignore the lump forming in my throat.

"I don't need to explain myself, but I can't tell him. You know why I can't." I can't make him see my side if he doesn't want to.

"Can you even comprehend how difficult this must be for him?" There's no point arguing back because he's right.

"The way you all are messing with him as if he's a puppet. Don't you think he deserves to know the whole truth?" His voice is low and sympathetic.

"I do," I agree quietly.

"Then why won't you tell him?" He seems bewildered, having to state the obvious but knowing I won't oblige and tell him the whole truth.

"I did, and he lost it again." I try to think of any excuse to save me from the hole I'm digging myself. "What do you think will happen when he finds out?" I question, but he doesn't answer.

"He will be more unstable than he already is"—Reece clears his throat—"regardless of how he'll react, who are you to dictate his life about what he can and cannot know?"

He's right, but what can I do?

"I called him," he confesses.

"You called? What do you mean you called him?"

I try to keep my voice from rising. This is the last thing I want Asher to be involved in.

"You know full well who. He deserves to know," he says in a serious tone.

"Who the fuck are you to decide that?"

I don't have time. I have to get him out of here.

"The same dickhead who thinks it's okay to dictate someone's life?" Why can't he understand?

"Can't you see what I'm doing?" I yell.

"You've led him on long enough. I don't know what way you think you're helping him, but he needs this." I run my hands through my hair and try to think about how to leave.

"You don't know what he fucking needs." This can't be happening, not now.

"Neither do you, it seems." I can't fight him, not here, not now.

"I'm trying to save the damn guy." Panic begins to rise, and my palms start to get sweaty. I've kept him away for this long, and now he decides to come back.

"What's all the commotion about?"

It's Asher. Of course it's fucking him. Why is this happening? Now he is going to have more damn questions.

"We're leaving." I expect him to move, but he doesn't.

"Didn't you hear me? I said we're leaving."

Before he can resist, I take him by the arm and attempt to pull him towards the door.

"I heard you pretty clearly, actually. Now stop pulling me. It's obvious I'm not going to move," he snaps, his expression daring me to push him.

"Do you need to be difficult every single time?" Frustration begins to brew. How am I meant to get him to leave?

"Yes. It's kind of my trademark."

Why can't he see I'm doing this for him?

"Again with the sarcasm. Move your ass." I try to be sterner and angrier, but he doesn't care.

"Why? What happened? Someone questioned you, and you got mad about it?" Defiance masks his words.

If Reece is telling the truth, then we don't have much time.

"You can't hide it from him forever. You treat him like a kid. He is capable of handling it," he protests.

"Why does this guy seem to know more than I do?" Asher says, seeming puzzled.

"You think I hate you, but I swear, I don't," I beg him to reason.

"I didn't say you did," he says lightly.

"You think you're standing your ground, but believe me, this is the last thing you want." He can't find out, not yet.

"Somehow, I doubt that." He frowns.

"Were you there every time he broke down? Let me answer it for you. No, you weren't. You can't blame me based on someone else's story. You may not see it or anyone else, but this is for the best. Why can't you see that?" I question Reece. He doesn't say anything and stands there calmly. Why am I explaining myself to him? Whatever it is I am doing is with the purest of intentions. I can't make them understand if they have already decided I'm wrong, no matter what I say.

"Why are you both talking about me as if I am not literally standing right here? I'm literally taller than both of you fuckers. There is no way I'm invisible. If anything, it would be you two," Asher snaps. He takes a seat where Reece sits and inhales the tension.

Both our gazes turn towards him as he smiles back at us in amusement.

"Not now."

I can't keep telling him off like a child, but if he would listen for once in his life, it would make my life a hell of a lot easier. He has every reason to protest and go against everything I say. Honestly, I wouldn't put up with half the shit I've put him through. The shit all of us have put him through.

"I told you to grab your shit, we're leaving." I urge him to move fast; he couldn't move slower if he tried.

"And I said no, what part of that aren't you understanding?" His tone tests my patience.

"Look, we've been over this, trust me. I keep saying it, but you're the one who made me promise," I confess.

"I made you promise to lie to me?" His expression twisting into disbelief.

"Yes, you fucker!" I yell.

Reece laughs. "Now you're really digging yourself a hole." Someone, just fucking shoot him already.

"I think it's time I tell him the truth." We turn to face each other, but it didn't come from any of us.

Now, there is nothing I can do to stop him from drowning. Asher's eyes widen as he stares. The little colour he has in his skin is fading by the second, his face pale as his words come out in a low whisper, slow and pained.

"Tyler."

CHAPTER TWENTY-EIGHT
ASHER

"Tyler."

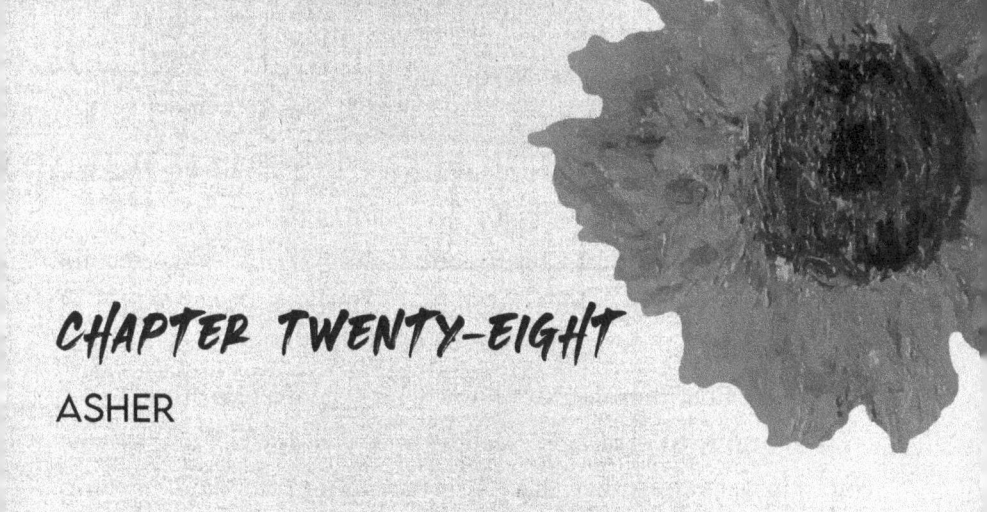

His name comes out as a whisper, his name refusing to be uttered out loud, my mind drowning in searching for an explanation. Any explanation. This can't be real, can it? I'm really insane. This can't be real. I look to the side of Nate where the Tyler I know stood, but he morphs into this man standing before me.

Numb doesn't begin to describe the betrayal seeping through my blood, my mind laughing loud and obnoxious at how blinded I've been. Everything seems to have frozen. My body refuses to move.

"You're alive?" is all I can muster myself to say. I can feel my throat closing.

It's like someone set it on fire. I can't stop it from burning, and my chest begins to tighten. I can't cry. I can't show him how weak I've become. He's alive? Has he been alive all this time? They all fucking played me.

"I can e—"

I cut him off. "Let me guess, you can explain?"

All this time, I felt so burdened, so heavy and fucking broken. I thought I was the reason for his death. For as long as I can remember, the guilt has been eating away at me every second of every day, and here he is, standing before me, clear as day, in perfect health.

"You're fine," I exclaim. "I know what you must be thinking—"

He begins to stammer. "Believe me, you don't. I don't know you." He was my brother, but the guy standing before me, he's not. The Tyler I know wouldn't do this. He was kind. He would never be this cruel.

"It's so good to see you again," his voice is light and careful.

His eyes fill up with tears. He almost seems happy to see me. He steps forward and studies me, waiting for a reaction. I stand back. I don't know why I'm so hesitant. How is anyone meant to react in this situation? I wonder if I should kill him fast or slowly so I can enjoy his fucking pain.

"I bet it is. It must be pretty tiring having faked being dead for so long." What does he want? A hug?

"I deserve that."

"You haven't even begun to receive what you deserve, but don't worry. I'll give you exactly that," I threaten. He glances towards Nate, who's refusing to make eye contact. He shifts nervously before directing his attention back to me. Even though he's standing right here, I can't help but wonder if what Nate said was true.

Have I really imagined Alessia all this time?

Does she even exist?

When I say nothing, he clears his throat. "You look well."

Now, I really can't help bursting out in laughter. "Really?" I ask. "Here you are. God, I would have done anything to see you again. I've missed you more than you could possibly understand. Yet here you are, fine. You were here all this time, and I've been suffering."

I can't keep the tears in any longer. My eyes begin to sting, and the droplets begin to stain my skin, softly rolling down my cheeks, gradually falling faster and harder. I wipe my eyes. "You bastard. I've been suffering because I felt so guilty about what happened to you, how I couldn't fucking save you!" I shout.

He steps back.

"Yeah, step back. Come closer, and I'll snap your fucking neck!" I yell.

I don't care if I seem pathetic. I don't care for any of this shit anymore. I'm done.

"I wanted to come. Believe me, I did. I know what you went through, but I couldn't stand seeing you hurt," he tries to explain.

"Aw, I didn't realise how caring everyone is, so understanding."

I must have missed the training that's made everyone so fucking empathetic. "Ash, please," Tyler begins to say.

"No, no. I mean, it must be hard for everyone to have so much love and compassion and not be able to handle it. I mean to make you feel faint at the sight of me because of how 'hurt' I am. I understand."

His expression churns. "You're twisting it."

Of course I am. If what I say doesn't suit them, I'm always in the wrong. Always the misunderstood, irresponsible mess who has a field day making everyone else's lives shit.

"No, I get it. You're all saints, and I should be so thankful for how much everyone cares for me." I dramatically gesture to myself. "Look at us, all so loving." I beam.

"It's not that, you know it isn't." He sucks in a breath and kisses his teeth, trying to bite his tongue to hold back, not saying anything he regrets.

"You're here. You're actually here," I remind myself. Tyler is really standing in front of me, his black curls overgrown and his skin clear and warm-toned.

"I am." His voice is cautious.

"Do you not realise how fucked up that is?"

He's here, he's actually fucking here. They wonder why I've supposedly lost my mind? It's because of them.

"What's that?" I gesture towards his cheek.

"This?" He's taken off guard by the change of subject. He ponders for a moment and points to the scar embedded in his left cheek.

"I got this a long time ago." This scar seems familiar, tugging at a part of me to remember.

"I don't know why you're here. Why now? All this time, you let me become this"—I gesture to myself—"and you didn't feel guilty once? You left, and you didn't care?" I cut in.

"If you let me explain, I can tell you."

"Did you know?" I direct my attention to Nate, but the room tenses and falls silent. "This was what you couldn't tell me?"

I wait for an answer. "What? You've gone mute? I'm asking you a fucking question!" I shout, his body still.

"Yes," he says, ashamed.

"You all lied to me."

"It's not what you think," Nate says defensively.

"Nothing I think seems to be right, does it?" Apparently, I can't seem to comprehend anything.

"Asher," Tyler says, his voice deep and soft. "Don't be mad at him. It wasn't his fault."

My attention resorts back to him. "Who gave you permission to talk?" I snap.

"Don't you know how much I needed you? It must be nice to have each other's back. What? Do you guys have a scorecard? Who can fuck me up the most?"

They both exchange looks, defeat smeared all over their faces. Their eyes are embarrassed and sad. "Give me one reason why I shouldn't kill you right now." Prison doesn't seem like such a bad alternative.

Nate opens his mouth slightly. "Don't say anything. You're lucky you're not the one my attention is on right now," I say quickly, shutting him down.

"We can leave," Nate says, "right now. We can go and forget about this."

Does he think he can make this disappear that easy?

"Easy for you to say, I just found out my supposed brother has risen from the dead, and everyone knows but me." I don't know how they thought this was ever okay. How they thought they could play this game long enough that it would never come to light.

"No, okay? Listen," Tyler interjects.

"No, you listen." I grab him by the collar of his coat. "I'm not playing your game anymore."

I'm so tired, I'm so fucking tired. Of this, of everyone. Tired of being a burden, tired of being a mess, tired of being me. He was supposed to be my rock, the person I looked up to. He was the person I always thought deserved to live, but it turns out he was always alive.

I'm like this for nothing. I've been trapped in the past for nothing. I could have lived. I could have been free. I didn't need to feel shame. I didn't need to feel burdened. I've been caged to the darkness for what seems like an eternity, waiting for a light, only to find out Tyler was always in it.

I throw him against the wall, debating what part of his body to break first. "You want to play dead? There's no need to pretend. I can make it happen for you." I linger over him. His brown eyes don't back down as he stares up at me and stands up.

"Asher." Nate holds me back. "You can't keep doing this," he warns me.

"You think I like being like this?" Every part of me wants to scream, scream until my lungs give out.

"No," Nate says, his voice straining.

"He thinks I'm pathetic." I bite my tongue. I can feel my throat closing up. "Why me, huh?" I try to push past Nate as Tyler sympathetically watches me.

"No, you don't get to look at me like that. You don't get to pity me. You did this to me!" I yell as I tighten my grip. I don't feel angry. I'm hurt. Hurt because he was the last person I thought would do this to me. I don't remember doing anything to make him want to do this to me.

"How sick can you be?" My eyes still refuse to register, Tyler is here, *he's here*.

"Asher, listen to me." His eyes plead to find reason within mine.

"I needed you." My voice starts to crack even more. "I know you did. You do. That's why I'm here." He nods to Nate, and he lets go of me.

"Now. Now, you're here," I remind him. "You weren't here when I needed you most. When I was deciding how to end my life, you weren't here when my life fell apart."

He sighs, hanging his head low in shame. "I'm sorry it's taken me so long." He throws his arms around me.

"I'm sorry I did this to you, but I swear to you, it's going to end differently this time. I'm not going to let you go this time, not me, not Nate. Nobody." He tightens his hug. I hesitantly reciprocate the hug; he starts to ease, and I look towards Nate, who's trying to hide his smile.

"You're not pathetic. How could I find someone who loves my sister as much as you do, pathetic?" he says, his voice a hushed whisper. I break up the hug, standing back.

"Your sister?"

"Alessia."

CHAPTER TWENTY-NINE
ASHER

His sister? She's his sister?

I don't know how much time seems to have passed or at what point I let go of him, but it seems to be getting light. Tyler brushes himself off as he looks around, realising everyone is still here.

I still can't comprehend how he's in front of me. I never thought this was possible; not even in my wildest dreams would I have ever envisioned this. He coughs, and I can tell he's deciding whether to approach me or not. It's weird seeing how much he's aged yet still looks exactly the same.

Seeing the hesitation and watching him assess how to go forward, wondering how to approach me, is weird. "Walk with me, and I'll explain everything. It's been long enough."

He clears his throat. "Nate, you coming?" he calls after him.

"Nah, I think we've spent enough time with each other today. Or our lifetimes, for that matter." His smile is genuine and hopeful.

Is this how it's going to be from now on? Is he really back? How can everything turn so casual so fast? Tyler nods, and I head towards him. Nate moves aside with no protest.

His demeanour is unfazed but comfortable as he lowers his gaze and begins to clear up the mess around him. I should really clean up when I'm back. Minutes pass by, and we're walking down a road. The lights are dim, and everything seems dark, which is strange since it's supposed to be getting light, but perhaps I imagined that, too. Who knows what's real and what's not? I don't think I know the answer anymore.

One thing for sure is Nate wasn't kidding. We really are in the middle of nowhere. He runs his hand through his hair, and I can't help but stare, but he seems so much healthier, better. Perhaps pretending to be dead finally set him free. He clears his throat, and words start pouring out.

"That night, it all happened so fast. You blame yourself, and I've let you live like that ever since I last saw you. I tried to remind you. Let you know it wasn't your fault, but you never believed me. You never saw me." There's a deep sadness and regret embracing his words. He might be free, but that doesn't mean he wouldn't change the outcome.

"You've come back before?" I try to remember, but I can't even process the last time I saw him. "Yes, many times, and we go through this whole process. Sometimes, you honestly don't see me, so I decided it was better that I left." I'm listening, and the familiarity of his words makes me shiver.

"You loved her so much, you still do. You need to remember it wasn't your fault. You couldn't have saved her." I stand still, letting my ears digest the words he's saying, but my heart won't accept it.

She really is dead.

My Alessia, she's really gone, and I'm never going to see her again.

He turns me towards him, his hand gripping my shoulder. "Believe me," he tries to snap me out of my daze and stop the remainder of my soul from ripping to shreds. "It hurts me every day what happened. The blood, her scream, her. It all haunts me. It should have been me that night, but she got in the way." His voice cracks.

I don't say anything. How am I meant to comfort him? "I came to spend the day with you. We both did. Every Friday, it was movie night, but we spent it at mine instead. It was a traditional thing." His fractured smile seeps through his haunted features. "Do you remember?" He lets out a low chuckle.

I do, I remember it clearly. I remember her. I really remember her.

Tyler lets his arm drop and lowers himself to his knees, inhaling the air. I follow him to the floor and lean against the brown picket fence that follows the road all the way to the end.

"I went outside because I heard his car pull up, but I didn't think he would come round. My dad wasn't supposed to be in town. I went out back, and as soon as he got out of the car, we started arguing. I don't remember what it was about. It was so ridiculous and petty that I can't even remember what started it. Dad always hated me. Dad always started fights and blamed me for making his life hell," he explains.

I remember. His father clearly truly hated him. If hate was a man, he was the perfect mould for it. Every little thing Tyler did was never good enough. His dad would always find a way to make him feel worthless. I never understood why. He didn't even try to hide his resentment in front of anyone.

"Ever since Mum, Dad hated every second of my existence. As if it was my fault that she died. That it wouldn't have happened if it wasn't for me, if I didn't call her saying I was ready to be picked up and she wouldn't be headed towards me. She got hit by that drunk driver, and that night everything went down... nothing has been the same for me since." He pauses, maintaining the crack in his voice.

"You, Alessia, Nate, and your dad were the only real family I had," Tyler carries on, "and I was content with that. You reminded me I was still loved. You didn't make me feel like an outsider, no matter what Dad would say. I think that's what pissed him off more, the fact you didn't hate me like he did. That you guys loved me when he thought I didn't deserve to be."

I try to recall what happened, but slowly, it starts to make sense. The missing pieces of the puzzle start to bind together. "Dad started getting more serious and saying I deserved to die, shouting about if I hadn't said I was ready, she wouldn't have left the house that night. She would still be alive."

He let out sobs, his breathing becoming heavier. "I didn't deny it," he says quietly, his brown eyes glistening with the pain he holds.

"He started beating me, and I let him. I thought I would finally let him get it out of his system. I remember I felt the life I had slowly escaping me, and his eyes lit up with accomplishment. It was terrifying. I hadn't seen him so hopeful before." He pauses. "It was as if he had been envisioning this moment for as long as he can remember," I say nothing and let him carry on.

"I saw you, and I told you to stay where you were, but you didn't listen. You ran, and then you fell. That's the part I remember. I was so glad you weren't coming any closer. I can't even begin to express the relief I felt when I knew he wasn't going to hurt you," he confesses.

Flashes of my memory plague my mind, becoming undone in the darkness I've caged them in for so long, "I got up, didn't I? I made it?" I question, my soul shattering by the second.

His gaze is pitiful at me. "You did." He squeezes my shoulder as he wipes his tears.

"Then why are you crying?"

Tyler takes a deep breath and exhales as he looks into the distance. "You got up anyway. You ran towards me. You tackled him to the ground, starting to beat him. I was too lifeless to move, but I managed. I had to. I didn't want him to hurt you.

"Dad saw me stand up, and he twisted your leg and pushed it all the way back before he pushed you on the ground. I heard something snap, and you screamed in pain, holding onto your leg." That explains why I limp half the time. I never understood why my leg would go numb and ache as if someone was stabbing me repeatedly.

"I tried to come to you, but you saw him grab for his gun, and you tried to move. You knew he was going to shoot me. He grabbed his gun, and I remember thinking, this is it. This is how I'll die." His features burrow, burdened. "I closed my eyes, and I heard the trigger. I didn't feel anything. And when I heard her scream, my eyes opened, and you stumbled towards her body."

Alessia. *I remember.*

It was her.

"You started to cry, screaming, doing everything to start

applying pressure to the wound to stop her from bleeding out, and you started screaming for help. I won't ever forget the expression you wore." He doesn't look towards me. "I remember her blood staining your cheeks as she tried to comfort you. She kept on caressing your face. She was so weak. I knew we were going to lose her." He sniffles, coughing before he carries on.

"She told you she loved you and wouldn't stop crying. You held her so tight. Her hand dropped from your cheek, and her lifeless body dangled in your arms. You knew she was gone, and your screams still haunt me. You cried. You cried so much and wouldn't let go of her."

I held her, lifting my hands. I remember the red covering them. I really have lost her.

"You needed her more than you needed me. That's why you let go of me and held onto her," he says. "You were willing to lose me if it meant you got to keep her," his voice is mournful.

"After the funeral, you didn't look back there, you never visited her, you refused to acknowledge anything about her. You disappeared for a while, and then you turned up again one day. None of us knew what had happened to you." I remember I gave up. I didn't know how to visit her because then I knew she would really be dead.

I just lost it; the love of my life left me, and I didn't know how to be without her, how to live a life without her.

"When you came back, we thought you were pretending at first when you started asking for her, but then we realised you weren't kidding. You'd call for her and try to see her. We tried to take you to therapy, but I don't think anything worked. We thought it had finally started to work because, one day, you randomly stopped. But then we would see you in public talking to yourself, and everyone would be wary of you because, well, it's a small town, and news travels fast. We knew you weren't pretending, so we would try to tell you about her, but you stopped seeing me."

"I stopped seeing you?" Only I could do that.

"Yeah, one day, you refused to acknowledge me. You were already so hopelessly depressed. But you kept saying I was dead and how you missed me; you refused to see me. I really thought you were kidding, but you wouldn't come by me. You'd refuse to talk to me."

How does someone refuse to see someone?

"I don't know why exactly. I guess because I was there that night and I was the one about to get shot, you remembered a way where it was me in the end, not her." His voice is regretful. "You didn't link her to me. I don't know if it made it easier for you, but that's when you would always meet her.

"Yet you'd fall in love with her, and then you'd forget her again when you realised you loved her. I think it's different this time because you found out yourself. Normally, you last a day before you start again. I don't know how you do it. How you fall so madly in love with her. How you search endlessly for her. It's always when you realise your feelings, when a part of you starts to remember her, that you break every time. You torture yourself because it's better than being in a world where you've lost her, then knowing you'll never see her again."

We let a moment of silence pass between us, the emotions too heavy.

"I love her. I love her more than she could ever know. I don't think she realises just how much I love her that I'd give up my entire life for her if it meant I got to see her one last time." I don't know how I'm meant to be without her, truly be without her. How am I meant to accept this?

My love isn't coming back, and there's really nothing I can do. Nothing I do will bring her back.

"Is this why Dad is always watching over me?"

He lets out a deep sigh. "Yeah, you do a lot of stupid shit," he says. "I've never known someone could love so much the way you love her." He laughs. "You fall in love with her every time. How do you manage that?" Admiration masks his words.

"She was perfect. She is perfect." He coughs. "I felt so guilty it took me so long to realise there wasn't anything I could have done." He's right. It wasn't his fault. It wasn't hers or mine. It was his father's.

"I'm sorry," I sincerely say.

I pretended he was dead all this time. I couldn't face him because I knew if he was here, then I would be faced with the truth that Alessia wasn't. I don't want to live in a world where she doesn't exist.

I remember her. I remember everything.

I really lost her. I lost the only woman I'll ever love. The purest soul I've ever known taken in a way that nobody deserves.

I really lost her.

"What happened after she died?" That part I really don't remember.

"Dad tried to get to her, but you wouldn't let him. You finally let go of her and held him to the ground, wrapping your hands around his neck and started strangling him. His face started turning blue, and you stopped. You picked up his gun and placed the pistol in his mouth, and if I hadn't pushed you off him, you would have shot him. Your clothes were covered in her blood, and you cried. You limped towards her body while Dad was unconscious, and you held her until you started to black out and you fainted."

He inhaled a deep breath and slowly exhaled.

His words slowly piece together the memories I've buried deep for so long. I was ready to commit murder. I still am if I ever see him again. Hours pass by, and I don't realise how fast time is slipping by. It's hard to focus on anything at the moment; everything seems painfully fake, but I know it's not, and it's killing me.

I unlock the door and make my way through to the double doors of my apartment building, Tyler and Nate bickering about how irritating they've become, and they dare to call me a child. It doesn't feel real to see Nate and Tyler together arguing like we used to. It feels surreal, and it's a comfort I didn't think I'd have the privilege of experiencing again.

I guess I'm to blame for that. "We're going to grab food if you want anything," Tyler asks.

It feels weird seeing him. "I'm good." My stomach growls in betrayal.

"I'll get you something anyway," he dismisses my reply and pulls on Nate. "Come on, you're driving."

Nate reluctantly follows. "Why me?" he groans.

"Because I came in a taxi," Tyler says flatly.

"Fair enough," he says as he waves to me. "Wait... are you sure you'll be okay?"

They don't need to worry about me anymore. "Yeah," I answer truthfully.

"Okay." He scans me, and once he's satisfied, he waves again and runs off.

I get out my keys and try to find the one to unlock my door, but then I see her door. I've been thinking about going back in. Now, things are different. I guess maybe it'll be different this time. I'll see everything instead of seeing nothing. I walk up to her door and unlock it, revealing the lifeless walls which overwhelm the room.

Everything about her is gone.

I guess this means I was seeing everything right the first time after she left. I run to the floor gap I put there. I have the photos. But there's something else, something I'm missing.

I dig further, and there's still nothing. I remember there is something here. It's been bugging me for hours.

I lean towards the abandoned fireplace and put my arm up on the mantle. I feel the bricks for something, anything, and there it is. I grip the corners and pull it down. I open the white envelope covered in dust and place it in my stained hands. I turn it upside down, letting a silver floral ring fall into my palm.

I put this here to remind myself. So, it's true. I really did do this. I put clues in here to remind myself of her, to remember she died. The ring is the one I promised I would marry her with.

I wear a ring, a silver one. I don't remember why I wore it. It felt wrong to take off, so I never did.

I got her a rose gold butterfly ring first, but it didn't look the right match, so I got her a silver butterfly one, crystals filling the wings. It sparkles just the way she likes it. It was not nearly as beautiful as she was. Nothing was. She loved butterflies. Damn, she was obsessed. It was the most adorable thing.

I got her a promise ring when we carved our stupid picket fence, the house I promised to make into her dream home, our forever home. It was our dream, a place to grow old together. It was our promise to each other. It sounds so silly, but it was the most wholesome moment of my life.

We were so happy.

"You found it?" I look up at the soft voice hovering over me.

"Cyra?"

Part of me wants to strangle her, but she had her reasons.

"Hi," she says awkwardly. "I know what you're going to say, but I don't know what else I can say other than I'm sorry. Nate told me to stay away because I was trying to tell you the truth."

"I'm not mad." it's not her fault I lost my mind.

"You're not?" she says, confused, fidgeting with her hair,

"I'm not mad," I say again. Honestly, if anything, I'm happy to see her. "Wait, you are real, right?" I question. It sounds dumb, but I don't trust myself these days. I have to be sure.

"I'm real." She giggles as she throws her arms around me, the floor creaking.

"Sorry, I saw the door open," Nate says nervously.

"You?" Cyra says, looking displeased.

"Yeah, I'm not too thrilled to see you either," he sulks.

"Well, lucky for you, I don't have to hide anymore."

"How's that lucky?" Genuine confusion invades his features.

"Because I'm a blessing? I didn't think I could be clearer," she states.

"As entertaining as this is, do you guys mind if I can spend some time alone here?" They both stop their bickering and agree as they take their leave. Cyra gives me a last hug and tells me she'll catch me later when I leave. For the first time, I've seen the girl in normal clothing, and it's weird. I mean, it's freezing, and she's wearing a blue sweater. I'm kind of proud.

I watch them leave as I fixate on the ring, watching it glisten. I sink, and time passes me by, drowning me in my sorrows. I reminisce about her soft whispers and her precious smile. Her need to always be so vibrant. I miss her.

I let the tears that I've kept trapped for so long fall as I remember. The ones truly meant for her.

Nothing can explain how much I miss her. Nothing in this world can replace her.

CHAPTER THIRTY
SUMMER

I'm trying to pull my bag wedged between the branches of the nestle. Why do I have to have a balance of a jelly substance that walking in a straight line seems to be impossible for me.

"That's stuck," a voice startles me from behind.

"You're kidding," I say over enthusiastically, exaggerating my gestures as I point towards the bushes. "It's stuck there? Oh, well, thank you for pointing that out for me. I would have never guessed." I roll my eyes as I turn back around and start pulling again.

I take one last tug as I launch backwards into him. Shit. I quickly stand up, brushing myself off as I dust off my bag,

"You're welcome?" he says, getting up steadily. I must look puzzled as he sighs and says, "For cushioning your fall? Oh, and don't mind me, I'm fine, thanks for asking." He smirks to himself. I wonder if he finds himself hilarious. I probably should have apologised, but I feel like the moment has passed, and it does not make it okay.

Clearing my throat, I manage to choke out a quiet apology, "I'm sorry." I cough to hide my awkwardness. I have no idea why I'm like this.

"You're Alessia, right?" he says, still standing there waiting for my acknowledgement. Why does he know my name? I look up and notice how his eyes are the bluest I've ever seen, and I try to remember what he asked me.

"Alessia?" he repeats my name again, breaking me out of my daze.

"Uh… yeah, that's me." I conjure up a smile that must look like the most constipated thing in the universe. I don't even smile like this. I feel like I'm trying to imitate a hamster.

"I got to say, you have a beautiful smile." I'm suddenly mortified.

"Get lost," I scoff as I walk past him. "You asked me if my name was Alessia first, but still called me it when I never told you it was." I still don't know how he knew my name.

"You didn't need to. The way you blushed was confirmation enough," he teases.

"Please don't confuse my cheeks flaring because of the frustration of trying to make you leave me alone with signs of endearment," I remark quickly, maybe too quick for him to see it as something else.

"You're rather rude, aren't you? I cushioned your fall, I told you your bag was stuck, and oh, I told you, you had a beautiful smile, but you gave me the cold shoulder instead." His sarcasm is evident enough to slap someone in the face as he counts three fingers, showing me trying to empathise with his 'broken wound'.

"What's your name?"

"I'm Asher, Asher Scott." I already know who he is, but he doesn't need to know that.

"Well, Asher, Asher Scott, leave me alone." I smile coldly as I carry on. I expect him to stay, at least be consumed with enough pride not to carry on the conversation and follow me further, but no. He runs up beside me and grabs my bag. "Hey, what are you doing?!" I try to pull my bag back, but he's already got it. "Don't think I won't push you into oncoming traffic if you don't let go within the next two seconds."

"I'd be scared if there were actual cars around us instead of trees. It would have made more sense to push me into the nettles." He laughs at his own joke.

Who is this clown?

"This is heavy, I'm going to carry it, and you just tell me where we're heading." I bite my cheek to stop myself from smiling, or he'll take it as an invitation that we're somewhat friends.

It takes me a lot not to ask him why he's suddenly trying to talk to me. I don't think we've ever spoken until today. His dark curls fall across his forehead as he lugs the bag over his shoulder. He's a lot taller than me, and I know this is completely random, but I really hope he trips, or perhaps a branch swats him in the face. I can't help but grin at the thought of his face planting the pavement.

"So, are you new?" he asks curiously. I can't figure out whether he is being serious or not.

"You're kidding me, right?" I don't even need to look at his face to see he's already kind of sweating.

"I didn't mean—" he begins to say.

"Relax," I interrupt him before he can carry on. "I'm not going to break down in tears if that's what you're thinking." He laughs nervously, probably contemplating why he's walking with me to begin with.

"I'm in your art class and history class," I say, trying not to show

how he may have hurt my feelings slightly. 'Am I new?' Please. I've been here since Year Nine. We're literally halfway through the year. I can't remember the last time I rolled my eyes this much. It's starting to become a workout.

"Oh, right. I knew that." He shrugs.

"Sure," I say, plastering on my fakest smile just for him. "I'm sorry. Is there a reason you're bothering me?" I can't help but wonder why he's even talking to me in the first place. We've never spoken, and it seems odd how he suddenly appeared to be following me.

"Listen, I don't know why you're being so defensive. There's a thing called a conversation where people can talk to one another without a motive? You realise how paranoid you sound, right?"

He's not making fun of me because his voice is soft, and he seems genuine. I realise I do seem a bit overly paranoid, but I can't help it. Ever since I moved here, it's been so hard to make friends. I can't say that I'm not a little jealous of all those big friendship groups in classes and how everyone seems to have someone. I wonder what it's like, that's all.

"Did I offend you?" he randomly blurts and shatters my daydream. Sometimes, I feel like I forget to actually talk out loud, and it's the most mortifying thing ever because, in reality, I'm silent or staring really intensely, which makes everyone uncomfortable.

"No, you're kind of right, I suppose, but I haven't told you where we're heading, and I'm pretty much home. I don't know how far this is from you and why you're still here, to be honest," I question, now that I realise we're walking the way to my apartment building.

He laughs a little. "And you're offended by me. You're funny." He didn't answer my question.

"Okay?" I don't get it.

"Seriously?" He starts laughing more. He stops to breathe, taking a deep breath as he nudges me. "I live three doors down from you."

"No, you don't." I try to take my bag back, but he pulls away instead.

"Yes, I do." His tone is not mocking me in the slightest.

"You're telling me"—I look him straight in the face, trying to call him out on his bluff—"you live three doors down from me, and I've never seen you walking this way before today? Not only that, but I've never seen you leave to go to school, or at all, for that matter."

"Yes, I'm telling you exactly that, except I don't really like you spying on me. That I find kind of creepy." I kind of agree with him there.

"Do you normally take this many breaks when you walk? You've had us stop four times already in the past ten minutes, and we're going at a very slow pace, even though we live only fifteen minutes away from this park." He gestures. This time, he is teasing me. I haven't wished for someone to face-plummet in the ground more than this guy.

"Will you go out with me?"

I can feel my face flaring as my cheeks burn red. "I'm sorry, what?" I'm trying not to choke.

"Will you go out with me?" he says as sternly as he did the first time, and it takes everything not to laugh in his face, but I break.

"Oh please, you don't even know me, and now you want to date me? Are you okay?"

I wonder if he truly is okay. "I know you. I know you well," he says, stepping closer towards me.

"I don't know if puberty has just hit you and you're not sure what is happening to your body, but I recommend you read a book and find out. Or you're really plain weird and desperate."

Asher puts a hand over his chest. "Now that one stings," he says as he pretends to be deeply wounded.

"Okay, listen, Alessia. I know you, I know you really well, and you definitely know me. Now, see, this is where it gets kind of awkward because I've wanted to ask you out for a long time because, quite frankly, you're a force to be reckoned with, and I find you undeniably breathtaking. Now, here is the awkward part." Asher pauses.

"This is the awkward part?" I question. I don't know why my body won't move.

"I don't know if you've blocked the memory out or something, but I was there when you tried to jump. When we met the first time and now see, the thing is…" He takes a deep breath. This guy talks an awful lot, doesn't he? And if anything, I should be running now.

Of course he was there, wasn't he? Why wouldn't the universe spare me a smidge of embarrassment? But why does he keep staring at me like that? Is this how it's going to be every time I talk to him?

Oh shit, he was! Oh crap. I had a whole conversation with this guy and blocked it out like it was nothing, hoping perhaps if I had no recollection of it, then… well, it didn't happen. I guess that stuff only works in cartoons, not in reality.

"I like you, I like you a lot. But because of that situation, I don't want you twisting it, making it seem like I'm pitying or something because, like I said, I want you to go out with me. I've actually been practising how to ask you, and believe me, it was nothing like this," Asher rambles.

MARYAM A.H.

"What I'm trying to say is, will you go out with me?" Asher's gaze is heavy with an intense yearning ache, which, to be honest, is the most frightening yet beautiful thing I've ever seen.

"No."

What and which species is this human?

CHAPTER THIRTY-ONE
ASHER

I've lost count of how many days have flown by. I've finally stopped counting and made amends with Nate and Tyler. I can't hate him. How can I? He was only trying to save me. But you can't save someone who doesn't want to be saved, no matter what you do.

I get that now.

I've even made up with Dad. Everything seems okay now. Nothing is left undone, and now is the right time. I should have done what I did before. He was so happy I'm not bitter. To everyone's surprise, I haven't lost my mind this time.

This time really is different.

Looking over the town, I let the breeze caress my skin as I stand on the ledge.

I let the luminous lights fill my vision and accept my fate. This is how it should end. I'm not scared anymore, I thought I would be, but I'm not. I've done it right this time. No one can be mad at me. But honestly, now that I know the truth, I remember why I was living the lie for so long.

No one told me healing would hurt as much as living in the

past. Somehow, being aware makes your heart ache more. It breaks you to the point that you don't know if it's worth it anymore. I'm scared that if I stay, I'll break their hearts, and I'll go back to my old self. I think I'm healing, or so they say. This is what healing is meant to be like.

I don't feel healed. I feel more broken.

I feel empty.

Waking up didn't heal me. It just made me realise how empty I really am.

"You're not really going to leave, are you?" a soft whisper enchants my hearing. Finally, she has come to see me.

"I've missed you, my love," I confess. This is a lie, but I don't want it to stop. It feels so real.

I stand down and turn to face her, her perfectly fallen hair brushing against her skin. "You've come back," I cry.

I'm terrified that she'll leave when I take my eyes off her. If I blink, I'll never see her again.

"Remember? This is how we met? When we got a little bit older? I saved you. You were trying to jump, your eyes filled with so much sadness, and you tried to push me away. I was terrified you were going to jump again, so I followed you around like a lost puppy, and you tried everything to avoid me," I say to her.

I remember it so clearly. The next time I met her again was on the ledge, when I really met her, and I plucked up the courage to talk to her, except I wasn't the one trying to jump. It was her.

We both let out a laugh. Her laugh is seemingly as angelic as she appears. Her soft chuckle soothes my pain. What I would give to hear her laugh forever.

"You couldn't stand me," I say. The memories of our time together dig my wound so deep, desperately trying to tear apart the pieces of my soul she's trying to keep together.

"No, I couldn't, but it's not all bad. We fell in love in the end, didn't we?" she says.

"It's weird. When you came back this time, I couldn't stand you, but then you showed me everything was worth living for. You showed me that every problem has a solution and nothing is left unsolved. When I saw the world as black and white, you made me see everything in colour."

As her hand wipes away my tears, I say, "Tell me, how am I supposed to live without you?"

"Live as you taught me to live." She kisses my cheek and smiles, her wholesome aura attempting to stitch every broken wound I have.

"I miss you so much. I don't know how I'm meant to live without you. You were my dream, my purpose. Without you, I don't have one."

Her eyes stare deep into my soul. I still don't know how eyes can reveal so much. Yet, at this moment, I believe they could reveal everything.

"My whole life, you protected me. You never knew, but I always knew who you were. From the moment I met you, I knew who you were. I recognised you the second I met you again. My whole life, I've never had eyes for anyone other than you. My heart belonged to you the second I laid my eyes on you. You were my first for everything. You made me brave, and you made me believe in myself when I needed it the most. My light, always helping me find my way out of the darkness, if and whenever I got lost. You're my star," I say, reaching for the token attached to my wrist and showing it to her. "See? I still have it."

Her eyes linger across the star. She lifts her eyes to meet mine. "You fool. I always knew it was you. How could I not?" Her words are so painfully serenading. "What a story, huh?" She laughs.

"I guess. Deep down, I knew you weren't here anymore, but I didn't want it to be real. I can't let go of you. I'm so scared to live a life without you. Every time I imagine you, I make you real. I finally get to see you. I hate getting to the stage where I remember what happened. I hate that I couldn't save you. I wish I died with you," I admit. My heart feels less heavy.

"I hate that you're not real." I pause. "I hate that I still think of you as someone I can grasp within my reach. I hate that I let myself fall when I knew better. I hate that I gave in." I watch as her gaze lovingly watches me, her hazel eyes absorbing my pain. "I hate how I don't hate you even though I feel like I should." I clear my throat, the words fleeing.

I try not to let my tears run. "It would make things easier, but deep down, I know 'hate' couldn't diminish the love I have for you. It makes my heart ache knowing I'll never get to embrace you, hold you, but most of all, be with you." I reach for her hand, and I gently squeeze it and shut my eyes as I remember her feel and warmth.

"I gave you my heart and told you never to return it to me, but you did. You gave it back to me, hoping I could move on, but I couldn't. I didn't know how to be me because, for the longest time, I thought of myself as a part of you. And without you, there is no me, and I don't know how to live a life where you're not a part of it."

This time, I don't hold back the tears and let them run. I feel her hand wipe them away, and it's killing me. It's not real, I open my eyes, and I see her, but she's not real. Why couldn't she be real?

"I thought, I-I-I..." I start to stammer, taking a deep breath. "I thought I would be better. Now that I know the truth, I thought I could move on, but it's harder now than it was before. I'm finally living the truth of my lie, and I wish I could go back to being oblivious. Go back to when I could reach you, because even though you were a trick, you were real for a moment, and for a moment, I was content. I was me. Like now"—I reach for her and softly caress her cheek—"I can feel you, and I don't want to stop." My eyes blur, stinging with the velocity of the wind, but I don't care.

"I'm awake, but I want to be blinded again. I want to be hurt. Hurt enough that you were real enough for me to hold. You were my downfall, but you were my greatest comfort, and for that, I wouldn't change it for the world."

I know this means I'm healing, but I didn't know healing meant I would still hurt. I didn't know I would be looking back to everything that happened. I thought healing meant that my wounds would finally close, but I guess life doesn't work like that."

"It wasn't your fault, but Asher, I think it's time." Her soft hands take mine into hers. "It's time to let me go."

Let go?

"I can't do that, I don't know how to..." I begin to panic.

"Don't leave me," I desperately plead. "I can't do that. You know I can't. I'm so sorry for everything. If I ever brought a single tear to your eye or made your heart ache in any way, I am so terribly sorry.

I love you wholeheartedly, with every fibre of my being."

"I know you do, and I love you, but can't you see? I'm killing you," she says remorsefully.

"You're not. I'm not like this because of you," I argue.

"But you are. You can't lie to me. I can't be the reason for your downfall. I don't want to be the reason why you can't live," she says, her hazel eyes piercing with flickers of gold light and warmth.

"If the roles were reversed, and it was you instead of me, is this how you would want me to be? Would you want the love of your life to be void of everything she once found happiness in? Would you want to be the reason I try to kill myself over and over again? This isn't living, and I can't be your anchor. Please stop holding onto me, hoping you find solace in drowning. If you hold on any longer, I don't know how many more times I can save you until you finally loosen my grip."

"I want to be with you. I'll do anything to be with you again. It wasn't meant to be you." I don't know how I can carry on like this, what I'm meant to feel anymore. I try to latch onto her, plead and beg for her to stay. Grasp anything, just something, so she doesn't leave me.

Not again.

"Please," I choke, begging.

"Asher, listen to me. I know it's hard, I know it hurts, but I can't be the reason you're in pain anymore. It was my time, but it's not yours yet. You still have time to live, to laugh. To love."

"Are you insane—"

"You will find love again, but just know they can have you in this lifetime, but in the next, you're mine. Just mine." Her voice is a soft whisper, laughing as tears stream down her cheeks, her forehead pressed against mine.

Alessia sighs deeply. "You can't live life like this. You know you can't, my love. I'm not real anymore. It's time to let go. I promise you, you'll be okay." Her fingertips brush my cheeks, her touch igniting my skin. I stop trying to fight for something to hold onto.

"How do you know?" How can she be so sure?

"Because if anyone knows how to live, it's you. If it wasn't for you helping me find my purpose, I wouldn't have lived the life I lived, the life you showed me. Asher, I'm not your purpose. I'm not the reason for you being alive. You are. You want to live, and you can. You don't have to run anymore. I promise you'll be okay."

"You promise?"

Her hand is steady against my heart. "I promise." She lifts her hand, gently caressing my cheek.

"You have a letter, don't you? One you haven't opened yet?" she questions.

"Yes, I do," I answer, I found it when I was rummaging through my box.

"Open it when you come to visit me. Don't you think it's time to see your wife?"

"My wife?" I question.

"Oh, you couldn't have forgotten, could you? The last time you held me, didn't I say, 'I do, a thousand times I do'?" She beams while showing me the butterfly ring glistening on her finger. I remember.

"I miss you so much." I hope she knows how much I love her.

"I miss you." Her voice is so delicate. "But you know I have to go now, don't you? This time, it's for good. It's your time to live, not mine. So please, for me, for us. Please live."

"I love you," I say, meaning it with every ounce of my existence.

"And I love you. I'll be waiting for you."

With her final words said, she leaves as quickly as she came. I can't stop the tears from falling, and this time, I can't see a thing. I'm silently pleading for her return, begging to be blinded just one more time. I fall to the ground and cry because everything has truly changed.

I cry because I'll never see her again, and before I know it, I'm screaming, screaming because it hurts. Everything hurts too much, and I don't think it'll ever stop hurting.

CHAPTER THIRTY-TWO
ASHER

"Have you wondered what happens when we die?" Alessia asks curiously.

"Why such a grim thought?" I shift closer to her.

Why does she always say the most random things? I wonder if she says everything that comes into her mind. Does she think before she says things? I don't think she has the ability to do that.

I don't mind. Her random thoughts always send me spiralling. She keeps me busy, and I like that. She's picking the pineapple off my pizza slice; she thinks I hate them, but I don't. But she loves them, so she can always have them.

"You're eating your favourite, but death is what's on your mind?"

"Well, I was thinking about it before, but then I got distracted." She shrugs.

"I'm sorry, I didn't realise I hold so much power over you like that."

She pauses and laughs, almost choking and leans forward, planting a soft kiss on my lips. "I'll kiss you more if you promise never to say that again." She grins.

"Okay." I laugh. "But to answer your question, I can't say that I have. I don't really think about it," I admit. It's not something I think about often.

"Not even once?" she questions accusingly, obviously not believing me.

"No, I mean... I've thought about it, but I don't really know what happens." I guess this is Alessia's topic of the day. I don't care. As long as she's here, I'll listen to her babble all day.

"What would you want to be?" She wipes the sauce off her mouth with a tissue. How does she do that? Look so effortlessly beautiful without trying?

"What do you mean?" I finally question.

"I mean stupid, what would you come back as if you could," she says, getting more comfortable.

"You tell me." I lean closer.

"A butterfly. When I die, I'll come back as a butterfly, like this." She excitedly shakes her wrist in front of my face.

"Your butterfly?"

She shakes her head. "Our butterfly," she corrects me. "It's funny, I still remember when you gave me this, and it's been my favourite ever since."

"You're cute, you know that?" She should. I tell her every day. I'm surprised she's not sick of me.

"Let's not make me sick." She laughs, I knew I spoke too soon. But I kiss her anyway.

"Tell me," she moans. "What do you want to be?"

I hadn't really thought about that either. But I know exactly what I would be. "It's only fair I become a star," I say, dangling my wrist in front of her face like she did with mine.

"I like that." She tries to hide her smile, trying to fight the blush rushing to fill her cheeks.

"I know you do." I steal the last piece of the pizza out of her hands. Alessia playfully tries to take it back. She never fails to remind me of how food-aggressive she is.

"Oh, come on, you had most of it. We were meant to share."

Alessia wraps her arms around my neck and kisses my cheek repeatedly. "I love you. Let's not kid ourselves. I never said I was going to share with you." Her brows furrow. "But I'm hungry," I groan.

"So am I!" She surprises herself at the sudden crack in her voice.

"How? You just ate everything!" I will never understand this girl. "By the way, I know why I'm always covered in paint, but why are you?" Alessia questions, taking in my appearance as suspicion highlights her features.

"Because you keep hitting me with your brushes."

"I see, that would make sense," she teases.

"Of course it does." I pull her into my embrace and hold her. "You smell like heaven, do you know that?"

She giggles. "Heaven? That's a bit much." Her lips curve.

"I don't think so. Let's stay like this."

I squeeze her tighter. Her curls brush my face as I lean back and cup her face. "What are you doing? You weirdo." She teasingly hits me, honey swirling in her eyes.

"I'm looking at you." She begins to grow shy, her face starting to go red as she breaks free from my hold and turns around to pick her paint back up. It's always warm in her den, no matter the season. I don't think I've ever felt cold in here.

"Here, the pizza is yours." She hands me the slice. "Truce?" she bargains.

I'll take it. I take a bite and hand it back to her. "Truce." I kiss her forehead.

"Come outside for a moment," I say. She looks intrigued but follows me as she undoes her apron and throws it on the beanbag, pulling down the sleeves of her yellow sweater.

"I've kind of been working on something for you." I've never been more ready in my life.

"Oh yeah?" She seems really intrigued now.

I grab the canvas I had hidden behind the bench. "Um, here you go."

Alessia hesitantly takes it off me and turns it around. "You did this for me?" Her expression is wonderful and pure. How does she snatch the air from my lungs every time? I see her every day, but somehow, she always manages to steal my breath.

"Yeah, you see, the sunflower is half full," I say, pointing towards the floating flower. "The petals are floating even though the flower is trying to sink. It hasn't yet. It's not meant to drown, no matter how hard it tries. It's kind of like you. You see everything wrong with yourself, and sometimes you feel overwhelmed."

I lean in closer and point towards the centre where the flower is afloat. "But see how the flower is still beautiful even though it's not whole? No matter what, the water refuses to let something so precious, genuine, and warm sink."

Alessia stares at the painting in admiration, her eyes starting to tear up. "You think this is me?" Her voice cracking.

"Of course I do." I cup her face to wipe her escaped tears. "Even though it's got every reason to let go, it doesn't, and still, it's the most beautiful thing I've ever seen."

"You fool," she says softly, "but you hate to paint."

I would do anything for her. "I know." I sweep her into my arms. "But for you, my love, I'll do anything."

I kiss her forehead. She's wiping her eyes as she lets go of me, clutching hard onto the painting. I get onto my knee as her eyes are blurred by her sleeve.

"Alessia?"

"Yes?" She's lowering her arm. She takes in the sight and gasps. "Are you...?" Disbelief underlies her words.

"Shush, let me finish," I teasingly say. "Alessia, I always said I don't understand how a man can love someone so wholeheartedly and pure. To love someone that they would do anything and everything for them, but then I met you. You are the only person I'd let hold my heart for as long as we live. Even after that, I don't ever want you to return it. It's fate that you're in my life. When we were kids, what were the chances you were the star to guide me home? Since then, believe me when I say I've had eyes for no one but you. Since I knew you existed. Sometimes, things can get hard, and marriage is a lifetime commitment and isn't a fairy tale like people think. It's a journey I don't see myself taking with anyone but you. I want to grow old with you. I want children with you. I want everything with you. The good and the bad, give me all of it.

"Alessia, I will love you always and unconditionally, in this life and the next, I swear to you. Now, all there is to ask is for you to say yes. Will you do the honour of marrying me?"

She throws herself onto me as I fall backwards, clinging to her tight, "Yes, yes, a thousand times yes." Tears stain her cheeks as she beams so brightly.

She holds out her left hand as I gently grasp it, sliding the silver butterfly ring that sparkles as brightly as her.

"I love you," she says.

"I love you." I tuck her loose strands behind her ears and press my lips against hers, embracing her warmth. I'll love her for as long as I breathe. Even death couldn't stop me from loving her.

CHAPTER THIRTY-THREE
ASHER

"Nice to see you here, son," a familiar voice cradles my hearing.

"I thought it was about time," I say. I've kept her waiting long enough.

"You remember me?" he says, surprised.

"You're her grandfather. How could I forget? Plus, I did wreck your car once."

"Nice. You finally admit it," he says jokingly.

"Yeah," I laugh as he playfully nudges me. "By the way, thanks for the coat. You were right. I was freezing my ass off," I say.

"Anytime, son." He rests his hand on my shoulder. "It's good to have you back." I smile, and he squeezes my shoulder as he takes his leave.

Days have passed since I last saw her, and this time is different. No matter how hard I've tried, I haven't seen her since. I can't seem to conjure her up anymore. I'm not imagining her again; I haven't created a reality where she's alive. I can't do it anymore; I don't know how to.

I guess everyone is on edge waiting until I let my imagination take over again. Where I let my pain blindfold me and make me see a world where I must lose her all over again. I'm awake this time. This is different. Yes, I'm still broken, but I'm finally awake, and I'll do whatever it takes to find myself again.

I'm holding a bouquet of sunflowers, which have always been her favourite.

"I'm wearing yellow for you," I say as I gesture towards my sweater and blue jeans. "I can feel you smiling. Is that weird?"

I place them down in front of her headstone. "I've finally come back, my love," I whisper. "I'm sorry I never came. I finally visited you after I lost you. I'm so sorry it's taken me this long. I won't make you wait anymore, but um… I got the letter you reminded me about. I found it in my box. It was supposed to be a gift to me, but you never let me read it. You were adamant it had to be ready. I guess now I'll read it to you, as I should have done long ago. Is it weird I'm nervous?"

I carefully undo the envelope where her final piece remains, in black ink, her letters delicately crafted. It reads:

To Asher,

I hold back the tears as the familiarity of her writing embraces my soul.

As soon as you asked me to be your wife, I was overwhelmed with joy. I couldn't have wanted anything more. I wouldn't change anything about the way we met, not a single thing. I would keep everything the same, whatever heartache I went through, every struggle, every broken piece of mine which led me to you.

    I don't know if I ever thanked you, but you set me free of the burdens I carried for so long. I love you and everything to do with you. When I saw nothing but black and white, you showed me the world for its wondrous glory. You helped me love everything to do with myself.

    I knew that in order to love you to the fullest as you truly deserve, I had to learn to love myself, and I finally did. You helped me achieve the impossible and lift me higher than I had ever imagined. You gave me a new lease of life I didn't think I could have, and I am truly thankful for that. I love everything about you, your jokes that don't make sense.

    How you get excited when you see the most unexpected things. The little things about you have me thanking God for you. You wouldn't ever see me praying, but when I started falling, I found myself praying for you. Praying you were safe, for every little thing about you, I found myself doing what I thought I never could.

    You are the reason I believe someone up there is looking out for us. After all, it led me to you.

    I give my heart to you to hold for always and forever, and it is yours to eternally keep, as

I hope yours is mine. Thank you for everything. Thank you for teaching me how to live again. Thank you for being my other half.

I promise to always be with you through any hurdles we face together. I promise to always stand by you in this life and the next. I'll love you for eternities to come. This is my vow to you:) to always be your star as you are mine. I love you, Asher Scott. Thank you for being the better half of us.

My legs give up as I fall to the ground, kneeling in front of her grave. My tears cloud my vision.

"I'll let you go. I'll do it for you. How you always manage to save me, I'll always wonder," I whisper.

I'll love you now and for eternities to come.

Always and forever. Wait for me, my love.

"I will see you again. I promise no one will ever take your place." As I start to stand, I notice a bright and warm butterfly planted on top of the sunflowers I had just laid.

My heart feels momentarily full and whole. "I guess you really did come back as a butterfly."

My vow to you, my love; for you, I will live.

You will always be my star.

Thank you for existing, for being you, unapologetically you. But most of all, thank you for letting me love you and for loving me.

For helping me to be someone all over again.

ACKNOWLEDGEMENTS

First and foremost, I want to thank you—the readers. Whether you've loved this book or disliked it, your time and support mean everything to me. Thank you for giving my story a chance. I hope my words have reached you in some way—whether they made you laugh, cry, or simply escape reality for a moment. Asher and Alessia's journey exists because of you, and for that, I am endlessly grateful.

To my mother—thank you, Ma, for always being there for me. For listening to me ramble about a story you didn't entirely understand but still indulged me anyway. For supporting my dreams, even when they didn't always make sense to you. For letting me take risks, and for believing in me no matter what. You're the reason I fell in love with books and storytelling—starting with that first Barbie movie, *Rapunzel*, and its lesson about finding freedom in creativity. And, for taking me to buy my first book even though I couldn't read that great. I wouldn't be the person I am today without you. I couldn't have got this far without you. Even if I'm not always appreciative I know how blessed I am to have you. This book wouldn't exist without you. Thank you for always being my rock and my biggest cheerleader.

To my Aunty Bena, who would have been so proud that I did this. I wish you were here.

To Rasikhah—thank you for being the first to read this book. For reading it *several* times. For all the so-called "editing" sessions we had. And most importantly, for believing in the story and in me enough to never let me give up. Even though you don't read much, you still made this happen. You made me believe I could make my dreams come true.

To my editor, Imogen—thank you for your hard work, insight, and feedback. You helped bring the final pieces of this book together, and I truly appreciate everything you've done to make it the best it can be.

To my beta readers—Ru, Ifer, and Sahar—thank you for being among the first to give my book a chance. Your feedback, your love for the story, and your time meant the world to me. I'm so grateful for each of you.

To BookTok—thank you for the motivation, the encouragement, and the belief that this book could become a reality. Your support has meant everything.

And finally, to my friends and family—thank you for listening to me ramble, for hyping me up endlessly, and for pretending to understand when I explained the same plan *hundreds* of times. And pretending it was the most amazing thing you've ever heard.

I love you all. Thank you again. It truly means the world that you picked up my novel and gave it a chance. Thank you for reading my words.

With love,
Maryam

ABOUT THE AUTHOR

Maryam is a British Pakistani author with a background in Forensic Psychology. She writes character-driven stories for those who long to lose themselves in words—to escape, to feel, to heal. *To Be Someone All Over Again* is her debut novel: a tender exploration of love, grief, and the quiet hope that lingers after everything falls apart.

Find her on TikTok and Instagram: **@maryamahauthor**

www.ingramcontent.com/pod-product-compliance
Ingram Content Group UK Ltd.
Pitfield, Milton Keynes, MK11 3LW, UK
UKHW040048180925
7957UKWH00007B/100